WAR IN HEAVEN

WAR IN HEAVEN

Charles Williams

William B. Eerdmans Publishing Company
Grand Rapids, Michigan / Cambridge, U.K.

This edition first published in 1967 by
Wm. B. Eerdmans Publishing Co.
2140 Oak Industrial Drive N.E., Grand Rapids, Michigan 49505 /
P.O. Box 163, Cambridge CB3 9PU U.K.

Printed in the United States of America

12 11 10 09 08 07   22 21 20 19 18 17

ISBN 978-0-8028-1219-8

www.eerdmans.com

CONTENTS

Chapter One

THE PRELUDE

The telephone bell was ringing wildly, but without result, since there was no-one in the room but the corpse.

A few moments later there was. Lionel Rackstraw, strolling back from lunch, heard in the corridor the sound of the bell in his room, and, entering at a run, took up the receiver. He remarked, as he did so, the boots and trousered legs sticking out from the large knee-hole table at which he worked, but the telephone had established the first claim on his attention.

"Yes," he said, "yes. . . . No, not before the 17th. . . . No, who cares what he wants? . . . No, who wants to know? . . . Oh, Mr. Persimmons. Oh, tell him the 17th. . . . Yes. . . . Yes, I'll send a set down."

He put the receiver down and looked back at the boots. It occurred to him that someone was probably doing something to the telephone; people did, he knew, at various times drift in on him for such purposes. But they usually looked round or said something; and this fellow must have heard him talking. He bent down towards the boots.

"Shall you be long?" he said into the space between the legs and the central top drawer; and then, as there was no answer, he walked away, dropped hat and gloves and book on to their shelf, strolled back to his desk, picked up some papers and read them, put them back, and, peering again into the dark hole, said more impatiently, "Shall you be long?"

No voice replied; not even when, touching the extended foot with his own, he repeated the question. Rather reluctantly

7

he went round to the other side of the table, which was still darker, and, trying to make out the head of the intruder, said almost loudly: "Hallo! hallo! What's the idea?" Then, as nothing happened, he stood up and went on to himself: "Damn it all, is he dead?" and thought at once that he might be.

That dead bodies did not usually lie round in one of the rooms of a publisher's offices in London about half-past two in the afternoon was a certainty that formed now an enormous and cynical background to the fantastic possibility. He half looked at the door which he had closed behind him, and then attempted the same sort of interior recovery with which he had often thrown off the knowledge that at any moment during his absence his wife *might* be involved in some street accident, some skidding bus or swerving lorry. These things happened—a small and unpleasant, if invisible, deity who lived in a corner of his top shelves had reminded him—these things happened, and even *now* perhaps. . . . People had been crushed against their own front doors; there had been a doctor in Gower Street. Of course, it was all untrue. But this time, as he moved to touch the protruding feet, he wondered if it were.

The foot he touched apparently conveyed no information to the stranger's mind, and Lionel gave up the attempt. He went out and crossed the corridor to another office, whose occupant, spread over a table, was marking sentences in newspaper cuttings.

"Mornington," Lionel said, "there's a man in my room under the table, and I can't get him to take any notice. Will you come across? He looks," he added in a rush of realism, "for all the world as if he was dead."

"How fortunate!" Mornington said, gathering himself off the table. "If he were alive and had got under your table and wouldn't take any notice I should be afraid you'd annoyed him somehow. I think that's rather a pleasant notion," he went on as they crossed the corridor, "a sort of modern *King's Threshold*—get under the table of the man who's insulted you and simply sulk there. Not, I think, starve—that's for more romantic ages than ours—but take a case filled with sandwiches and a thermos. . . . What's the plural of thermos? . . ." He stared at the feet, and then, going up to the desk, went down on one knee and put a hand over the disappearing leg. Then he looked up at Lionel.

"Something wrong," he said sharply. "Go and ask Dalling to come here." He dropped to both knees and peered under the table.

Lionel ran down the corridor in the other direction, and returned in a few minutes with a short man of about forty-five, whose face showed more curiosity than anxiety. Mornington was already making efforts to get the body from under the table.

"He must be dead," he said abruptly to the others as they came in. "What an incredible business! Go round the other side, Dalling; the buttons have caught in the table or something; see if you can get them loose."

"Hadn't we better leave it for the police?" Dalling asked. "I thought you weren't supposed to move bodies."

"How the devil do I know whether it is a body?" Mornington asked. "Not but what you may be right." He made investigations between the trouser-leg and the boot, and then stood up rather suddenly. "It's a body right enough," he said. "Is Persimmons in?"

"No," said Dalling; "he won't be back till four."

"Well, we shall have to get busy ourselves, then. Will you get on to the police-station? And, Rackstraw, you'd better drift about in the corridor and stop people coming in, or Plumpton will be earning half a guinea by telling the *Evening News*."

Plumpton, however, had no opportunity of learning what was concealed behind the door against which Lionel for the

9

next quarter of an hour or so leant, his eyes fixed on a long letter which he had caught up from his desk as a pretext for silence if anyone passed him. Dalling went downstairs and out to the front door, a complicated glass arrangement which reflected every part of itself so many times that many arrivals were necessary before visitors could discover which panels swung back to the retail sales-room, which to a waiting-room for authors and others desiring interviews with the remoter staff, and which to a corridor leading direct to the stairs. It was here that he welcomed the police and the doctor, who arrived simultaneously, and going up the stairs to the first floor he explained the situation.

At the top of these stairs was a broad and deep landing, from which another flight ran backwards on the left-hand to the second floor. Opposite the stairs, across the landing, was the private room of Mr. Stephen Persimmons, the head of the business since his father's retirement some seven years before. On either side the landing narrowed to a corridor which ran for some distance left and right and gave access to various rooms occupied by Rackstraw, Mornington, Dalling, and others. On the right this corridor ended in a door which gave entrance to Plumpton's room. On the left the other section, in which Lionel's room was the last on the right hand, led to a staircase to the basement. On its way, how-ever, this staircase passed and issued on a side door through which the visitor came out into a short, covered court, having a blank wall opposite, which connected the streets at the front and the back of the building. It would therefore have been easy for anyone to obtain access to Lionel's room in order, as the inspector in charge remarked pleasantly to Mornington, "to be strangled."

For the dead man had, as was evident when the police got the body clear, been murdered so. Lionel, in obedience to the official request to see if he could recognize the corpse, took one glance at the purple face and starting eyes, and with a choked negative retreated. Mornington, with a more contemplative, and Dalling with a more curious, interest, both in turn considered and denied any knowledge of the stranger. He was a little man, in the usual not very fresh clothes of the lower middle class; his bowler hat had been crushed in under the desk; his pockets contained nothing but a cheap watch, a few coppers, and some silver—papers he appeared to have none. Around his neck was a piece of stout cord, deeply embedded in the flesh.

So much the clerks heard before the police with their proceedings retired into cloud and drove the civilians into other rooms. Almost as soon, either by the telephone or some other means, news of the discovery reached Fleet Street, and reporters came pushing through the crowd that began to gather immediately the police were seen to enter the building. The news of the discovered corpse was communicated to them officially, and for the rest they were left to choose as they would among the rumours flying through the crowd, which varied from vivid accounts of the actual murder and several different descriptions of the murderer to a report that the whole of the staff were under arrest and the police had had to wade ankle-deep through the blood in the basement.

To such a distraction Mr. Persimmons himself returned from a meeting of the Publishers' Association about four o'clock, and was immediately annexed by Inspector Colquhoun, who had taken the investigation in charge. Stephen Persimmons was rather a small man, with a mild face apt to take on a harassed and anxious appearance on slight cause. With much more reason he looked anxious now, as he sat opposite the inspector in his own room. He had recognized the body as little as any of his staff had, and it was about them rather than it that the inspector was anxious to gain particulars.

"This Rackstraw, now," Colquhoun was saying: "it was his room the body was found in. Has he been with you long?"

"Oh, years," Mr. Persimmons answered; "most of them

have. All the people on this floor—and nearly all the rest. They've been here longer than me, most of them. You see, I came in just three years before my father retired—that's seven years ago, and three's ten."

"And Rackstraw was here before that?"

"Oh, yes, certainly."

"Do you know anything of him?" the inspector pressed. "His address, now?"

"Dalling has all that," the unhappy Persimmons said. "He has all the particulars about the staff. I remember Rackstraw being married a few years ago."

"And what does he do here?" Colquhoun went on.

"Oh, he does a good deal of putting books through, paper and type and binding, and so on. He rather looks after the fiction side. I've taken up fiction a good deal since my father went; that's why the business has expanded so. We've got two of the best selling people to-day—Mrs. Clyde and John Bastable."

"Mrs. Clyde," the inspector brooded. "Didn't she write *The Comet and the Star?*"

"That's the woman. We sold ninety thousand," Persimmons answered.

"And what are your other lines?"

"Well, my father used to do, in fact he began with, what you might call occult stuff. Mesmerism and astrology and histories of great sorcerers, and that sort of thing. It didn't really pay very well."

"And does Mr. Rackstraw look after that too?" asked Colquhoun.

"Well, some of it," the publisher answered. "But of course, in a place like this things aren't exactly divided just—just exactly. Mornington, now, Mornington looks after some books. Under me, of course," he added hastily. "And then he does a good deal of the publicity, the advertisements, you know. And he does the reviews."

"What, writes them?" the inspector asked.

"Certainly not," said the publisher, shocked. "Reads them and chooses passages to quote. Writes them! Really, inspector!"

"And how long has Mr. Mornington been here?" Colquhoun went on.

"Oh, years and years. I tell you they all came before I did."

"I understand Mr. Rackstraw was out a long time at lunch to-day, with one of your authors. Would that be all right?"

"I daresay he was," Persimmons said, "if he said so."

"You don't *know* that he was?" asked Colquhoun. "He didn't tell you?"

"Really, inspector," the worried Persimmons said again, "do you think my staff ask me for an hour off when they want to see an author? I give them their work and they do it."

"Sir Giles Tumulty," the inspector said. "You know him?"

"We're publishing his last book, *Historical Vestiges of Sacred Vessels in Folklore.* The explorer and antiquarian, you know. Rackstraw's had a lot of trouble with his illustrations, but he told me yesterday he thought he'd got them through. Yes, I can quite believe he went up to see him. But you can find out from Sir Giles, can't you?"

"What I'm getting at," the inspector said, "is this. If any of your people are out, is there anything to prevent anyone getting into any of their rooms? There's a front way and a back way in and nobody on watch anywhere."

"There's a girl in the waiting-room," Persimmons objected.

"A girl!" the inspector answered. "Reading a novel when she's not talking to anyone. She'd be a lot of good. Besides, there's a corridor to the staircase alongside the waiting-room. And at the back there's no-one."

"Well, one doesn't expect strangers to drop in casually," the publisher said unhappily. "I believe they do lock their doors sometimes, if they have to go out and have to leave a lot of papers all spread out."

"And leave the key in, I suppose?" Colquhoun said sarcastically.

"Of course," Persimmons answered. "Suppose I wanted something. Besides, it's not to keep anyone out; it's only just to save trouble and warn anyone going in to be careful, so to speak; it hardly ever happens. Besides——"

Colquhoun cut him short. "What people mean by asking for a Government of business men, I don't know," he said. "I was a Conservative from boyhood, and I'm stauncher every year the more I see of business. There's nothing to prevent anyone coming in."

"But they don't," said Persimmons.

"But they have," said Colquhoun. "It's the unexpected that happens. Are you a religious man, Mr. Persimmons?"

"Well, not—not exactly religious," the publisher said hesitatingly. "Not what you'd call religious unpleasantly, I mean. But what——"

"Nor am I," the inspector said. "And I don't get the chance to go to church much. But I've been twice with my wife to a Sunday evening service at her Wesleyan Church in the last few months, and it's a remarkable thing, Mr. Persimmons, we had the same piece read from the Bible each time. It ended up—'And what I say unto you I say unto all, Watch.' It seemed to me fairly meant for the public. 'What I say unto you,' that's us in the police, 'I say unto all, Watch.' If there was more of that there'd be fewer undiscovered murders. Well, I'll go and see Mr. Dalling. Good day, Mr. Persimmons."

Chapter Two

THE EVENING IN THREE HOMES

I

Adrian Rackstraw opened the oven, put the chicken carefully inside, and shut the door. Then he went back to the table, and realized suddenly that he had forgotten to buy the potatoes which were to accompany it. With a disturbed exclamation, he picked up the basket that lay in a corner, put on his hat, and set out on the new errand. He considered for a moment as he reached the garden gate to which of the two shops at which Mrs. Rackstraw indifferently supplied her needs he should go, and, deciding on the nearest, ran hastily down the road. At the shop, "Three potatoes," he said in a low, rather worried voice.

"Yes, sir," the man answered. "Five shillings, please."

Adrian paid him, put the potatoes in the basket, and started back home. But as at the corner he waited for the trams to go by and leave a clear crossing, his eye was caught by the railway station on his left. He looked at it for a minute or two in considerable doubt; then, changing his mind on the importance of vegetables, went back to the shop, left his basket with orders that the potatoes should be sent at once, and hurried back to the station. Once in the train, he saw bridges and tunnels succeed one another in exciting succession as the engine, satisfactorily fastened to coal-truck and carriages, went rushing along the Brighton line. But, before it reached its destination, his mother, entering the room with her usual swiftness, caught the station with her foot and sent it flying across the kitchen floor. Her immediate flood of

15

apologies placated Adrian, however, and he left the train stranded some miles outside Brighton in order to assist her in preparing the food for dinner. She sat down on a chair for a moment, and he broke in again hastily.

"Oh, mummie, don't sit down there, that's my table," he said.

"Darling, I'm so sorry," Barbara Rackstraw answered. "Had you got anything on it?"

"Well, I was going to put the dinner things," Adrian explained. "I'll just see if the chicken's cooked. Oh, it's lovely!"

"How nice!" Barbara said abstractedly. "Is it a large chicken?"

"Not a very large one," Adrian admitted. "There's enough for me and you and my Bath auntie."

"Oh," said Barbara, startled, "is your Bath auntie here?"

"Well, she may be coming," said Adrian. "Mummie, why do I have a Bath auntie?"

"Because a baby grew up into your Bath auntie, darling," his mother said. "Unintentional but satisfactory, as far as it goes. Adrian, do you think your father will like cold sausages? Because there doesn't seem to be anything else much."

"I don't want any cold sausages," Adrian said hurriedly.

"No, my angel, but it's the twenty-seventh of the month, and there's never any money then," Barbara said. "And here he is, anyhow."

Lionel, in spite of the shock that he had received in the afternoon, found himself, rather to his own surprise, curiously free from the actual ghost of it. His memory had obligingly lost the face of the dead man, and it was not until he came through the streets of Tooting that he began to understand that its effect was at once more natural and more profound than he had expected. His usual sense of the fantastic and dangerous possibilities of life, a sense which dwelled persistently in a remote corner of his mind, never showing itself in full, but stirring in the absurd alarm which shook him if his wife were ever late for an appointment—this sense now escaped from his keeping, and, instead of being too hidden, became too universal to be seized. The faces he saw, .the words he heard existed in an enormous void, in which he himself—reduced to a face and voice, without deeper existence—hung for a moment, grotesque and timid. There had been for an hour some attempt to re-establish the work of the office, and he had initialled, before he left, a few memoranda which were brought to him. The "L. R." of his signature seemed now to grow balloon-like and huge about him, volleying about his face at the same time that they turned within and around him in a slimy tangle. At similar, if less terrifying, moments, in other days, he had found that a concentration upon his wife had helped to steady and free him, but when this evening he made this attempt he found even in her only a flying figure with a face turned from him, whom he dreaded though he hastened to overtake. As he put his key in the lock he was aware that the thought of Adrian had joined the mad dance of possible deceptions, and it was with a desperate and machine-like courage that he entered to dare whatever horror awaited him.

Nor did the ordinary interchange of greetings do much to disperse the cloud. It occurred to him even as he smiled at Barbara that perhaps another lover had not long left the house; it occurred to him even as he watched Adrian finding pictures of trains in the evening paper that a wild possibility —for a story perhaps; not, surely not, as truth—might be that of a child whose brain was that of the normal man of forty while all his appearance was that of four. An infant prodigy? No, but a prodigy who for some horrible reason of his own concealed his prodigiousness until the moment he expected should arrive. And when they left him to his evening meal, while Barbara engaged herself in putting Adrian to bed, a hundred memories of historical or fictitious crimes entered his mind in which the victim had been carefully poisoned under the shelter of a peaceful and happy domesticity. And not that alone or chiefly; it was not the possibility of administered poison that occupied him, but the question whether all food, and all other things also, were not in themselves poisonous. Fruit, he thought, might be; was there not in the nature of things some venom which nourished while it tormented, so that the very air he breathed did but enable him to endure for a longer time the spiritual malevolence of the world?

Possessed by such dreams, he sat listless and alone until Barbara returned and settled herself down to the evening paper. The event of the afternoon occupied, he knew, the front page. He found himself incapable of speaking of it; he awaited the moment when her indolent eyes should find it. But that would not be, and indeed was not, till she had looked through the whole paper, delaying over remote paragraphs he had never noticed, and extracting interest from the mere superfluous folly of mankind. She turned the pages casually, glanced at the heading, glanced at the column, dropped the paper over the arm of her chair, and took up a cigarette.

"He's beginning to make quite recognizable letters," she said. "He made quite a good K this afternoon."

This, Lionel thought despairingly, was an example of the malevolence of the universe; he had given it, and her, every chance. Did she never read the paper? Must he talk of it himself, and himself renew the dreadful memories in open speech?

"Did you see," he said, "what happened at our place this afternoon?"

"No," said Barbara, surprised; and then, breaking off, "Darling, you look so ill. Do you feel ill?"

"I'm not quite the thing," Lionel admitted. "You'll see why, in there." He indicated the discarded *Star*.

Barbara picked it up. "Where?" she asked. " 'Murder in

City publishing house.' That wasn't yours, I suppose? Lionel, it was! Good heavens, where?"

"In my office," Lionel answered, wondering whether some other corpse wasn't hidden behind the chair in which she sat. Of course, they had found that one this afternoon, but mightn't there be a body that other people couldn't find, couldn't even see? Barbara herself now: mightn't she be really lying there dead? and this that seemed to sit there opposite him merely a projection of his own memories of a thousand evenings when she had sat so? What mightn't be true, in this terrifying and obscene universe?

Barbara's voice—or the voice of the apparent Barbara—broke in. "But, dearest," she said, "how dreadful for you! Why didn't you tell me? You must have had a horrible time." She dropped the paper again and hurled herself on to her knees beside him.

He caught her hand in his own, and felt as if his body at least was sane, whatever his mind might be. After all, the universe had produced Barbara. And Adrian, who, though a nuisance, was at least delimited and real in his own fashion. The fantastic child of his dream, evil and cruel and vigilant, couldn't at the same time have Adrian's temper and Adrian's indefatigable interest in things. Even devils couldn't be normal children at the same time. He brought his wife's wrist to his cheek, and the touch subdued the rising hysteria within him. "It was rather a loathsome business," he said, and put out his other hand for the cigarettes.

II

Mornington had on various occasions argued with Lionel whether pessimism was always the result of a too romantic, even a too sentimental, view of the world; and a slightly scornful mind pointed out to him, while he ate a solitary meal in his rooms that evening, that the shock which he undoubtedly had felt was the result of not expecting people to murder

other people. "Whereas they naturally do," he said to himself. "The normal thing with an unpleasant intrusion is to
try and exclude it—human or not. So silly not to be prepared
for these things. Some people, as De Quincey said, have a
natural aptitude for being murdered. To kill or to be killed
is a perfectly reasonable thing. And I will not let it stop me
taking those lists round to the Vicar's."

He got up, collected the papers which he had been analysing
for reports on parochial finance, and went off to the Vicarage
of St. Cyprian's, which was only a quarter of an hour from
his home. He disliked himself for doing work that he disliked,
but he had never been able to refuse help to any of his friends;
and the Vicar might be numbered among them. Mornington
suspected his Christianity of being the inevitable result of
having moved for some time as a youth of eighteen in circles
which were, in a rather detached and superior way, opposed
to it; but it was a religion which enabled him to despise himself and everyone else without despising the universe, thus
allowing him at once in argument or conversation the advantages of the pessimist and the optimist. It was because the
Vicar, a hard-worked practical priest, had been driven by
stress of experience to some similar standpoint that the two
occasionally found one another congenial.

That evening, however, he found a visitor at the Vicarage,
a round, dapper little cleric in gaiters, who was smoking a
cigar and turning over the pages of a manuscript. The Vicar
pulled Mornington into the study where they were sitting.

"My dear fellow," he said, "come in, come in. We've been
talking about you. Let me introduce the Archdeacon of Castra
Parvulorum— Mr. Mornington. What a dreadful business
this is at your office! Did you have anything to do with
it?"

Mornington saluted the Archdeacon, who took off his eye-
glasses and bowed back. "Dreadful," he said, tentatively
Mornington thought; rather as if he wasn't quite sure what

the other wanted him to say, and was anxious to accommodate himself to what was expected. "Yes, dreadful!"

"Well," Mornington answered, rebelling against this double sympathy, "of course, it was a vast nuisance. It disturbed the whole place. And I forgot to send the copy for our advertisement in the *Bookman*—so we shan't get in this month. That's the really annoying part. I hate being defeated by a murder. And it wasn't even in my own room."

"Ah, that's the trade way of looking at it," the Vicar said. "You'll have some coffee? But this poor fellow . . . is it known at all who he was?"

"Nary a know," Mornington answered brightly. "The police have the body as the clue, and that's all. Rather large, and inconvenient to lug about, and of course only available for a few days. Nature, you know. But it's the *Bookman* that annoys me—you wouldn't believe how much."

"Oh, come, not really!" the Vicar protested. "You wouldn't compare the importance of an advertisement with a murder."

"I think Mr. Mornington's quite right," the Archdeacon said. "After all, one shouldn't be put out of one's stride by anything phenomenal and accidental. The just man wouldn't be."

"But, still, a *murder*——" the Vicar protested.

The Archdeacon shrugged. "Murders or mice, the principle's the same," he answered. "To-morrow is too late, I suppose?"

"Quite," Mornington answered. "But I needn't worry you with my phenomenal and specialist troubles."

"As a matter of fact," the Archdeacon went on placidly, "we were talking about your firm at first rather differently." He pointed with his glasses to the manuscript on the table, and looked coyly at Mornington. "I dare say you can guess," he added.

Mornington tried to look pleased, and said in a voice that almost cracked with doubt: "Books?"

The Evening in Three Homes

"A book," the Vicar said. "The Archdeacon's been giving a series of addresses on Christianity and the League of Nations, and he's made them into a little volume which ought to have a good sale. So, of course, I thought of you."

"Thank you so much," Mornington answered. "And you'll excuse me asking—but is the Archdeacon prepared to back his fancy? Will he pay if necessary?"

The Archdeacon shook his head. "I couldn't do that, Mr. Mornington," he said. "It doesn't seem to me quite moral, so to speak. You know how they say a book is like a child. One has a ridiculous liking for one's own child—quite ridiculous. And that's all right. But seriously to think it's better than other children, to *push* it, to 'back' its being better, as you said—that seems to me so silly as to be almost wicked." He shook his head sadly at the manuscript.

"On the general principle I don't agree with you," Mornington said. "If your ideas are better than others' you ought to push them. I've no patience with our modern democratic modesty. How do you know the publisher you send it to is a better judge than you are? And, if he rejects it, what do you do?"

"If I send it to all the publishers," the Archdeacon answered, "and they all reject it, I think I should believe them. *Securus iudicat*, you know."

"But it doesn't," Mornington said. "Not by any manner of means. The *orbis terrarum* has to be taught its business by the more intelligent people. It has never yet received a new idea into its chaotic mind unless imposed by force, and generally by the sword."

He picked up the MS. and turned over the pages. " 'The Protocol and the Pact,' " he read aloud, " 'as Stages in Man's Consciousness.' 'Qualities and Nationalities.' 'Modes of Knowledge in Christ and Their Correspondences in Mankind.' 'Is the League of Nations Representative?' "

"I gather," he said, looking up, "that this is at once

specialist and popular. I don't for a moment suppose we shall take it, but I should like to have a look at it. May I carry it off now?"

"I think I'd like to keep it over the week-end," the Archdeacon answered. "There's a point or two I want to think over and a little Greek I want to check. Perhaps I might bring it down to you on Monday or Tuesday?"

"Do," Mornington said. "Of course, I shan't decide. It'll go to one of our political readers, who won't, I should think from the chapter-headings, even begin to understand it. But bring it along by all means. Persimmons' list is the most muddled-up thing in London. *Foxy Flossie's Flirtations* and *Notes on Black Magic Considered Philosophically*. But that, of course, is his father, so there's some excuse."

"I thought you told me the elder Mr. Persimmons had retired," the Vicar said.

"He is the Evening Star," Mornington answered. "He cuts the glory from the grey, as it were. But he pops in a good deal so as to do it. He hovers on the horizon perpetually, and about once a fortnight lightens from the east to the west, or at least to Persimmons' private office. A nice enough creature —with a perverse inclination towards the occult."

"I'm afraid," the Vicar said gloomily, "this interest in what they call the occult is growing. It's a result of the lack of true religion in these days and a wrong curiosity."

"Oh, wrong, do you think?" Mornington asked. "Would you say any kind of curiosity was wrong? What about Job?"

"Job?" the Archdeacon asked.

"Well, sir, I always understood that where Job scored over the three friends was in feeling a natural curiosity why all those unfortunate things happened to him. They simply put up with it, but he, so to speak, asked God what He thought He was doing."

The Vicar shook his head. "He was told he couldn't understand."

"He was taunted with not being able to understand—which isn't quite the same thing," Mornington answered. "As a mere argument there's something lacking perhaps, in saying to a man who's lost his money and his house and his family and is sitting on the dustbin, all over boils, 'Look at the hippopotamus.' "

"Job seemed to be impressed," the Archdeacon said mildly.

"Yes," Mornington admitted. "He was certainly a perfect fool, in one meaning or other of the words." He got up to go, and added: "Then I shall see you in the City before you go back to . . . Castra Parvulorum, was it? What a jolly name!"

"Unfortunately it isn't generally called that," the Archdeacon said. "It's called in directories and so on, and by the inhabitants, Fardles. By Grimm's Law."

"Grimm's Law?" Mornington asked, astonished. "Wasn't he the man who wrote the fairy tales for the *parvuli*? But why did he make a law about it? And why did anyone take any notice?"

"I understand it was something to do with Indo-European sounds," the Archdeacon answered. "The Castra was dropped, and in *parvulorum* the p became f and the v became d. And Grimm discovered what had happened. But I try and keep the old name as well as I can. It's not far from London. They say Cæsar gave it the name because his soldiers caught a lot of British children there, and he sent them back to their own people."

"Then I don't see why Grimm should have interfered," Mornington said, shaking hands. "Fardles . . . it sounds like an essay by Maurice Hewlett. Castra Parvulorum . . . it sounds like . . . it sounds like Rome. Well, good night, sir. Good night, Vicar. No, don't come to the door."

III

Actually at the moment when Mornington was speaking of him the elder Mr. Persimmons was sitting in a comfortable chair in an Ealing flat, listening to his son's account of the afternoon's adventure. He was a large man, and he lay back watching Stephen with amused eyes, as the younger man grew more and more agitated over the incredible facts.

"I'm so afraid it'll be bad for business," he ended abruptly.

The other sighed a little and looked at the fire. "Business," he said. "Oh, I shouldn't worry about business. If they want your books, they'll buy your books." He paused a little, and added: "I called in to see you to-day, but you were out."

"Did you?" his son said. "They didn't tell me."

"Just as well," Mr. Persimmons answered, "because you needn't know now. You won't be called at the inquest. Only, if anybody ever asks you, say you'll ask me and find out. I tell you because I want to know what you are doing and saying."

Stephen was looking out of the window, and a minute went by before he spoke. Then he said absently, "What did you want? Anything important?"

"I wanted to talk about the balance sheet," his father answered. "There are a few points I don't quite understand. And I still incline to think the proportion of novels is too high. It fritters money away, merely using it to produce more novels of the same kind. I want a definite proportion established between that and the other kind of book. You could quite well have produced my *Intensive Mastery* instead of that appalling balderdash about Flossie. Stephen, are you listening?"

"Yes," Stephen said half-angrily.

"I don't believe you mean to produce my book," his father went on equably. "Did you read it?"

"Yes," Stephen said again, and came back into the room. "I don't know about it. I told you I didn't quite like it—I don't think other people would. Of course, I know there's a great demand for that sort of psycho-analytic book, but I didn't feel at all sure——" He stopped doubtfully.

"If you ever felt quite sure, Stephen," the older man said, "I should lose a great deal of pleasure. What was it you didn't feel quite sure about this time?"

"Well, all the examples—and the stories," Stephen answered vaguely. "They're all right, I suppose, but they seemed so—funny."

"*Funny Stories I Have Read*, by Stephen Persimmons," his father gibed. "They weren't stories, Stephen. They were scientific examples."

"But they were all about torture," the other answered. "There was a dreadful one about—oh, horrible! I don't believe it would sell."

"It will sell right enough," his father said. "You're not a scientist, Stephen."

"And the diagrams and all that," his son went on. "It'd cost a great deal to produce."

"Well, you shall do as you like," Persimmons answered. "But, if you don't produce it by Christmas, I'll print it privately. That will cost a lot more money, Stephen. And anything else I write. If there are many more it'll make a nasty hole in my accounts. And there won't be any sale then, because I shall give them away. And burn what are over. Make up your mind over the week-end. I'll come down next week to hear what you decide. All a gamble, Stephen, and you don't like to bet except on a certainty, do you? You know, if I could afford it, I should enjoy ruining you, Stephen. But that, Stephen——"

"For God's sake, don't keep on calling me Stephen like that," the wretched publisher said. "I believe you like worrying me."

"But that," his father went on placidly, "wasn't the only reason I came to see you to-day. I wanted to kill a man, and your place seemed to me as good as any and better than most. So it was, it seems."

Stephen Persimmons stared at the large, heavy body

opposite lying back in its chair, and said, "You're worrying me . . . aren't you?"

"I may be," the other said, "but facts, I've noticed, do worry you, Stephen. They worried your mother into that lunatic asylum. A dreadful tragedy, Stephen—to be cut off from one's wife like that. I hope nothing of the sort will ever happen to you. Here am I comparatively young—and I should like another child, Stephen. Yes, Stephen, I should like another child. There'd be someone else to leave the money to; someone else with an interest in the business. And I should know better what to do. Now, when you were born, Stephen——"

"Oh, God Almighty," his son cried, "don't talk to me like that. What do you mean—you wanted to kill a man?"

"Mean?" the father asked. "Why, that. I hadn't thought of it till the day before, really—yesterday, so it was; when Sir Giles Tumulty told me Rackstraw was coming to see him —and then it only just crossed my mind. But when we got there, it was all so clear and empty. A risk, of course, but not much. Ask him to wait there while I get the money, and shut the door without going out. Done in a minute, Stephen, I assure you. He was an undersized creature, too."

Stephen found himself unable to ask any more questions. Did his father mean it or not? It would be like the old man to torment him: but if he had? Would it be a way of release?

"Well, first, Stephen," the voice struck in, "you can't and won't be sure. And it wouldn't look well to denounce your father on chance. Your mother *is* in a lunatic asylum, you know. And, secondly, my last will—I made it a week or two ago—leaves all my money to found a settlement in East London. Very awkward for you, Stephen, if it all had to be withdrawn. But you won't, you won't. If anyone asks you, say you weren't told, but you know I wanted to talk to you about the balance sheet. I'll come in next week to do it."

The Evening in Three Homes

Stephen got to his feet. "I think you want to drive me mad too," he said. "O God, if I only knew!"

"You know me," his father said. "Do you think I should worry about strangling you, Stephen, if I wanted to? As, of course, I might. But it's getting late. You know, Stephen, you brood too much; I've always said so. You keep your troubles to yourself and brood over them. Why not have a good frank talk with one of your clerks—that fellow Rackstraw, say? But you always were a secretive fellow. Perhaps it's as well, perhaps it's as well. And you haven't got a wife. Now, can you hang me or can't you?" The door shut behind his son, but he went on still aloud. "The wizards were burned, they went to be burned, they hurried. Is there a need still? Must the wizard be an outcast like the saint? Or am I only tired? I want another child. And I want the Graal."

He lay back in his chair, contemplating remote possibilities and the passage of the days immediately before him.

Chapter Three

THE ARCHDEACON IN THE CITY

The inquest was held on the Monday, with the formal result of a verdict of "Murder by a person or persons unknown," and the psychological result of emphasizing the states of mind of the three chief sufferers within themselves. The world certified itself as being, to Lionel more fantastic, to Mornington more despicable, to Stephen Persimmons more harassing. To the young girl who lived in the waiting-room and was interrogated by the coroner, it became, on the contrary, more exciting and delightful than ever; although she had no information to give—having, on her own account, been engaged all the while so closely indexing letter-books that she had not observed anyone enter or depart by the passage at the side of her office.

On the Tuesday, however, being, perhaps naturally, more watchful, she remarked towards the end of the day, three, or rather four, visitors. The offices shut at six, and about half-past four the elder Mr. Persimmons, giving her an amiable smile, passed heavily along the corridor and up to his son's room. At about a quarter past five Barbara Rackstraw, with Adrian, shone in the entrance—as she did normally some three or four times a year—and also disappeared up the stairs. And somewhere between the two a polite, chubby, and gaitered clergyman hovered at the door of the waiting-room and asked her tentatively if Mr. Mornington were in. Him she committed to the care of a passing office-boy, and returned to her indexing.

Gregory Persimmons, a little to his son's surprise and greatly to his relief, appeared to have shaken off the mood of tantalizing amusement which had possessed him on the previous

Friday. He discussed various financial points in the balance sheet as if he were concerned only with ordinary business concerns. He congratulated his son on the result of the inquest as likely to close the whole matter except in what he thought the unlikely result of the police discovering the murderer; and when he brought up the subject of *Intensive Mastery* he did it with no suggestion that anything but the most normal hesitation had ever held Stephen back from enthusiastic acceptance. In the sudden relief from mental neuralgia thus granted him, Stephen found himself promising to have the book out before Christmas—it was then early summer—and even going so far as to promise estimates during the next week and discuss the price at which it might reasonably appear. Towards the end of an hour's conversation Gregory said, "By the way, I saw Tumulty yesterday, and he asked me to make sure that he was in time to cut a paragraph out of his book. He sent Rackstraw a postcard, but perhaps I might just make sure it got here all right. May I go along, Stephen?"

"Do," Stephen said. "I'll sign these letters and be ready by the time you're back." And, as his father went out with a nod, he thought to himself: "He couldn't possibly want to go into that office again if he'd really killed a man there. It's just his way of pulling my leg. Rather hellish, but I suppose it doesn't seem so to him."

Lionel, tormented with a more profound and widely spread neuralgia than his employer's, had by pressure of work been prevented from dwelling on it that day. Soon after his arrival Mornington had broken into the office to ask if he could have a set of proofs of Sir Giles Tumulty's book on *Vessels of Folklore.* "I've got an Archdeacon coming to see me," he said—"don't bow—and an Archdeacon ought to be interested in folklore, don't you think? I always used to feel that Archdeacons were a kind of surviving folklore themselves—they seem pre-Christian and almost prehistoric: a lingering and bi-sexual tradition. Besides, publicity, you know. Don't Archdeacons charge? 'Charge, Archdeacons, charge! On, Castra Parvulorum, on! were the last words of Mornington.'"

"I wish they were!" Lionel said. "There are the proofs, on that shelf: take them and go! take them all."

"I don't want them all. Business, business. We can't have murders and Bank Holidays every day."

He routed out the proofs and departed; and when by the afternoon post an almost indecipherable postcard from Sir Giles asked for the removal of a short paragraph on page 218, Lionel did not think of making the alteration on the borrowed set. He marked the paragraph for deletion on the proofs he was about to return for Press, cursing Sir Giles a little for the correction—which, however, as it came at the end of a whole division of the book, would cause no serious inconvenience—and much more for his handwriting. A sentence beginning—he at last made out—"It has been suggested to me" immediately became totally illegible, and only recovered meaning towards the end, where the figures 218 rode like a monumental Pharaoh over the diminutive abbreviations which surrounded it. But the instruction was comprehensible, if the reason for it was not, and Lionel dispatched the proofs to the printer.

When, later on, the Archdeacon arrived, Mornington greeted him with real and false warmth mingled. He liked the clergyman, but he disliked manuscripts, and a manuscript on the League of Nations promised him some hours' boredom. For, in spite of his disclaimer, he knew he would have to skim the book at least, before he obtained further opinions, and the League of Nations lay almost in the nadir of all the despicable things in the world. It seemed to him so entire and immense a contradiction of aristocracy that it drove him into a positive hunger for mental authority imposed by force. He desired to see Plato and his like ruling with power, and remembered with longing the fierce inquisition of the *Laws*. However, he welcomed the Archdeacon without showing this, and settled down to chat about the book.

The Archdeacon in the City

"Good evening, Mr.—Archdeacon," he said rapidly, suddenly remembering that he didn't know the other's name, and at the same moment that it would no doubt be on the manuscript and that he would look at it immediately. "Good of you to come. Come in and sit down."

The Archdeacon, with an agreeable smile, complied, and, as he laid the parcel on the desk, said: "I feel a little remorseful now, Mr. Mornington. Or I should if I didn't realize that this is your business."

"That," Mornington said, laughing, "is a clear, cool, lucid, diabolical way of looking at it. If you could manage to feel a little remorse I should feel almost tender—an unusual feeling towards a manuscript."

"The relation between an author and a publisher", the Archdeacon remarked, "always seems to me to partake a little of the nature of a duel, an abstract, impersonal duel. There is no feeling about it——"

"Oh, isn't there?" Mornington interjected. "Ask Persimmons; ask our authors."

"Is there?" the Archdeacon asked. "You astonish me." He looked at the parcel, of which he still held the string. "Do you know," he said thoughtfully, "I don't *think* I have any feeling particularly about it. Whether you publish it or not, whether anyone publishes it or not, doesn't matter much. I think it might matter if I made no attempt to get it published, for I honestly think the ideas are sound. But with that very small necessary activity my responsibility ends."

"You take it very placidly," Mornington answered, smiling. "Most of our authors feel they have written the most important book of the century."

"Ah, don't misunderstand me," the Archdeacon said. "I might think that myself—I don't, but I might. It wouldn't make any difference to my attitude towards it. No book of ideas can matter so supremely as that. 'An infant crying in the night,' you know. What else was Aristotle?"

"Well, it makes it much pleasanter for us," Mornington said again. "I gather it's all one to you whether we take it or leave it?"

"Entirely," the Archdeacon answered, and pushed the bundle towards him. "I should, inevitably, be interested in your reasons so far as they bear stating."

"With this detachment," the other answered, undoing the parcel, "I wonder you make any reservation. Could any abominable reason shatter such a celestial calm?"

The Archdeacon twiddled his thumbs. "Man is weak," he said sincerely, "and I indeed am the chief of sinners. But I also am in the hands of God, and what can it matter how foolish my own words are or how truly I am told of them? Pooh, Mr. Mornington, you must have a very conceited set of authors."

"Talking about authors," Mornington went on, "I thought you might be interested in looking at the proofs of this book we've got in hand." And he passed over Sir Giles's *Sacred Vessels*.

The Archdeacon took them. "It's good work, is it?" he asked.

"I haven't had time to read it," the other said, "But there's one article on the Graal that ought to attract you." He glanced sideways at the first page of the MS., and read "*Christianity and the League of Nations*, by Julian Davenant, Archdeacon of Castra Parvulorum." "Well, thank God I know his name now," he reflected.

Meanwhile the third visitor, with her small companion, had penetrated to Lionel's room. They had come to the City to buy Adrian a birthday present, and, having succeeded, had gone on according to plan to the office. This arrangement—as such arrangements by such people tend to be—had been made two or three weeks earlier, and the crisis of the previous Friday had made Lionel only the more anxious to see if Barbara's presence would in any way cleanse the room from the slime that seemed still to carpet it. He had been a little doubtful whether she her-self would bear the neighbourhood, but, either because in effect the murder had meant little to her or because she guessed something of her husband's feelings, she had made no difficulty, had indeed assumed that the visit was still to be paid. Adrian's persistent interest in the date-stamp presented itself for those few minutes to Lionel as a solid reality amid the fantasies his mind made haste to induce. But Barbara's own presence was too much in the nature of a defiance to make him entirely happy. He kissed her as she sat on his table, with a sense of almost heroic challenge; neither he nor she were ignorant, and their ignoring of the subject was a too clear simulation of the ignorance they did not possess. But Adrian's ignorance was something positive. Lionel felt that a dead body beneath the desk would have been to this small and intent being something not so much unpleasant as dull and un-necessary; it might have got in the way of the movements of his body, but not of his mind. This was what he needed; his unsteady thought needed weighting, but with what, he asked himself, of all the shadows of obscenity that moved through the place of shadows which was the world—with which of all these could he weight it? From date-stamp to waste-paper basket, from basket to files, from files to telephone Adrian pursued his investigations; and Lionel was on the point of giving an exhibition of telephoning by ringing up Mornington, when the door opened and Gregory Persimmons appeared.

"I beg your pardon," he said, stopping on the threshold, "I really beg your pardon, Rackstraw."

"Come in, sir," Lionel said, getting up. "It's only my wife."

"I've met Mrs. Rackstraw before," Persimmons said, shaking hands. "But not, I think, this young man." He moved slowly in Adrian's direction.

"Adrian," Barbara said, "come and shake hands."

The child politely obeyed, as Persimmons, dropping on one knee, welcomed him with a grave and detached courtesy equal to his own. But when he stood up again he kept his eyes fixed on Adrian, even while saying to Barbara, "What a delightful child!"

"He is rather a pet," Barbara murmured. "But, of course, an awful nuisance."

"They always are," Persimmons said. "But they have their compensations. I've always been glad I had a son. Training them is a wonderful experience."

"Adrian trains himself, I'm afraid," Barbara answered, a little embarrassed. "But we shall certainly have to begin to teach him soon."

"Yes," Gregory said, his eyes still on Adrian. "It's a dreadful business, teaching them what's wrong. It has to be done all the same, and he's too fine a child to waste. I beg your pardon again—but I do think children are so wonderful, and when one meets the grown-ups one feels they've so often been wasted." He smiled at Barbara. "Look at your husband; look at me!" he said. "We were babies once."

"Well," Barbara said, smiling back, "I wouldn't say that Lionel had been altogether wasted. Nor you, Mr. Persimmons."

He bowed a little, but shook his head, then turned to Lionel. "All I came for, Rackstraw," he said, "was to say that I saw Tumulty yesterday, and he was rather anxious whether you could read a postcard he sent you about his book."

"Only just," Lionel answered, "but I managed. He wanted a paragraph knocked out."

"And you got it in time to make the correction?" Gregory asked again.

"Behold the proof," Lionel said, "*in* the proof. It goes off to-night." He held the sheet out to the other man, who took it with a word of thanks and glanced at the red-ink line. "That's it," he said, "the last paragraph on page 218." He stood for a moment reading it through.

In the room across the corridor the Archdeacon turned over page 217 and read on.

The Archdeacon in the City

"It seems probable therefore," the book ran, "if we consider these evidences, and the hypothetical scheme which has been adduced, not altogether unreasonably, to account for the facts which we have—a scheme which may be destroyed in the future by discovery of some further fact, but till then may not unjustifiably be considered to hold the field—it seems probable that the reputed Graal may be so far definitely traced and its wanderings followed as to permit us to say that it rests at present in the parish church of Fardles."

"Dear me!" the Archdeacon said; and, "Yes, that was the paragraph," said Mr. Gregory Persimmons; and for a moment there was silence in both offices.

The Archdeacon was considering that he had, in fact, never been able to find out anything about a certain rarely used chalice at Fardles. A year or two before the decease of the last Vicar a very much more important person in the neighbourhood had died—Sir John Horatio Sykes-Martindale, K.V.O., D.S.O., and various other things. In memory of the staunch churchmanship of this great and good man, his widow had presented a complete set of altar fittings and altar plate to the parish church, which was then doing its best with antique but uncorresponding paten and chalice. These were discarded in favour of the new gift, and when the Archdeacon succeeded to the rectory and archdeaconry he followed his predecessor's custom. He had at different times examined the old chalice carefully, and had shown it to some of his friends, but he had had no reason to make any special investigation, nor indeed would it have been easy to do so. The new suggestion, however, gave it a fresh interest. He was about to call Mornington's attention to the paragraph, then he changed his mind. There would be plenty of time when the book was out: lots of people —far too many—would hear about it then, and he might have to deal with a very complicated situation. So many people, he reflected, put an altogether undue importance on these exterior and material things. The Archbishop might write—and

The Archdeacon in the City

Archæological Societies—and perhaps Psychical Research people: one never knew. Better keep quiet and consider.

"I should like", he said aloud, "to have a copy of this book when it comes out. Could you have one sent to me, Mr. Mornington?"

"Oh, but I didn't show it to you for that reason," Mornington answered. "I only thought it might amuse you."

"It interests me very deeply," the Archdeacon agreed. "In one sense, of course, the Graal is unimportant—it is a symbol less near Reality now than any chalice of consecrated wine. But it is conceivable that the Graal absorbed, as material things will, something of the high intensity of the moment when it was used, and of its adventures through the centuries. In that sense I should be glad, and even eager," he added precisely, "to study its history."

"Well, as you like," Mornington answered. "So long as I'm not luring or bullying you into putting money into poor dear Persimmons's pocket."

"No one less, I assure you," the Archdeacon said, as he got up to go. "Besides, why should one let oneself be lured or bullied?"

"Especially by a publisher's clerk," Mornington added, smiling. "Well, we'll write to you as soon as possible, Mr. Davenant. In about forty days, I should think. It would be Lent to most authors, but I gather it won't be more than the usual Sundays after Trinity to you."

The Archdeacon shook his head gravely. "One is very weak, Mr. Mornington," he said. "While I would do good, and so on, you know. I shall wonder what will happen, although it's silly, of course, very silly. Good-bye and thank you."

Mornington opened the door for him and followed him out into the corridor. As they went along it they saw a group, consisting of Gregory and the Rackstraws outside Stephen Persimmons's room at the top of the stairs, and heard Gregory say to Barbara, "Yes, Mrs. Rackstraw, I'm sure that's the best way. You can't teach them what to want and go for because you don't know their minds. But you can teach them what *not* to do—just a few simple rules about what's wrong. Be afraid to do wrong—that's what I used to tell Stephen.''

"*Le malheureux!*" Mornington murmured as he bowed to the group, and let his smile change from one of respect to Gregory to one of friendliness for Barbara. The Archdeacon's foot was poised doubtfully for a moment over the first stair. But, if he had been inclined to go back, he changed his mind and went on towards the front door, with the other in attendance.

"Yes," Barbara said, distracted by Mornington's passing, "yes, I expect you're right."

"I suppose," Gregory remarked, changing the conversation, "that you've settled your holiday plans by now. Where are you going?"

"Well, sir," Lionel said, "we weren't going away this year at all. But Adrian had a slight attack of measles a month or so ago, so we decided we ought to, just to put him thoroughly right. Only every place is booked up and we don't seem able to get anything."

"I don't want to seem intrusive," Gregory said hesitatingly, "but, if you really want a place, there's a cottage—not a very grand one—down near where I live. It's on my grounds actually, and it's quite empty just now . . . if it's any good to you."

"But, Mr. Persimmons, how charming of you!" Barbara cried. "That would be delightful and just the thing. Where do you live, by the way?"

"I've just taken a place in the country," Gregory answered, "in Hertfordshire, near a little village called Fardles. Indeed, I've only just moved in. It belonged to a Lady Sykes-Martindale, but she's been advised to go to Egypt for her health, and I took the house. So it's quite new to me. Adrian and I could explore it together."

"How splendid!" Barbara said. "But are you quite sure, Mr.

Persimmons? I did want to get away, but we were giving up hope. Are you quite sure we shan't be intruding?"

"Not if you will let me see something of you there," Gregory assured her. "And, if Adrian liked me enough," he smiled at the boy, "you and your husband——" A motion of his hand threw England open to their excursions.

"It's very good of you, sir," Lionel began.

"Nonsense, nonsense," the other answered. "There's the cottage and here are you. I'll write about it. When do you go, Rackstraw? July? I'll write in a week or two, then. And now I must go and look at more figures. Good night, Mrs. Rackstraw. I shall see you again in five weeks or so. Good night, Adrian." He bowed down to shake the small hand. "Good night, Rackstraw. I'm delighted you'll come." He waved his hand generally and departed.

"What a divine creature!" Barbara said, going down the stairs. "Adrian darling, we're really going away. Would you like to go into the country?"

"Where is the country?" Adrian said.

"Oh—out there," Barbara said. "Away from the streets. With fields and cows."

"I don't like cows," Adrian said coldly.

"I daresay you won't see any," Lionel put in. "It does seem rather fortunate, Barbara."

"I think it's perfectly splendid," Barbara said joyously.

"Can I take my new train?" Adrian asked. And, in a whirl of assurances that he should take anything he liked or needed or had the slightest inclination to take, they came out into the hot June evening.

Chapter Four

THE FIRST ATTEMPT ON THE
GRAAL

The Archdeacon of Castra Parvulorum returned to
Fardles and his rectory on the next morning, for a
few days' clearing up before he went on his holiday.
After he had spent an hour or two in his study, he got up
suddenly, and, going out of the house, took the private path
that led through his garden and the churchyard to the small
Norman Church. The memory of the article he had read in
Mornington's office had grown more dominating as he returned to the place where, if Sir Giles Tumulty were right,
the Graal, neglected and overlooked, stood in his sacristy. No-
one had ever seen the Archdeacon excited, not even when, in
the days of his youth, he had assisted his friends to break up a
recruiting meeting in the days of the Boer War; and even now
he yielded to himself as he might have yielded to a friend's
importunities, and went along the path rather with an air of
humouring a pleasant but persistent visitor than with any
eagerness of his own.

The church stood open, as it always did, from the early
celebration till dusk. The verger was at the moment engaged
on the Archdeacon's roses, and, since Fardles lay off the main
road, it was rarely that it was visited by strangers. Fardles itself indeed lay a little way distant from the church, the nearest
houses being about a quarter of a mile off and the main street
of the village beginning another quarter of a mile beyond them.
The railway station formed the third corner of an equilateral
triangle, with the village and the church at the angles of its
base. On the other side of the base a similar triangle was

formed by the grounds of the late Sir John Horatio Sykes-Martindale's house. The house itself—Cully, as it was called, to the Archdeacon's secret and serious delight, and without any distress to the naturally ignorant Sir John—lay in the middle of its grounds; an enormous overbuilt place, of no particular age and no particular period. And beyond it, towards the apex of this second triangle, lay the empty cottage of which Mr. Gregory Persimmons had spoken to Lionel.

The Archdeacon went into the church and passed on into the sacristy. He unlocked and opened the tall and antique chest in which the sacred vessels were kept, lifted one of them out, and, carrying it back into the church, set it upon the altar. Then he stood and looked at it carefully.

It was old enough, that appeared certain; it was plain enough too, almost severe. The drinking cup itself was some six inches in depth, with a stem in proportion, and a small pedestal which was carried by slowly narrowing work up some distance of the stem. The whole was about fifteen or sixteen inches high. There were, so far as the Archdeacon could see, no markings, no ornamentation, except for a single line, about half an inch below the rim. It was made of silver, so far as he could tell, slightly dented here and there, but still apparently good for a considerable amount of use. It stood there on the altar, as it had done so many mornings, until the grief of Lady Sykes-Martindale had enriched the late Vicar's sacristy with a new gold chalice. And the Archdeacon stood and considered it.

Of course, the thing was not impossible. He did not remember Sir Giles's article accurately enough to know the stages by which the archæologist had traced the Graal from Jerusalem to Fardles: here a general tradition, there a local rumour, a printed paragraph or an unpublished MS., even the remnants of an old tapestry or a carving in a remote Town Hall. He could see clearly that it might all be nothing but a fantasy of peculiar neatness, and he attached little importance to the vessel itself. But he was conscious that a great many people might attach a good deal of importance to it if there were any truth in the story. If it were the Graal, what would they want to do with it? He considered with pleasure that at least it was in the hands of the officials of the Church, and that there were some things that even officials of the Church could not do. They could not, for example, sell it to a millionaire. But why, the Archdeacon asked himself, should he object to it being sold to a millionaire?

He was about to restore the vessel to the sacristy when he asked himself this question, and stayed for a moment or two with it in his hands. Then he changed his mind, went and locked the door of the cabinet, and came back to the altar. "Ah, fair sweet Lord," he said half-aloud, "let me keep this Thy vessel, if it be Thy vessel; for love's sake, fair Lord, if Thou hast held it in Thy hands, let me take it into mine. And, if not, let me be courteous still to it for Thy sake, courteous Lord; since this might well have been that, and that was touched by Thee." He smiled a little, took up the chalice, and went back to the Rectory.

There he passed straight to his own pleasant bedroom and opened an inner door which led to a small room, once perhaps a dressing-room. It was furnished now with a pallet-bed, a hard chair or two, a table, and a kneeling-desk. On one otherwise empty wall a crucifix hung; a small shelf in one corner held a few books, and there were one or two more on the table. The window in one of the pair of shorter walls looked out over the graveyard towards the church. The Archdeacon went across to the mantelshelf, set down his burden, looked at it for a minute or two, murmured a prayer, and went down to lunch.

After lunch he walked for a little while in his garden. His *locum tenens*, a rather elderly clergyman whom the Archdeacon thoroughly disliked, but who needed the money that the temporary post would bring him, was not due till the next day. The Archdeacon felt a pang, slight but definite, at the idea that this tall, lean, harassed, talkative, and inefficient priest would sit in his chair and sleep in his bed; not so much that they were his chair and his bed as that it seemed a shame that such ready and pleasant things should be subjected to the invasion of human futility. He put out his hand and touched a flower, then withdrew it. "I am becoming sentimental," he thought to himself. "How do I know that a chair is full of goodwill, or a bed anxious to please? They may be, but they mayn't. Their life is hidden with Christ in God. Oh, give thanks to the God of all gods," he sang softly, "for His mercy endureth for ever."

"Mr. Davenant?" said a voice at his back.

The Archdeacon, a little startled, turned. A large man whose face he dimly remembered was looking over the garden gate.

"Er—yes," he said vaguely, "that is, yes. I am Mr. Davenant."

"Mr. Archdeacon, I suppose I ought to say," the other went on agreeably. "I knew I was wrong as soon as I'd spoken."

"Not at all," the Archdeacon answered. "You wanted to see me? Come in, won't you?" He opened the gate for the stranger, who, as he entered, uttered a word of thanks and went on: "Well, I did, rather. My name is Persimmons, Gregory Persimmons. I've just bought Cully, you know, so we shall be neighbours. But I understand from the village talk that you're going away to-morrow, and I didn't come to-day merely for a neighbourly call."

"Whatever the reason——" the Archdeacon murmured. "Shall we go inside or would you rather sit down over there?" He indicated a garden-seat among the flowers.

"Oh, here, by all means," Persimmons said. "Thank you." He accepted a cigarette. "Well the fact is, Mr. Archdeacon, I have come as a beggar and yet not a beggar. I have come to beg for another and pay for myself."

The Archdeacon put a finger to his glasses. The word Persimmons had taken him back to the previous day's visit to

43

Mornington; and he was asking himself whether this was the voice that had been offering advice on how to train children. There was something about this last sentence also that offended him.

"I know a priest," Persimmons proceeded, "who is in bad need of some altar furniture, especially the sacred vessels, for a new mission church he's starting. Now, I was talking to one and another down here—the grocer's an ardent churchman, I find. And one of your choir-boys, and so on—as one does. And I gathered—you'll tell me if I'm wrong—that you had an extra chalice here which you didn't often use. So I wondered, as you have the set that Lady Sykes-Martindale gave, whether you'd consider letting me have it at a reasonable price, for my friend."

"I see," the Archdeacon said. "Yes, quite. I see what you mean. But, if you'll forgive me asking, Mr. Persimmons, surely a new chalice would be better than a—shall I say, second-hand one?" He threw a deprecating smile at Gregory and loosed an inner secret smile to Christ at the epithet.

"My friend," Persimmons said, leaning comfortably back and lazily smoking, "my friend hates new furniture for an altar. He has some kind of theory about stored power and concentrated sanctity which I, not being a theologian, don't profess to understand. But the result of it is that he infinitely prefers things that have been used for many years in the past. Perhaps you know the feeling?"

"Yes, I know the feeling," the Archdeacon said. "But in this instance I'm afraid it can't be rewarded. I'm afraid the chalice is not to be parted with."

"It's natural you should say that," the other answered, "for I expect I've put it clumsily, Mr. Archdeacon. But I hope you'll think it over. Of course, I know I'm a stranger, but I want to feel part of the life here, and I thought if I could send out a—a sort of magnetic thrill by buying that chalice for my friend . . . and I'd be glad to buy another for you if

you wanted it replaced . . . I thought . . . I don't know . . .
I thought . . ."

His voice died away, and he sat looking half-wistfully out
over the garden, the portrait of a retired townsman trying to
find a niche for himself in new surroundings, shy but good-
hearted, earnest if a little clumsy, and trying not to touch too
roughly upon subjects which he seemed to regard with a
certain ignorant alarm. The Archdeacon shot a glance at him,
and after a minute's silence shook his head. "No," he said,
"I'm sorry, Mr. Persimmons, but that chalice is not for sale.
But perhaps I can do something for you. Over in your
direction, some eight miles beyond you, there's a church
which I think has exactly the kind of thing you want. I know
that recently they had an altar set up in their Lady Chapel,
replaced the vessels at the High Altar, and bought fresh ones
for the other two. If the Vicar hasn't given his old ones away
yet, he's the very man for you—and he hadn't a week ago,
because I was over there. I'll give you a note of introduction
to him if you like—he's a nice fellow; he's one of the old
Rushforths, you know: they're a side branch of the Herberts.
A good old Anglican family, one might say. His Christian
name's Herbert—a very pleasant fellow. Devoted to the
Church, too. Fasts in Lent and all that kind of thing, I believe;
and they do say he hears confessions—but I don't want to
take any notice of that unless I'm driven to. It wouldn't
matter, of course, I couldn't do anything—that's the great
charm of being an Archdeacon, one never can. But there's a
certain prestige and so on, and I don't want to throw that, for
what it's worth, against him. Herbert Rushforth, yes, I'll
certainly give you a note. Or, even better—I have to go out
that way—probably—possibly—this evening, and I'll call on
him and ask him myself. And, if he has them still, he'll be
delighted for you to have them; you needn't mind in the
least—he's extremely well-to-do. He'll want to leave them at
Cully to-morrow, and perhaps he will. Even if you don't want

45

to take them over personally, as, of course, you may, he could have them sent to your friend. Where did you say his church was?" The Archdeacon, a fountain-pen in his hand, a slip of paper on his knee, looked pleasantly and inquiringly at Mr. Persimmons, and all round them the flowers gently stirred.

Mr. Persimmons was a little taken back. There had not appeared to him to be any conceivable reason why the Archdeacon should refuse to part with the old chalice, and if by any chance there had been any difficulty he had still expected to be able to obtain sight of it, to see what it looked like and where it was kept. He found himself at the moment almost, it seemed, on the other side of the county from Fardles, and he did not immediately see any way of getting back. He thought for a moment of making his imaginary clerical friend a native of Fardles, in order to give him a special delight in things that came from there, but that was too risky.

"Oh, well," he said, "if you don't mind, I think I won't give you his name. He might be rather ashamed of not being able to buy the necessary things. That was why, I thought, if you and I could just quietly settle it together, without bringing other people in, it would be so much better. A clergyman doesn't like to admit that he's poor, does he? And that was why——"

Damnation! he thought, he was repeating himself. But the Archdeacon's fantastic round face and gold glasses were watching him with a grave attention, and where but now had been a steady flow of words there was an awful silence. "Well," he said, with an effort at a leap across the void, "I'm sorry you can't let me have it."

"But I'm offering it to you," the Archdeacon said. "You didn't want the Fardles chalice *particularly*, did you?"

"Only as coming from the place where I was going to live," Persimmons said, and added suddenly: "It just seemed to me as if, as I was leaving my friend myself, I was

46

sending him something better instead, something greater and stronger and more friendly."

"But you were talking about a chalice," the Archdeacon objected perplexedly. "How do you mean, Mr. Persimmons —finer and stronger and so on?"

"I meant the chalice," Gregory answered. "Surely that——"

The Archdeacon laughed good-naturedly and shook his head. "Oh, no," he said, "no. Not the chalice alone. Why, if it were the Holy Graal itself," he added thoughtfully, replacing the cap on his fountain-pen and putting it away, "you could hardly say that about it." He stood up, a little disappointed at not having noticed any self-consciousness about the other when he had mentioned the Graal. "Well," he said, "I must apologise, but you will understand I have some work to do; I'm going to-morrow, as you say. Will you forgive me? And shall I speak to Rushforth?"

"If you will be so good," Persimmons answered. "Or, no, don't let me take up your time. I will go and see him, if I may mention you name? Yes, I assure you I would rather. Good afternoon, Mr. Archdeacon."

"Good afternoon," the Archdeacon said. "I shall see you often when I return, I hope."

He accompanied his visitor to the gate, chatting amicably. But when Persimmons had gone he walked slowly back towards the house, considering the discussion thoughtfully. Was there a needy mission church? and was his visitor to be its benefactor? And the chalice? It seemed possible, and even likely, in this fantastic dream of a ridiculous antiquary, that the Graal of so many romances and so long a quest, of Lancelot and Galahad and dim maidens moving in antique pageants of heraldry and symbolism and religion, the desire of Camelot, the messenger of Sarras, the relic of Jerusalem, should be resting neglected in an English village. "Fardles," he thought, "Castra Parvulorum, the camp of the children: where else should the Child Himself rest?" He re-entered the Rectory, singing again to himself: "Who alone doeth marvellous things; for his mercy endureth for ever."

It was the custom of the parish that there should be a daily celebration at seven, at which occasionally in summer a small congregation assembled. Before this, at about a quarter to seven, the Archdeacon was in the habit of saying Morning Prayer publicly, as he was required to do by the rubrics. Once a week, on Thursday mornings, he was assisted by the sexton; on the other mornings he assisted himself. As, however, the sexton with growing frequency overslept himself, the Archdeacon preferred to keep the key of the church himself, and it was with this in his hand that he came to the west door about half-past six the next morning. At the door, however, he stopped, astonished. For it hung open and wrenched from the lock, wrenched and broken and pushed back against the other wall. The Archdeacon stared at it, went closer and surveyed it, and then hastened into the church. A few minutes gave him the extent of the damage. The two boxes, for the Poor and for the Church, that were fixed not far from the font, had also been opened, and their contents, if they had any, looted; the candlesticks on the altar had been thrown over, the candles in them broken and smashed, and the frontal pulled away and torn. In the sacristy the lock of the cabinet had been forced and the gold chalice which commemorated the late Sir John had disappeared, together with the gold paten. On the white-washed wall had been scrawled a few markings—"Phallic," the Archdeacon murmured, with a faint smile. He came back to the front door in time to see the sexton at the gate of the churchyard, and, judiciously lingering on the footpath beyond, two spasmodically devout ladies of the parish. He waved to them all to hurry, and when they arrived informed them equably of the situation.

"But, Mr. Archdeacon——" Mrs. Major cried.

"But, Mr. Davenant——" Miss Willoughby, who, as being

older, both in years and length of Fardles citizenship, than most of the ladies of the neighbourhood, permitted herself to use the personal name. And "Who can have done it?" they both concluded.

"Ah!" the Archdeacon said benignantly. "A curious business, isn't it?"

"Isn't it sacrilege?" said Mrs. Major.

"Was it a tramp?" asked Miss Willoughby.

"What we want is Towlow," the sexton said firmly. "Towlow isn't at all bad at finding things out, though, being a Wesleyan Methodist, as he calls himself, he can't be expected to want to find out these bloody murderers. I'll go and get him, shall I, sir?"

"How fortunate my brother's staying with me," Mrs. Major cried out. "He's in the Navy, you know, and quite used to crime. He even sat on a court-martial once."

Miss Willoughby, out of a wider experience, knew better than to commit herself at once. She watched the Archdeacon's eyes, and, as she saw them glaze at these two suggestions, ventured a remote and disapproving "H'm, h'm!" Even the nicest clergymen, she knew, were apt to have unexpected fads about religion.

"No," the Archdeacon said, "I don't think we'll ask Towlow. And though, of course, I can't object to your brother looking at these damaged doors, Mrs. Major, I shouldn't like him to want to make an arrest. Sacrilege is hardly a thing a priest can prosecute for—not, anyhow, in a present-day court."

"But——" Mrs. Major and the sexton began.

"The immediate thing," the Archdeacon flowed on, "is the celebration, don't you think? Jessamine"—this to the sexton—"will you move those candlesticks and get as much of the grease off as you can? Mrs. Major, will you put the frontal straight? Miss Willoughby, will you do what you can to set the other ornaments right? Thank you, thank you. Fortunately the other chalice is at the rectory; I will go and get it." Then he paused a moment. "And perhaps," he said gravely, "as these two boxes have been robbed, we may take the advantage to restore something." He moved from one box to the other, dropping in coins, and a little reluctantly the two ladies imitated him. Jessamine was already at the altar.

As the Archdeacon walked up to the house he allowed himself to consider the possibilities. The breaking open of the west door pointed to a more serious attack than that of a casual tramp; tramps didn't carry such instruments as this success must have necessitated. But, if a tramp were not the burglar, then the money in the boxes had not been the aim. The gold chalice, then? Possible, possible: or the other chalice, the one of whose reputed history, except for that quarter of an hour in Mornington's room, he would have known nothing —could that be the aim? After all, the man who wrote the book—what was his name?—might have mentioned it, mentioned it to anyone, to a collector, to a millionaire, to a frenzied materialist. But one wouldn't expect them to try burglary at once. He saw in the distance the garden-seat where he had sat in talk the previous afternoon. And had they? Or had they tried purchase? Persimmons—Stephen Persimmons, publisher—*Christianity and the League of Nations*—a mission church in need—sacrilege—phallic scrawls.

He came into the inner room where he had looked at the chalice before he went out that morning, and as he came in it seemed to meet him in sound. A note of gay and happy music seemed to ring for a moment in his ears as he paused in the entrance. It was gone, if it had been there, and gravely he genuflected in front of the vessel and lifted it from its place. Carrying it as he had so often lifted its types and companions, he became again as in all those liturgies a part of that he sustained; he radiated from that centre and was but the last means of its progress in mortality. Of this sense of instrument-ality he recognized, none the less, the component parts—the ritual movement, the priestly office, the mere pleasure in ordered, traditional, and almost universal movement. "Neither is this Thou," he said aloud, and, coming to the garden door, looked round him. In the hall the clock struck seven; he heard his housekeeper moving upstairs; as he came out into the garden he saw on the road a few men on their way to work. Then suddenly he saw another man leaning over the gate as Persimmons had leant the previous afternoon; only this was not Persimmons, though a man not unlike him in general height and build. The man opened the gate and came into the garden, though not directly in the path to the churchyard gate, and on the sudden the Archdeacon stopped.

"Excuse me, mister," a voice said, "but is this the way to Fardles?" He pointed down the road.

"That is the way, yes," the Archdeacon answered. "Keep to the right all the way."

"Ah, thankee," the stranger said. "I've been walking almost all night—nowhere to go and no money to go with." He was standing a few yards off. "Excuse me coming in like this, but seeing a gentleman——"

"Do you want something to eat?" the Archdeacon asked.

"Ah, that's it," said the other, eyeing him and the chalice curiously. "Reckon you've never been twenty-four hours without a bite or sup." He took another step forward.

"If you go round to the kitchen you shall be given some food," the Archdeacon said firmly. "I am on my way to the church and cannot stop. If you want to see me I will talk to you when I come back." He lifted the chalice and went on down the path and through the churchyard.

The Mysteries celebrated, he returned, still carefully carrying the chalice, and set it out of sight in a cupboard in the breakfast-room. When his housekeeper came in with coffee he asked after the stranger.

"Oh yes, sir, he came round," she said, "and I gave him some food. But he didn't eat much, to my thinking, and he was off again in ten minutes. Those folk don't want breakfast,

money's what they're after. He wouldn't stop to see you, not
after I told him you might get him a job. Money, that's what
he wanted, not a job, nor breakfast, either."

But the Archdeacon absurdly continued to doubt this. He
had felt, all through the short conversation in the garden,
that it was not himself, but the vessel that the stranger had
been studying—and that not with any present recognition, but
as if he were impressing it on his memory. His train went at
half-past nine; it was now half-past eight. But the train was
out of the question; he had to explain the state of the church
to the *locum tenens*; he had to go over to Rushforth, not now
for Persimmons, but for his own needs. And, above all, he
had to decide what to do with that old, slightly dented chalice
that was hidden in the cupboard of the breakfast-room of an
English rectory.

The first thing that occurred to him was the bank; the
second was the Bishop. But the nearest bank was five miles
off; and the Bishop was probably thirty-five, at the cathedral
city. He might be anywhere, being a young and energetic and
modern Bishop, who organized the diocese from railway
stations, and platforms at public meetings before and after
speaking, and public telephone-boxes, and so on. The Archdeacon foresaw some difficulty in explaining the matter. To
walk straight in, and put down the chalice, and say: "This
is the Holy Graal. I believe it to be so because of a paragraph
in some proofs, a man who tried to buy it for a mission church
and said that children ought to be taught not to do wrong,
a burglary at my church, and another man who asked the
way to Fardles"—would a young, energetic, modern Bishop
believe it? The Archdeacon liked the Bishop very much, but he
did not believe him to be patient or credulous.

The bank first then, and Rushforth next. And, in a day or
two, the Bishop. Or rather first a telegram to Scotland. He
sat down to write it, meaning to dispatch it from the station
when he took the train to town. Then he spent some time in

looking out a leather case which would hold the chalice, and had indeed been used for some such purpose before. He ensconced the Graal—if it were the Graal—therein, left a message with his housekeeper that he would be back some time in the afternoon, and by just after nine was fitting his hat on in the hall.

There came a knock at the door. The housekeeper came to open it. The Archdeacon, looking over his shoulder, saw the stranger who had invaded his garden that morning standing outside.

"Excuse me, ma'am," the stranger said, "but is the reverend gentleman in? Ah, to be sure, there he is. You see, sir, I didn't want to worry you over your breakfast, so I went for a bit of a walk. But I hope you haven't forgotten what you said about helping me to find work. It's work I want, sir, not idleness."

"You didn't seem that keen on it when you were talking to *me* about it," the housekeeper interjected.

"I didn't want to forestall his reverence," the stranger said. "But anything that he could do I'd be truly grateful for."

"What's your name?" the Archdeacon asked.

"Kedgett," the other answered, "Samuel Kedgett. I served in the war, sir, and here——"

"Quite," the Archdeacon answered. "Well, Mr. Kedgett, I'm sorry I can't stop now; I have to go to town most unexpectedly. Call"—he changed "this evening" into "to-morrow morning"—"and I'll see what can be done."

"Thank you, sir," the other said, with a sudden alertness. "I'll be there. Good-bye, sir." He was out of the porch and down the garden path before his hearers were clear that he was going.

"What a jumpy creature!" the housekeeper said. "Dear me, sir, I hope you're not going to give him work here. I couldn't stand a man like that."

"No," the Archdeacon said absently, "no, of course, you couldn't. Well, good-bye, Mrs. Lucksparrow. Explain to Mr.

Batesby when he comes, won't you? I shall be back in the afternoon probably."

Along the country lane on the other side of the churchyard there was little to be seen beyond the fields and pleasant slopes of the country twenty miles out of North London. The Archdeacon walked along, meditating, and occasionally turning his head to look over his shoulder. Not that he seriously expected to be attacked but he did feel that there was something going on of which he had no clear understanding. "How vainly men themselves amaze," he quoted, and allowed himself to be distracted by trying to complete the couplet with some allusion to the high vessel. He produced at last, as he came to a space where four roads met and as he went on through what was called a wood, but was not much more than a copse—he produced as a result:

> *How vainly men themselves divert,*
> *Even with this chalice, to their hurt!*

and heard a motor-car coming towards him in the distance. It was coming very quietly from the direction of the station, and in a few minutes it came round the curve of the road. He saw someone stand up in it and apparently beckon to him, quickened his steps, heard a faint voice calling: "Archdeacon! Archdeacon!" felt a sudden crash on the back of his head, and entered unconsciousness.

The car drew up by him. "Quick, Ludding, the case," Mr. Persimmons said to the man who had slipped from the wood in the Archdeacon's rear. He caught it to him, opened it, took out the chalice, and set it in another case which stood on the seat by him. Then he gave the empty one back to Ludding. "Keep that till I tell you to throw it away," he said. "And now help me lift the poor fellow in. You have a fine judgement, Ludding. Just in the right place. You didn't hit *too* hard, I suppose! We don't want to attract attention. A little more this way, that's it. We have some brandy, I think.

I will get in with him." He did so, moving the case which held the Graal. "Can you put that with the petrol-tin, Ludding? Good! Now drive on carefully till we come to the cross-roads."

When, in a few moments, they were there, "Now throw the case into the ditch," Persimmons went on, "over by that clump, I think. Excellent, Ludding, excellent. And now round up to the Rectory, and then you shall go on to the village or even the nearest town for a doctor. We must do all we can for the Archdeacon, Ludding. I suppose he was attacked by the same tramp that broke into the church. I think perhaps we ought to let the police know. All right; go on."

Chapter Five

THE CHEMIST'S SHOP

For some three weeks the Archdeacon was in retirement, broken only by the useful fidelity of Mrs. Lucksparrow and the intrusive charity of Mr. Batesby, who, having arrived at the Rectory for one reason, was naturally asked to remain for another. As soon as the invalid was allowed to receive visitors, Mr. Batesby carried the hint of the New Testament, "I was sick and ye visited me" to an extreme which made nonsense of the equally authoritative injunction to be "wise as serpents." He was encouraged by the feeling which both the doctor and Mrs. Lucksparrow had that it was fortunate another member of the profession should be at hand, and by the success with which the Archdeacon, dizzy and yet equable, concealed his own feelings when his visitor, chatting of Prayer Book Revision, parish councils, and Tithe Acts, imported to them a high eternal flavour which savoured of Deity Itself. Each day after he had gone the Archdeacon found himself inclined to brood on the profound wisdom of that phrase in the Athanasian Creed which teaches the faithful that "not by conversion of the Godhead into flesh, but by taking of the manhood into God" are salvation and the Divine End achieved. That the subjects of their conversation should be taken into God was normal and proper; what else, the Archdeacon wondered, could one do with parish councils? But his goodwill could not refrain from feeling that to Mr. Batesby they were opportunities for converting the Godhead rather firmly and finally into flesh. "The dear flesh," he murmured, thinking ruefully of the way his own had been treated.

The Chemist's Shop

In London the tracing of the murderer seemed, so far as Stephen Persimmons and his people could understand, to be a slow business. Descriptions of the murdered man had been circulated without result. There had been no papers—with the exception, crammed into the corner of one pocket, of the torn half of a printed bill inviting the attendance of outsiders at a mission service to be held at some (the name was torn) Wesleyan church. The clothes of the dead man were not of the sort that yield clues—such as had any marks, collars and boots, were like thousands of others sold every day in London. There were, of course, certain minor peculiarities about the body, but these, though useful for recognition, were of no help towards identification.

Investigations undertaken among the vanmen, office boys, and others who had been about the two streets and the covered way about the time when the corpse entered the building resulted in the discovery of eleven who had noticed nothing, five who had seen him enter alone (three by the front and two by the side door), one who had seen him in company with an old lady, one with a young lad, three with a man about his own age and style, and one who had a clear memory of his getting out of a taxi, from which a clean-shaven or bearded head had emerged to give a final message and which had then been driven off. But no further success awaited investigations among taxi-drivers, and the story was eventually dismissed as a fantasy.

Mornington suspected that a certain examination into the circumstances of the members of the staff had taken place, but, if so, he quoted to his employer from Flecker, "the surveillance had been discreet." Discreet or not, it produced no results, any more than the interview with Sir Giles Tumulty that Inspector Colquhoun secured.

"Rackstraw?" Sir Giles had said impatiently, screwing round from his writing-desk a small, brown wrinkled face toward the inspector, "yes, he came to lunch. Why not?"

"No reason at all, sir," the inspector said, "I only wanted to be sure. And when did he leave you—if you remember?"

"About half-past two," Sir Giles said. "Is that what he ought to have done? I'll say two, if you like, if it'll help you catch him. Only, if you do, you must arrange for me to see the hanging."

"If he left at half-past two, that's all I want to know," the inspector said. "Did you happen to mention to anyone that he was coming?"

"Yes," said Sir Giles, "I told the Prime Minister, the Professor of Comparative Etymology at King's College, and the cook downstairs. Why the hell do you ask me these silly questions? Do you suppose I run round telling all my friends that a loathsome little publisher's clerk is going to muck his food about at my table?"

"If you felt like that," the inspector said, holding down his anger, "I wonder you asked him to lunch."

"I asked him to lunch because I'd rather him foul my table than my time," Tumulty answered. "I had to waste an hour over him because he didn't understand a few simple things about my illustrations, and I saved it by working it in with lunch. I expect he charged overtime for it, so that he'd be two shillings to the good, one saved on his food and another extra pay. I should think he could get a woman for that one night. How much do you have to pay, policeman?"

The inspector at the moment felt merely that Sir Giles must be mad; it wasn't till hours afterwards that he became slowly convinced that the question was meant as an insult beyond reach of pardon or vengeance. At the time he stared blankly and said soberly: "I'm a married man, sir."

"You mean you get her for nothing?" Sir Giles asked. "Two can live as cheaply as one, and your extras thrown in? Optimistic, I'm afraid. Well, I'm sorry, but I have to go to the Foreign Office. Come and chat in the taxi; that's what your

The Chemist's Shop

London taxis are for. When I want a nice long talk with anyone I get in one at Westminster Abbey after lunch and tell him to go to the Nelson Column. We nearly always get there for tea. Oh, good-bye, policeman. Come again some day."

The immediate result of this conversation was to cause Colquhoun to suspect Rackstraw more grievously than before. But no amount of investigation could prove the tale of the lunch unreliable or connect him in any way with an unexplained disappearance or even with any semi-criminal attitude towards the law. He owed no money; he seemed to do nothing but work and stop at home, and his connection with Sir Giles, which was the most suspicious thing about him, was limited apparently to the production of *Sacred Vessels in Folklore*. The inspector even went the length of procuring secretly through Stephen Persimmons an advance copy of this, and reading it through, but without any result.

Another of the advance copies Mornington had sent personally to the Archdeacon, and a few days before the official publication, and some four weeks after the archidiaconal visit to the publishing house he had a letter in reply.

DEAR MR. MORNINGTON, the Archdeacon wrote, I have to thank you very much for the early copy of *Sacred Vessels* which you were good enough to send me. It is a book of great interest, so far as anything intellectual can be, and especially to a clergyman; who has, so to speak, a professional interest in anything sacred, and especially to anything which has a bearing on Christian tradition—I mean, of course, Sir Giles Tumulty's study of the possible history of the Holy Graal.

There is one point upon which I should like information if you are able to give it to me—if it is not a private matter. This article on the Graal contained, when I glanced through it in the proofs you showed me, a concluding paragraph which definitely fixed the possibility (within the limitations imposed

59

by the very nature of Sir Giles's research) of the Graal being identified with a particular chalice in a particular church. I have read the article as it now stands with the greatest care, but I cannot find any such paragraph. Could you tell me (1) whether the paragraph was in fact deleted, (2) whether, if so, the reason was any grave doubt of the identification, (3) whether it would be permissible for me to get into touch with Sir Giles Tumulty on the subject?

Please forgive me troubling you so much on a matter which has only become accidentally known to me through your kindness. I am a little ashamed of my own curiosity, but perhaps my profession excuses it in general and in particular.

I hope, if you are ever in or near Castra Parvulorum, you will make a special point of calling at the Rectory. I have one or two early editions—one of the *Ascent of Mount Carmel*—which might interest you.

Yours most sincerely,

JULIAN DAVENANT.

"Bless him," Mornington said to himself as, coiled curiously round his chair, he read the letter, "bless him and damn him! I suppose Lionel will know." He dropped the letter on his desk, and was opening another, when Stephen Persimmons came into the office. After a few sentences had been exchanged, Stephen said: "When do you go for your holidays, Mornington?"

"I was going at the end of August—for some of them, anyhow," Mornington answered—"if that fits in all right. It fitted in when I fixed it. But I'm only walking a little, so, if there's any need, I can easily alter it."

"The fact is," Stephen went on, "I've been asked to go with some people I know to the South of France at the beginning of August, and I might stop six weeks or so if things didn't call me back. But I like you to be here while I'm away."

"The beginning of August—six weeks—" Mornington murmured, "and it's the fifth of July now. Well, sir, I'll go before or after, whichever you like. Rackstraw goes next Friday, and he'll be back by the end of the month."

"Are you sure it's convenient?" Stephen asked.

"Entirely," the other said. "I shall walk as long as I feel like it, and stop when and where I feel like it. And I can walk in July as well as in September. Anyhow, I'm only taking ten days or a fortnight now. I have to go to my mother in Cornwall in October for the rest."

"Well, what about now, then?" said Stephen.

"Now, then," Mornington answered. "Or at least Friday week, shall we say? Unless, of course, I'm arrested. I feel that's always possible. Didn't I see the inspector calling on you the other day, sir?"

"You did, blast him!" Stephen broke out. "Why that wretched creature got huddled up here I can't imagine. It's killing me, Mornington, all this worry!" He got up and wandered round the office.

Behind his back his lieutenant raised surprised eyebrows. It was a nuisance, of course, but, as Stephen Persimmons had for alibi the statement of every other reputable publisher in London, this agitation seemed excessive. It might be the murder in general, but why *worry*? Stephen was always reasonably decent to the staff, but to worry over whether any of them had committed a murder seemed to point to a degree of personal interest which surprised him.

"I know," he said sympathetically. "You feel you'd like to murder the fellow just for having *been* murdered. Some people always muddle their engagements. Probably he had arranged to be done in at a tea-shop or somewhere like that—he was just that kind of fellow—and then got mixed and came here first. Has the inspector any kind of clue? The body, by now, is past inspecting."

"I don't believe he knows anything, but one can't be sure,"

Persimmons answered. "And, of course, if he does it needn't—"
He became unhappily silent.

Mornington uncoiled himself and got up. "Are you sure you wouldn't like to go away now for a week or two, sir?" he said. "It's rather knocked you over, I expect."

"No," Stephen said, drifting to the door. "No, I can't go away now. I simply can't. We'll leave it at that then." He disappeared.

"We seem to be leaving it at a very undefined that," Mornington thought to himself, as he went back to his letters. "Stephen never was what the deceased would probably have called 'brainy'. But he seems rather cloudy even for him."

Later in the day he replied to the camp of the children.

MY DEAR MR. ARCHDEACON,—The fact is that the paragraph you refer to was cut out by Sir Giles Tumulty at the last moment. This puts us in a mild fix, because I suppose technically proofs in a publisher's office are private, till the book is published. And after, for that matter. I am given to understand by the people here who have met him that he is the nearest to a compound of a malevolent hyena and an especially venomous cobra that ever appeared in London, and I shrink therefore from officially confirming your remembrance of that paragraph. But you *were* here, and you saw the proofs, and, if you could conceal the unimportant fact that we showed them to you, write to Sir Giles by all means.

This sounds as if I were proposing an immorality. But it only means that, while I can't officially say 'Write,' I am reluctant to say 'Don't write.' Your tact will no doubt discover the wise road. Personally, I hope you'll find out.

Thank you for your invitation. I may conceivably turn up one day before the month ends.

Did you have a pleasant time in Scotland?

Yours very sincerely,
K. H. MORNINGTON.

The Chemist's Shop

At the moment when this letter was being dictated Sir Giles had, in fact, a visitor from Fardles sitting with him; not the Archdeacon, but Mr. Gregory Persimmons. They were speaking in subdued tones, both of them rather greedily, as if they each wanted something from the other, and the subject of their conversation might have eluded Mornington, had he heard it, for a considerable time. When Gregory had been shown in, Sir Giles got up quickly from his table.

"Well?" he said.

Gregory came across to him, saying: "Oh, I've got it—a little more trouble than I thought, but I've got it. But I don't quite like doing anything with it. . . . In fact, I'm not quite sure what it's best to do."

Sir Giles pushed a chair towards him. "You don't think," he said. "What do you want to do?" He sat down again as he spoke, his little eager eyes fixed on the other, with a controlled but excited interest. Persimmons met them with a sly anxiety in his own.

"I want something else first," he said. "I want that address."

"Pooh," Sir Giles said, "that won't help you. Tell me more about this other thing first. Do you notice anything about it? How does it affect you?"

Gregory considered. "Not at all, I think," he said. "It's just an ordinary piece of work—with a curious smell about it sometimes."

"Smell?" Sir Giles said. "Smell? What sort of smell?"

"Well," Persimmons answered, "it's more like ammonia than anything else; a sort of pungency. But I only notice it sometimes."

"I knew a cannibal chief in Nigeria who said the same thing," Sir Giles said musingly. "Not about that, of course, and not ammonia. It was a traditional taboo of the tribe—the dried head of a witch-doctor that was supposed to be a good omen to his people. He said it smelt like the fire that burned

63

the uneaten offal of their enemies. Curious—the same notion of cleansing."

Gregory sniggered. "It'll take Him a good deal of ammonia to clean things out," he said. "But it'd be like Him to use ammonia and the Bible and that kind of thing."

Sir Giles switched back to the subject. "And what are you going to do with it?" he asked alertly.

Gregory eyed him. "Never mind," he said. "Or, rather, why do you want to know?"

"Because I like knowing these things," Sir Giles answered. "After all, I saved it for you when you asked me, on condition that you told me about your adventures, or let me see them for myself. You're going mad, you know, Persimmons, and I like watching you."

"Mad?" Gregory said, with another snigger. "You don't go mad this way. People like my wife go mad, and Stephen. But I've got something that doesn't go mad. I'm getting everything *so*." He stretched out both arms and pressed them downwards with an immense gesture of weight, as if pushing the universe before and below him. "But I want the ointment."

"Better leave it alone," Sir Giles said tantalizingly. "It's tricky stuff, Persimmons. A Jew in Beyrout tried it and didn't get back. Filthy beast he looked, all naked and screaming that he couldn't find his way. That was four years ago, and he's screaming the same thing still, unless he's dead. And there was another fellow in Valparaiso who got too far to be heard screaming; he died pretty soon, because he'd forgotten even how to eat and drink. They tried forcible feeding, I fancy, but it wasn't a success: he was just continually sick. Better leave it alone, Persimmons."

"I tell you I'm perfectly safe," Gregory said. "You promised, Tumulty, you promised."

"My lord God," Sir Giles said, "what does that matter? I don't care whether I promised or not; I don't care whether you want it or not; I only wonder whether I shall get more satisfaction from——" He broke off. "All right," he said, "I'll give you the address—94, Lord Mayor Street, Finchley Road. Somewhere near Tally Ho Corner, I think. Quite respectable and all that. The man in Valparaiso was a solicitor. It's in the middle classes one finds these things easiest. The lower classes haven't got the money or the time or the intelligence, and the upper classes haven't got the power or intelligence."

Gregory was writing the address down, nodding to himself as he did so; then he looked at a clock, which stood on the writing-table, pleasantly clutched in a dried black hand set in gold. "I shall have time to-day," he said. "I'll go at once. I suppose he'll sell it me? Yes, of course he will, I can see to that."

"It'll save you some time and energy," Sir Giles said, "if you mention me. He's a Greek of sorts—I've forgotten his name. But he doesn't keep tons of it, you know. Now, look here, Persimmons. This is two things you have got out of me, and I've had nothing in return. You'd better ask me down to wherever you hatch gargoyles. I can't come till after Monday because I'm speaking at University College then. I'll come next Wednesday. What's the station? Fardles? Send me a card to tell me the best afternoon train and have it met."

Gregory promised in general terms to do this, and as quickly as he could got away. An hour after he had hunted out Lord Mayor Street.

It was not actually quite so respectable as Sir Giles had given him to understand. It had been once, no doubt, and was now half-way to another kind of respectability, being in the disreputable valley between two heights of decency. There were a sufficient number of sufficiently dirty children playing in the road to destroy privacy without achieving publicity: squalor was leering from the windows and not yet contending frankly and vainly with grossness. It was one of those sudden terraces of slime which hang over the pit of hell, and for which beastliness is too dignified a name. But the slime was still only oozing over it, and a thin cloud of musty pretence expanded over the depths below.

At one end of the road three shops huddled together in the thickest slime; a grocer's at the corner, flying the last standard of respectability in an appeal towards the Finchley Road some couple of yards away—like Roland's horn crying to Charlemagne. At the far end of the street a public house signalized the gathering of another code of decency and morals which might in time transform the intervening decay. Next to the grocer's was a sweet-shop, on which the dingy white letters ADBU OC A appeared like a charm, and whose window displayed bars of chocolate even more degradingly sensual than the ordinary kind. Next to this was the last shop, a chemist's. Its window had apparently been broken some time since and very badly mended with glass which must have been dirty when it was made, suggesting a kind of hypostatic union between clearness and dinginess. Nor, since the breakage, had the occupant, it seemed, troubled to re-dress the window; a few packets of soap and tooth-paste masked their own purpose by their appearance. Persimmons pushed open the door and, first looking to see that the shop was empty, went quietly in.

A young man was lounging behind the counter, but he did no more than look indolently at his customer. Persimmons tried to close the door and failed, until the other said "Push it at the bottom with your foot," when he succeeded, for the door shut with an unexpected crash. Gregory came to the counter and looked at the shopman. He might be Greek, as Sir Giles had said, he might be anything, and the name over the door had been indecipherable. The two looked at one another silently.

At last Persimmons said: "You keep some rather out of the way drugs and things, don't you?"

The other answered wearily: "Out of the way? I don't know what you mean—out of the way? Nothing's out of the way."

"Out of the ordinary way," Gregory said quickly and softly, "the way everyone goes."

"They go nowhere," the Greek said.

"But I go," Persimmons answered, with the same swiftness as before. "You have something for me."

"What I have is for buyers," the other said, "all I have is for buyers. What do you want and what will you pay?"

"I think I have paid a price," Gregory said, "but what more you ask you shall have."

"Who sent you here?" the Greek asked.

"Sir Giles Tumulty," said Gregory, "and others. But the others I cannot name. They say"—his voice began to tremble —"that you have an ointment."

"I have many precious things." The answer came out of an entire weariness which seemed to take from the adjective all its meaning. "But some of them are not for sale except to buyers."

"I have bought everything." Gregory leaned forward. "The time has come for me to receive."

Still the other made no movement. "The ointment is rich and scarce and strange," he said. "How do I know that you are worth a gift? And what will my master say if I mistake?"

"I cannot prove myself to you," Gregory answered. "That I know of it—is not that enough?"

"It is not enough," the other said. "But I have a friendship for all who are in the way. And priceless things are without any price. If you are not worth the gift, the gift is worth nothing to you. Have you ever used the ointment?"

"Never," Gregory said; "but it is time, I am sure it is time."

"You think so, do you?" the Greek said slowly. "There comes a time when there is nothing left but time—nothing. Take it if you like."

Still with the minimum of movement, he put out his hand, opened a drawer in the counter, and pushed on to it a little cardboard box, rather greasy and dented here and there.

"Take it," he said. "It will only give you a headache if you are not in the way."

Gregory caught up the box and hesitated. "Do you want money?" he asked.

"It is a gift, but not a gift," the other answered. "Give me what you will for a sign."

Gregory put some silver on the counter and backed toward the door. But the same difficulty that had met him in closing it now held it fast. He pulled and pushed and struggled with it, and the Greek watched him with a faint smile. Outside it had begun to rain.

Chapter Six

THE SABBATH

"I met Mr. Persimmons in the village to-day," Mr. Batesby said to the Archdeacon. "He asked after you very pleasantly, although he's sent every day to inquire. It was he that saw you lying in the road, you know, and brought you here in his car. It must be a great thing for you to have a sympathetic neighbour at the big house; there's so often friction in these small parishes."

"Yes," the Archdeacon said.

"We had quite a long chat," the other went on. "He isn't exactly a Christian, unfortunately, but he has a great admiration for the Church. He thinks it's doing a wonderful work— especially in education. He takes a great interest in education; he calls it the star of the future. He thinks morals are more important than dogma, and of course I agree with him."

"Did you say 'of course I agree' or 'of course I agreed'?" the Archdeacon asked. "Or both?"

"I mean I thought the same thing," Mr. Batesby explained. He had noticed a certain denseness in the Archdeacon on other occasions. "Conduct is much the biggest thing in life, I feel. 'He can't be wrong whose life is for the best; we needs must love the higher when we see Him.' And he gave me five pounds towards the Sunday School Fund."

"There isn't," the Archdeacon said, slightly roused, "a Sunday School Fund at Fardles."

"Oh, well!" Mr. Batesby considered. "I daresay he'd be willing for it to go to almost anything *active*. He was very keen, and I agr—thought just the same, on getting things *done*. He thinks that the Church ought to be a means of progress. He

69

quoted something about not going to sleep till we found a pleasant Jerusalem in the green land of England. I was greatly struck. An idealist, that's what I should call him. England needs idealists to-day."

"I think we had better return the money," the Archdeacon said. "If he isn't a Christian——"

"Oh, but he is," Mr. Batesby protested. "In effect, that is. He thinks Christ was the second greatest man the earth has produced."

"Who was the first?" the Archdeacon asked.

Mr. Batesby paused again for a moment. "Do you know, I forgot to ask?" he said. "But it shows a sympathetic spirit, doesn't it? After all, the second greatest——! That goes a long way. Little children, love one another—if five pounds helps us to teach them that in the schools. I'm sure mine want a complete new set of Bible pictures."

There was a pause. The two priests were sitting after dinner in the garden of the Rectory. The Archdeacon, with inner thoughts for meditation, was devoting a superficial mind to Mr. Batesby, who on his side was devoting his energies to providing his host with cheerful conversation. The Archdeacon knew this, and knew too that his guest and substitute would rather have been talking about his own views on the ornaments rubric than about the parishioners. He wished he would. He was feeling rather tired, and it was an effort to pay attention to anything which he did not know by heart. Mr. Batesby's ecclesiastical views he did—and thought them incredibly silly —but he thought his own were probably that too. One had views for convenience' sake, but how anyone could think they mattered. Except, of course, that even silly views . . .

A car went by on the road and a hand was waved from it. To Gregory Persimmons the sight of the two priests was infinitely pleasurable. He had met them both and summed them up. He could, he felt, knock the Archdeacon on the head whenever he chose, and the other hadn't got a head to be knocked. It was all very pleasant and satisfactory. There had been a moment, a few days ago, in that little shop when he couldn't get out, and there seemed suddenly no reason why he should get out, as if he had been utterly and finally betrayed into being there for ever—he had felt almost in a panic. He had known that feeling once or twice before, at odd times; but there was no need to recall it now. To-night, to-night, something else was to happen. To-night he would know what it all was of which he had read in his books, and heard—heard from people who had funnily come into his life and then disappeared. Long ago, as a boy, he remembered reading about the Sabbath, but he had been told that it wasn't true. His father had been a Victorian Rationalist. The Archdeacon, he thought, was exceedingly Victorian too. His heart beating in an exalted anticipation, he drove on to Cully.

Mr. Batesby was asleep that night, and the Archdeacon was, in a Victorian way, engaged in his prayers, when Gregory Persimmons stood up alone in his room. It was a little after midnight, and, as he glanced out of the window, he saw a clear sky with a few stars and the full moon contemplating him. Slowly, very slowly, he undressed, looking forward to he knew not what, and then—being entirely naked—he took from a table the small greasy box of ointment and opened it. It was a pinkish ointment, very much the colour of the skin, and at first he thought it had no smell. But in a few minutes, as it lay exposed to the air, there arose from it a faint odour which grew stronger, and presently filled the whole room, not overpoweringly, but with a convenient and irresistible assurance. He paused for a moment, inhaling it, and finding in it the promise of some complete decay. It brought to him an assurance of his own temporal achievement of his power to enter into those lives which he touched and twist them out of their security into a sliding destruction. Five pounds here, a clever jeer there—it was all easy. Everyone had some security, and he had only to be patient to find and destroy it. His father, when he had grown old and had had a good deal of trouble, had been inclined to wonder whether there was anything in religion. And they had talked of it; he remembered those talks. He had—it had been his first real experiment—he had suggested very carefully and delicately, to that senile and uneasy mind, that there probably was a God, but a God of terrible jealousy; God had driven Judas, who betrayed Him, to hang himself; and driven the Jews who denied Him to exile in all lands. And Peter, his father had said, Peter was forgiven. He had stood thinking of that, and then had hesitated that, yes, no doubt Peter was forgiven, unless God had taken a terrible revenge and used Peter to set up all that mystery of evil which was Antichrist and Torquemada and Smithfield and the Roman See. Before the carefully sketched picture of an infinite, absorbing, and mocking vengeance, his father had shivered and grown silent. And had thereafter died, trying not to believe in God lest he should know himself damned.

Gregory smiled, and touched the ointment with his fingers. It seemed almost to suck itself upward round them as he did so. He disengaged his fingers and began the anointing. From the feet upwards in prolonged and rhythmic movements his hands moved backward and forward over his skin, he bowed and rose again, and again. The inclinations gradually ceased as the anointing hands grew higher—around the knees, the hips, the breast. Against his body the pink smears showed brightly for a moment, and then were mingled with and lost in the natural colour of the flesh. All the while his voice kept up a slow crooning, to the sound of which he moved, pronouncing as in an incantation of rounded and liquid syllables what seemed hierarchic titles. He touched his temples and his forehead with both hands, and so for a moment stayed.

His voice grew deeper and charged with more intensity, though the sound was not noticeably quicker, as he began the second anointing. But now it was only the chosen parts that he touched—the soles of the feet, the palms of the hands, the inner side of the fingers, the ears and eyelids, the environs of nose and mouth, the secret organs. Over all these again and again he moved his hands, and again ceased and paused, and the intensity died from his voice.

For the third anointing was purely ritual. He marked various figures upon his body—a cross upon either sole, a cross inverted from brow to foot, and over all his form the pentagon reversed of magic. While he did so his voice rose in a solemn chant which entered with a strange power through those anointed ears, and flowed through his body as did the new faint light that seemed to shine through his closed eyelids. Light and sound were married in premonitions of approaching experience; his voice quivered upon the air and stopped. Then with an effort he moved uncertainly towards his bed, and stretched himself on it, his face towards the closed window and the enlarging moon. Silent and grotesque he lay, and the secret processes of the night began.

If it had been possible for any stranger to enter that locked room in the middle of his journeying they would have found his body lying there still. By no broomstick flight over the lanes of England did Gregory Persimmons attend the Witches' Sabbath, nor did he dance with other sorcerers upon some blasted heath before a goat-headed manifestation of the Accursed. But scattered far over the face of the earth, though not so far in the swiftness of interior passage, those abandoned spirits answered one another that night; and That beyond them (which some have held to be but the precipitation and tendency of their own natures, and others for the equal and perpetual co-inheritor of power and immortality with Good) —That beyond them felt them and shook and replied, sustained and nourished and controlled.

After Gregory had laid himself upon the bed he made the usual attempt at excluding from the attention all his surroundings. But to-night the powerful ointment worked so swiftly upon him, stealing through all his flesh with a delicious

venom and writhing itself into his blood and heart, that he
had scarcely come to rest before the world was shut out. He
was being made one with something beyond his consciousness; he accepted the union in a deep sigh of pleasure.

When it had approached a climax it ceased suddenly.
There passed through him a sense of lightness and airy
motion; his body seemed to float upwards, so unconscious
had it become of the bed on which it rested. He knew now
that he must begin to exercise his own intention, and in a
depth beyond thought he did so. He commanded and directed
himself towards the central power which awaited him.
Images floated past him; for his mind, rising as it were out
of the faintness which had overcome it, now began to change
his experiences into such sounds and shapes as it knew; so
that he at once experienced and expressed experience to
himself intellectually, and could not generally separate the
two. At this beginning, for example, as he lay given up to
that sensation of swift and easy motion towards some still
hidden moment of exquisite and destructive delight, it seemed
to him that at a great distance he heard faint and lovely
voices, speaking to him or to each other, and that out of
him in turn went a single note of answering glee.

And now he was descending; lower and lower, into a
darker and more heavy atmosphere. His intention checked
his flight, and it declined almost into stillness; night was about
him, and more than night, a heaviness which was like that
felt in a crowd, a pressure and intent expectation of relief.
As to the mind of a man in prayer might come sudden
reminders of great sanctities in other places and other periods,
so now to him came the consciousness, not in detail, but as
achievements, of far-off masteries of things, multitudinous
dedications consummating themselves in That which was
already on its way. But that his body was held in a trance
by the effect of the ointment, the smell of which had long
since become part of his apprehension, he would have turned

his head one way or the other to see or speak to those unseen companions.

Suddenly, as in an excited crowd a man may one minute be speaking and shouting to those near him, and the next, part of the general movement directed and controlled by that to which he contributes, there rose within him the sense of a vast and rapid flow, of which he was part, rushing and palpitating with desire. He desired—the heat about his heart grew stronger—to give himself out, to be one with something that should submit to him and from which he should yet draw nourishment; but something beyond imagination, stupendous. He was hungry—but not for food; he was thirsty —but not for drink; he was filled with passion—but not for flesh. He expanded in the rush of an ancient desire; he longed to be married to the whole universe for a bride. His father appeared before him, senile and shivering; his wife, bewildered and broken; his son, harassed and distressed. These were his marriages, these his bridals. The bridal dance was beginning; they and he and innumerable others were moving to the wild rhythm of that aboriginal longing. Beneath all the little cares and whims of mankind the tides of that ocean swung, and those who had harnessed them and those who had been destroyed by them were mingled in one victorious catastrophe. His spirit was dancing with his peers, and yet still something in his being held back and was not melted.

There was something—from his depths he cried to his mortal mind to recall it and pass on the message—some final thing that was needed still; some offering by which he might pierce beyond this black drunkenness and achieve a higher reward. What was the sacrifice, what the oblation that was greater than the wandering and unhappy souls whose ruin he had achieved? Heat as from an immense pyre beat upon him, beat upon him with a demand for something more; he absorbed it, and yet, his ignorance striking him with fear, shrunk from its ardent passions. It was not heat only, it was sound also, a rising tumult, acclamation of shrieking voices, thunder of terrible approach. It came, it came, ecstasy of perfect mastery, marriage in hell, he who was Satan wedded to that beside which was Satan. And yet one little thing was needed and he had it not—he was an outcast for want of that one thing. He forced his interior mind to stillness for a moment only, and in that moment recollection came.

From the shadowy and forgotten world the memory of the child Adrian floated into him, and he knew that this was what was needed. All gods had their missionaries, and this god also who was himself and not himself demanded neophytes. Deeply into himself he drew that memory; he gathered up its freshness and offered it to the secret and infernal powers. Adrian was the desirable sacrifice, an unknowing initiate, a fated candidate. To this purpose the man lying still and silent on the bed, or caught up before some vast interior throne where the masters and husbands and possessors of the universe danced and saw immortal life decay before their subtle power, dedicated himself. The wraith of the child drifted into the midst of the dance, and at the moment when Adrian far away in London stirred in his sleep with a moan a like moan broke out in another chamber. For the last experience was upon the accepted devotee; there passed through him a wave of intense cold, and in every chosen spot where the ointment had been twice applied the cold concentrated and increased. Nailed, as it were, through feet and hands and head and genitals, he passed utterly into a pang that was an ecstasy beyond his dreams. He was divorced now from the universe; he was one with a rejection of all courteous and lovely things; by the oblation of the child he was made one with that which is beyond childhood and age and time—the reflection and negation of the eternity of God. He existed supernaturally, and in Hell. . . .

When the dissolution of this union and the return began, he knew it as an overwhelming storm. Heat and cold, the

interior and exterior world, images and wraiths, sounds and
odours, warred together within him. Chaos broke upon him;
he felt himself whirled away into an infinite desolation of
anarchy. He strove to concentrate, now on that which was
within, now on some detail of the room which was already
spectrally apparent to him; but fast as he did so it was gone.
Panic seized him; he would have screamed, but to scream
would be to be lost. And then again the image of Adrian
floated before him, and he knew that much was yet to be
done. With that image in his heart, he rose slowly and through
many mists to the surface of consciousness, and as it faded
gradually to a name and a thought he knew that the Sabbath
was over and the return accomplished.

.   .   .

"He's very restless," Barbara said to Lionel. "I wonder if
the scone upset him. There, darling, there!"

"He's probably dreaming of going away," Lionel answered
softly. "I hope he won't take a dislike to the place or Persimmons or anything."

"Hush, sweetheart," Barbara murmured. "All's well. All's
well."

Chapter Seven

ADRIAN

The Archdeacon, as he considered matters, found himself confronted by several dilemmas. As, for example: (1) Was the stolen chalice the Holy Graal or not? (2) Had it or had it not been taken from him on the supposition that it was? (3) Had Mr. Persimmons anything to do with the supposition or with the removal? (4) Ought he or ought he not to take an active interest in retrieving it? (5) If so, what steps ought he to take?

He felt that, so far as the property itself was concerned, he was very willing to let it slip—Graal or no Graal. But he admitted that, if by any ridiculous chance Mr. Persimmons had had to do with its removal, he should have liked the suspicions he already entertained to be clear. On the other hand, it was impossible to call in the police; he had a strong objection to using the forces of the State to recover property. Besides, the whole thing would then be likely to become public.

He was revolving these things in his mind as he strolled down the village one evening in the week after the Rackstraws had occupied the cottage on the other side of Cully. Except that Barbara, in a rush of grateful devotion, had come to the early Eucharist on the Sunday morning, and he had noticed her as a stranger, the Archdeacon knew nothing of their arrival. He had been diplomatically manoeuvred by Mr. Batesby into inviting him to stop another week or two. Mr. Batesby thought the Archdeacon ought to go for a holiday; the Archdeacon thought that he would not trouble at present. For he felt curiously reluctant to leave the neighbourhood of Cully and perhaps of the Graal.

Adrian

As he came to the village he heard a voice calling him and looked up. Coming towards him was Gregory Persimmons, with a stranger. Gregory waved his hand again as they came up.

"My dear Archdeacon," he said, shaking hands warmly, "I'm delighted to see you about again. Quite recovered, I hope? You ought to go away for a few weeks."

"I owe you many thanks," the Archdeacon answered politely, "not only for rescuing me from the road and taking me to the Rectory, but for so kindly and so often inquiring after me. It has really been very thoughtful of you." He substituted "thoughtful" for "kind" at the last minute with an eye on truth.

"Not a bit, not a bit," Persimmons said. "So glad you're better. Have you met Sir Giles Tumulty by any chance? Sir Giles, 'meet' the Archdeacon of Fardles, as they say elsewhere."

"I hear you have been set on by tramps," Sir Giles said, as they shook hands. "Many about here?"

As the Archdeacon began to reply, Barbara Rackstraw came along the road with Adrian on their way home, and Persimmons, with a word of apology, skipped aside to meet them. The Archdeacon slurred over the subject of tramps, and proceeded casually: "I have just been reading your last book, Sir Giles. Most interesting." He became indefinitely more pompous, a slight clericalism seemed to increase in him, "But, you know, that article on the Graal—most interesting, most interesting. And you think, er—m'm, you think *true*?"

"True?" Sir Giles said, "true? What do you mean—true? It's an historical study. You might as well ask whether a book on the Casket Letters was true."

"Umph, yes," the Archdeacon answered, exuding ecclesiasticism. "To be sure, yes. Quite, quite. But, Sir Giles, as we happen to have met so pleasantly, I have a confession—yes, a confession to make, and a question to ask. You'll forgive me both, I'm sure."

Adrian

Sir Giles in unconcealed and intense boredom stared at the road. Persimmons, Adrian's hand in his, was walking slowly from them, chatting to Barbara. The Archdeacon went on talking, but the next thing that Sir Giles really heard was —"and it seemed most interesting. But it was my fault entirely, only, as I've kept it *quite* secret, I hope you won't mind. And, if you could tell me—in strict confidence, affecting me as it does—why you cut that last paragraph out, it would of course be a very generous act on your part, though I quite realize I have no right to ask it."

His voice ceased, but by this time Sir Giles was alert. The last paragraph cut out? There was only one last paragraph he had cut out lately. And how did this country clergyman know? His fault entirely, was it? He shook a reluctant head at the Archdeacon. "I'm rather sorry you've seen it," he said. "But there's no harm done, of course. After all, being your church, you have a kind of claim! But, as far as cutting it out——" He raised his voice. "Persimmons! Persimmons!"

The Archdeacon threw a hand out. "Sir Giles, Sir Giles, he is talking to a lady."

"Lady be damned," said Sir Giles. "A country wench, I suppose, or a county wench—it doesn't signify, anyhow. Persimmons!"

Gregory made his farewells to Barbara and Adrian near a turn in the road and returned. "Yes?" he said. "Why such particular excitement?"

Sir Giles grinned. "What do you think?" he said. "The Archdeacon saw that paragraph you made me cut out. So he knew it was his church the Graal was in. And it was Persimmons," he added to the priest, "who wanted it taken out. He pretended the evidence wasn't good enough, but that was all nonsense. Evidence good enough for anybody."

From the turn in the road Adrian shouted a final good-bye, and Gregory, remembering his work, turned and waved before he answered. Then he smiled at the Archdeacon, who was looking at him also with a smile. Sir Giles grinned happily, and a bicyclist who passed at the moment reflected bitterly on the easy and joyous time which such people had in the world.

"Dear me," the Archdeacon said. "And was that the cause of the needy mission church, Mr. Persimmons?"

"Well," Persimmons said, "I'm afraid it was. I have been something of a collector in my time, and—once I understood from Sir Giles what your old chalice might be—I couldn't resist it."

"It must be a wonderful thing to be a collector," the Archdeacon answered gravely. "Apparently you may be seized any time with a passion for anything. Have you a large collection of chalices, Mr. Persimmons?"

"None at all, since I didn't get *that*," Gregory answered. "To think it's in the hands of some thief now, or a pawnbroker perhaps. Have you put the police on the track yet, Archdeacon?"

"No," the Archdeacon answered. "I don't think the police would find it. The police sergeant here believes in letting his children run more or less wild, and I feel sure he wouldn't understand my clues. Well, good-day, Sir Giles. Good-day, Mr. Persimmons."

"Oh, but look here," Gregory said, "don't go yet. Come up to Cully and have a look at some of my things. You don't bear malice, I'm sure, since I didn't succeed in cheating you."

"I will come with pleasure," the Archdeacon said. "Collections are always so delightful, don't you think? All things from all men, so to speak." And, half under his breath, as they turned towards Cully, he sang to himself, "Oh, give thanks unto the Lord, for He is gracious; for His mercy endureth for ever."

"I beg your pardon?" Gregory asked at the same moment that Sir Giles said, "Eh?"

"Nothing, nothing," the Archdeacon said hastily. "Merely an improvisation. The fine weather, I suppose." He almost smirked at the others, with gaiety in his heart and curving his usually sedate lips. Gregory remembered the way in which the priest's monologue had carried him half over the county, and began almost seriously to consider whether he were not half-witted. Sir Giles, on the other hand, began to feel more interest than hitherto. He glanced aside at Gregory, caught his slight air of bewilderment, and grinned to himself. It appeared that his country visit might be of even more interest than he supposed. He always sought out—at home and abroad—these unusual extremists in religion; they wandered in a borderland, whatever their creed, of metaphysics, mysticism, and insanity which was a peculiarly fascinating spectacle. He had himself an utter disbelief in God and devil, but he found these anthropomorphic conceptions interesting, and to push or delay any devotee upon the path was entertainment to a mind too swiftly bored. The existence and transmission of the magical ointment had become gradually known to him during his wanderings. Of its elements and concoction he knew little; they seemed to be a professional mystery reserved to some remoter circle than he had yet touched. But the semi-delirium which it induced in expectant minds was undoubted, and whenever chance made him acquainted with suitable subjects and he could, without too much trouble to himself, introduce the method, he made haste to do so. Subjects were infrequent; it required a particularly urgent and sadistic nature; he was not at all sure that Persimmons was strong enough. However, it was done now, and he must gain what satisfaction he could from the result.

Of the Graal he thought similarly. That the chalice of Fardles was the Graal he had little doubt; the evidence was circumstantial, but good. He regretted only that the process of time had prevented him from studying its origin, its first user, and his circle, at close quarters. "All martyrs are masochists," he thought, "but crucifixion is a violent form." Yet, given in the Jew's mind the delusion that he loved the world, what else was the Passion but masochism? And the passion of the communicant was, of course, a corresponding sadism. Religion was bound to be one of the two; in extreme cases both. The question was, which was the Archdeacon?

The Archdeacon, ignorant that this question was being asked, strolled happily on between his two acquaintances, and with them turned up the drive to Cully. He promised himself opportunities of making clear to Persimmons that he guessed very clearly who had the Graal. He wished that in the early stages of his recovery he had not let out to Mr. Batesby that he had been robbed of the chalice. Mr. Batesby had, of course, passed the information on. If only it were still a secret! But why should anyone want it so much, he wondered. Collecting—well, collecting perhaps.

"Do you collect anything in particular, Mr. Persimmons?" he asked. "Or merely any unconsidered trifles?"

"I have a few interesting old books," Gregory said. "And a few old vestments and so on. I once took an interest in ecclesiology. But of late I have rather concentrated on old Chinese work—masks, for instance."

"Masks are always interesting," the Archdeacon said. "The Chinese mask, I think, has no beard?"

"None of mine have—long mustachios, but no beard," answered Gregory.

"False beards," the Archdeacon went on, "are never really satisfactory. A few weeks ago a man called to see me in what I suspect to have been a false beard, I can't imagine why. It seems such a curious thing to wear."

"I believe that many priesthoods make it a part of their convention not to wear beards," Gregory said conversationally. "Now what is the reason of that?"

"Obvious enough," Sir Giles put in. "They have dedicated their manhood to the god—they no longer possess virility. They are feminine to the god and dead to the world. Every priest is a kind of a corpse-woman . . . if you'll excuse me," he added after a pause to the Archdeacon, who said handsomely: "I wish it were more largely true."

"Not *every* priest," Persimmons said. "There are virile religions, adorations of power and strength."

"To adore strength is to confess weakness," Sir Giles said. "To *be* power is *not* to adore it. The very weakest only dream of being powerful. Look at the mystics."

"Don't, this evening," Gregory said to the Archdeacon, laughing. "Come in and look at some of my treasures."

Cully was a large, rambling house, with "the latest modern improvements". Gregory took his companions up a very fine staircase into a gallery from which his own rooms opened out. In the hall itself were a few noticeable things—a suit of armour, a Greek head, a curious box or two from the Minoan excavations, a cabinet of old china. The gallery was hung with the Chinese masks of which Gregory had spoken, and, having examined them on their way, the visitors were brought at last into their host's sitting-room. It was lined with books, and contained several cabinets and cases; a few prints hung on the walls.

"I suppose," Sir Giles said, glancing round him, "if you had succeeded in cheating the Archdeacon out of the Graal, you'd have kept it in here."

"Here or hereabouts," Gregory said. "The trouble is that in the alterations which earlier inhabitants of the house made the old chapel was converted, at least the upper part of it, into these rooms—my sitting-room, my bedroom, my bathroom, and so on. So far as I can understand, the bathroom— or what is almost the bathroom—is just over where the altar stood; so that to restore the chalice to its most suitable position would be almost impossible."

"As a matter of manners," the Archdeacon admitted, "perhaps. But surely not more so than achieving it—if I may say so—by throwing dust in the eyes of its keeper. No, I don't speak personally, Mr. Persimmons; I allude only to an example of comparative morals."

"What upsets the comparison," Sir Giles said, "is that in the one case you have a strong personal lust and action deflected in consequence. But in the second action is—comparatively—free."

"I shouldn't have thought that any action was freer than any other," the Archdeacon said as he followed Gregory across the room. "Man is free to know his destiny, but not free to evade his destiny."

"But he can choose his destiny," Gregory answered, taking a book from the shelves. "He may decide what star or what god he will follow."

"If you spell destiny and god with capital letters—no," the Archdeacon said. "All destinies and all gods bring him to One, but he chooses how to know *Him*."

"He may defy and deny him for ever," Gregory said, with a gesture.

"You can defy and deny the air you breathe or the water you drink," the Archdeacon answered comfortably. "But if you do you die. The difference in the parallels is that in the other case, though you come nearer and nearer to it, you never quite die. Almost—you are in the death-agony—but never quite."

Sir Giles interrupted the discussion. "I'm going to revise my last Monday's lecture," he said. "I know the orthodox creed and the orthodox revolt by heart. I don't quite know how the Archdeacon would put it, but I know your *apologia* inside out, Persimmons. I heard it put very well by a wealthy Persian once. I've got a note of it somewhere. What time do you dine in this bloody hole of yours?" he threw over his shoulder as he went towards the door.

"Half-past seven," Gregory called, and turned back to exhibit more of his possessions. These now were rare books, early editions, and bibliographical curiosities in which the Archdeacon took a definite and even specialized interest. The two bent over volume after volume, confirming and commenting, their earlier hostility quiescent, and a pleasant sense of intellectual intimacy established. After the examination had gone on for some time Gregory took from a drawer a morocco case in which was a thin square pamphlet. He drew it out and held it towards the priest. "Now this," he said, "may interest you. Look at the initials."

The Archdeacon took it carefully. It was a copy of the old pre-Shakespearean *King Leir*, stained and frayed. But on the front was scrawled towards the top and just against the title the two letters "W.S." and just under them in a precise, careful hand "J.M."

"Good heavens!" the Archdeacon exclaimed. "Do you mean——?"

"Ah, that's the point," Gregory said. "Is it or isn't it? There's very little doubt of the J.M. I've compared it with the King's College MS., and it's exact. But the W.S. is another matter. One daren't believe it! Alone—perhaps, but both together! And yet, why not? After all, it's very likely Shakespeare didn't take all his books back to Stratford, especially when he'd written a better play himself. And he may have known Milton the scrivener. *We* don't know."

There was a soft tap at the door. "Come in," Gregory called, and the door opened to show a man standing on the threshold.

"Excuse me, sir," he said, "but you're wanted on the telephone. A Mr. Adrian, I understood, sir."

"Damn!" Gregory said. "I forgot I told him to ring me up. It's a child staying near here," he went on, "who was frightfully interested in the telephone, so . . . And the telephone's in the hall."

"Please, please," the Archdeacon said. "Don't disappoint him, I shall be quite happy here." His eyes were on the books on the table. But so were Gregory's. He had heard and seen the interest the Archdeacon felt, and one or two of these treasures were small, compact things. Yet to disappoint Adrian might throw him back there. He moved to the door and caught the arm of the man who stood there.

"Ludding," he whispered, "keep your eye on him. Don't let him put anything in his pocket. Do something about the room till I get back."

"He may recognize me, sir," the man said doubtfully.

"Then look through the crack in the door, but watch him whatever you do. I shall only be two or three minutes." He went swiftly along the gallery and down the stairs, and Ludding softly manipulated the door till he was able to take in the leaning figure at the table.

The Archdeacon's eyes were on the books, but his attention was on the gallery. He heard Persimmons go, guessed the other was watching, and leaned still more awkwardly forward. Then suddenly he made a grotesque noise, dragged out his handkerchief, put it to his mouth, and rushed out of the room. Ludding, leaping back from the door as he came, received him with a stare.

"I'm going to be sick," the Archdeacon gurgled, leaning forward. "Where's the . . . Ouch!" He ended with a convulsive choke.

"Here, sir." Ludding ran and threw open a door. The Archdeacon shot by him, banged it, looked round. In a corner behind the door the Graal lay on its side. He caught it up and considered, looking at the window. For him to carry it off, he recognized, was impossible; he would be knocked on the head again before he got home, if he ever did get home. There were only two possibilities, to leave it where it was or to throw it out of the window. He made a loud, hideous noise for Ludding's benefit and peered out.

Terrace and lawns below, grounds and plantations beyond, but all the Cully domain. Could he by any chance recover it if he threw it out? But Persimmons would be bound to guess what had happened. He would search too, with the advantages all on his side. The Archdeacon preferred to keep the advantages and leave the Graal. After all, he would know and the other wouldn't. Certainty and uncertainty—certainty for him.

"Ouch," he said loudly, laid down the chalice where he had found it, and said in his heart: "Fair sweet Destiny, draw all men to the most happy knowledge of Thee." He leant against the wall for a minute till he heard a soft whispering outside, then he pulled the chain loudly, opened the door, and came rather staggeringly out. As he did so, Ludding slipped past him into the little room.

"My dear Archdeacon!" Gregory cried sympathetically. "I'm so sorry." But his eyes went hurrying past the other, after Ludding, and for the moment while the servant was absent he stood between his guest and the stairs. Ludding was out almost immediately, and behind the priest's back nodded at his master. Gregory, with a little sigh, looked directly at the Archdeacon, who looked as sorry for himself as his inexperience could contrive.

"It's the screwing myself up," he said faintly. "It's nothing; my stomach's a weak thing, Mr. Persimmons. But I think perhaps I had better be getting home."

"Bring the car round, Ludding," Gregory said. "Yes, I insist. Are you sure you won't stop here a little while?"

"No, really, really," the Archdeacon said, his reluctance sounding like weakness. "I'll just get out into the air."

"Do," Gregory exclaimed. "Take my arm." And with murmurs and distressed ejaculations and gentle protests the two dropped to the hall.

It was later in the evening, when dinner was over and the two were alone, that Gregory told Sir Giles of the incident.

"It may have been true," he said doubtfully, "but I didn't quite like it. But he hadn't touched the Cup. I went back to see."

"He'll know it's there," Sir Giles explained.

"He may know it as much as he likes," Gregory answered. "I'll get a whole pedigree for that Cup. Stephen gave it to me, I think. It's his word against half a dozen I can arrange for, if he makes a fuss. And a clergyman accusing his Good Samaritan of theft because he's got a chalice which the clergyman, after a knock on the head, thinks he recognizes. Oh, no, Tumulty, it wouldn't do."

"What should you have done if he'd taken it?" Sir Giles asked.

"Taken it back. I saw that when I was coming upstairs after that beastly baby had been taken away from the telephone," Gregory said spitefully. "Violence—real violence—wouldn't have been necessary. Taken it back and written to the Chief Constable."

"Who'd have wanted it traced, probably," said Sir Giles. "And would have found out about that damned book. Who was the accursed imbecile who let him see it?"

"Some fool at my son's," Gregory said. "But I'll have the pedigree all right. Don't worry, Tumulty."

"Don't worry!" Sir Giles cried. "Who the hell are you talking to, Persimmons? Don't worry! Me worry over your bastard murders, indeed. The thing that'll keep you safe is that no-one with more brains than a gutter-bred snipe like that Archdeacon would think your collection of middle-class platitudes worth adding to. Chinese masks—you might be a Jew financier. And, anyhow, what do you want to do with the thing?"

"Ah, now that's important," Gregory said. "I didn't quite know at first, but I do now. I'm going to talk to the child."

"Ungh?" Sir Giles asked.

"Say it's what we think it is, it's been as near the other

centre as anything in this world can get," Gregory went on. "And it's been kept pretty deep down in that world all the time. It's close to the place where all things meet and all souls—anyhow, their souls. And I can get at that baby there —the real baby—and make the thing easy up here. Not at first altogether perhaps, but I shall do it. I shall make the offering there when he agrees—till we go to the Sabbath together."

"You do talk pretty, Persimmons," Sir Giles said. "You believe that this damn Graal is more use than that coffee-cup?"

"I think it is the great chalice of their initiation," Gregory answered. "And I think we can use it—I and my people. I can meet Adrian there and separate and draw and convert him. It's got power in it; it's a gate. But anyone can use the power, and a gate is for coming out as well as going in."

"Pretty, pretty," Sir Giles murmured, his head on one side. "And when does your blessed child bleat out through the gate of the fold? Don't forget I want to see."

"You won't see anything; you'll be horribly bored," Gregory sneered.

"I shall see you," Sir Giles said, with a sweet mildness. "And I shan't be bored. I saw something like it in Brazil. But there they killed a slave. Are you going to kill Ludding, by any chance?"

"Don't be a fool," Gregory said. "Well, come, if you like. I don't mind, all this cleverness of yours is such universes away that it won't interfere. Only I warn you, absolutely nothing'll happen."

"Don't die, that's all I ask," Sir Giles said. "In Brazil one of them did, and it might be more difficult to bribe the police here."

They went from the dining-room to a small room next to Gregory's bedroom, which he unlocked with a key he carried on his own chain. There appeared in it only a cabinet in one corner, two or three cushions dropped beside it, and a low pedestal of wood in the centre on which lay an oblong slab of stone. On this slab stood two candlesticks, around the pedestal, at a good distance, had been drawn a white circle, in which at one point was a small gap. Before he entered the room Gregory had fetched the Graal from its corner; he passed through the gap, set it upright on the slab between the candlesticks, and turned to Sir Giles.

"You'd better sit down at once," he said, "and I should recommend you to keep within the circle. There are curious forces released sometimes on these occasions."

"I know all about that," Sir Giles said, as he brought two of the cushions into the circle, also taking care to pass through the gap. "I saw a man once in Ispahan who looked as if he'd been unable to breathe once he got outside. Atmospheric disturbances, but *why?* Why does your purely subjective industry disturb the air? Well, never mind. I won't say a word more." He settled himself comfortably on his cushions over against one of the shorter sides of the pedestal. Gregory went over to the cabinet, and there first changed from the clothes he was wearing into a white cassock, marked with esoteric signs. He then brought from it an antique vessel, from which he poured what was apparently wine into the Graal till it all but brimmed. He brought also a short rod and laid it on the slab in front of the Graal; he arranged and lit at what appeared to be the back of the altar a chafing-dish containing herbs and powders, scattered other powders upon it, and came back to the front of the altar. Lastly, with great care, he brought to it from the cabinet a parchment inscribed with names and writings, and a small paper from which he let fall on to the wine in the Graal what appeared to Sir Giles to be a few short hairs.

He considered the arrangements, went back and closed the cabinet, re-entered the circle, took the rod from the altar, and, bending down, with a strong concentration of countenance, closed the gap, drawing the rod slowly as if with an effort against the path of the sun. He came to the front of the altar, and immersed himself in a profound silence.

Sir Giles, curled upon the cushions, watched him intently, noting every change in his face and the growing remoteness of his eyes. Almost an hour had passed before those eyes, seeming to stir of their own volition, lowered themselves from the darkness of the room to the Graal standing in the steady light of the two candles. Very slowly he stretched his hands over the chalice and began to speak. Sir Giles, straining his ears, caught only an occasional phrase. "Pater Noster, qui fuisti in cælis . . . per te omnipotentem in sæcula sæculorum. . . . hoc est calix, hoc est sanguis tuus infernorum . . . in te regnum mortis, in te delectatio corruptionis, in te via et vita scientiæ maleficæ . . . qui non es in initio, qui eris in sempiternum. Amen." He took up the rod from the altar, still moving with extreme slowness and, resting it on the edge of the chalice, allowed it to touch the surface of the wine; his eyes followed its length and rested also there. "De corpore, de mente . . . mitte animum in simulacro . . . per potestatem tuam in omnibus . . . animum Adriani cujus nomen scripsi in sanguine meo dimitte in sanguine tuo . . . Adrianum oblationem pro me et pro seipsum . . . nomen tuum." The rod moved in magical symbols upon the wine. "De Cujus corpore hæc sunt . . . O Pastor, O Pater, O Nox et Lux infernorum et domus rejectionis."

The vibrating voice ceased, and it seemed to Sir Giles that the faintest of mists hung for a moment over the chalice and was dissolved; then, more urgently and in a lower tone the voice began again, but the phrases the listener caught were now far between. " . . . Adrianum filium tuum, ovem tuam . . . et omnia opera mea et sua . . . tu cujus sum et cujus erit . . . dimitte . . . dimitte." It paused again, and then in a murmur through which the whole force of the celebrant seemed to pass, it came again. "Adrian, Adrian, Adrian . . ."

Adrian

Faint, but certain, the mist rose again from the wine; and Sir Giles, absorbedly drinking in the spectacle, saw Gregory's eyes light up with recognition. He seemed without moving to draw near the altar and the chalice and the mist, his face was bent toward it; he spoke, carefully, quietly, and in English. "Adrian, it is I who speak, image to image, through this shadow of thee to thee. Adrian, well met. Know me again, O soul, and know me thy friend and master. In the world of flesh know me, in the world of shadows, and in the world of our lord. Many times I shall shape thine image thus, O child, my sacrifice and my oblation, and thou shalt come, more swiftly and more truly thou, when I desire thee. Image of Adrian, dissolve and return to Adrian, and may his soul and body, whence thou hast come, receive this message that thou bearest. I, dimissus es."

The mist faded again; the priest of these mysteries sank upon his knees. He laid the rod on the altar; he stretched out both hands and took the chalice into them; he lifted it to his lips and drank the consecrated wine. "Hic in me et ego in hoc et Tu, Pastor et Dominus, in utrisque." He remained absorbed.

The candles had burned half an inch more towards their sockets before, very wearily, he arose and extinguished them. Then he broke the circle, and slowly, in reverse order, laid away the magical implements. He took the Graal and set it inverted on the floor. He took off his cassock and put on— in a fantastic culmination—the dinner-jacket he had been wearing. Then he turned to Sir Giles. "Do what you will," he said. "I am going to sleep."

Chapter Eight

FARDLES

"I have read," said Kenneth Mornington, standing in the station of a small village some seven miles across country from Fardles, "that Paris dominates France. I wish London dominated England in the matter of weather."

Further letters exchanged between him and the Archdeacon had led to an agreement that he should spend the first Sunday of his holiday at the Rectory, arriving for lunch on the Saturday. The Saturday morning in London had been brilliant, and he had thought it would be pleasanter to walk along the chord of the monstrous arc which the railway made. But it had grown dull as the train left the London suburbs, and even as he jumped from his compartment the first drops of rain began to fall. By the time he had reached the outer exit they had grown to a steady drizzle, and the train had left the station.

Kenneth turned up his collar and set out; the way at least was known to him. "But why," he said, "do I always get out at the wrong times? If I had gone on I should have had to sit at Fardles station for an hour and a half, but I should have been dry. It is this sheep-like imitation of Adam which annoys me. Adam got out at the wrong time. But he was made to by the railway authorities. I will write," he thought, and took to a footpath, "the diary of a man who always got out at the wrong time, beginning with a Cæsarean operation. "And let the angel whom thou still hast served Tell thee Macduff was from his mother's womb Untimely ripped." *A Modern Macduff*, one might call it. And death? He might die inopportunely, before the one in advance had been moved on, so that all the angels on the line of his spiritual progress found themselves crowded with two souls instead of the one they were prepared for. "Agitation in Heaven. Excursionist unable to return. Trains to Paradise overcrowded. Strange scenes at the stations. Seraph Michael says rules to be enforced." Stations . . . stages . . . it sounds like Theosophy. Am I a Theosophist? Oh, Lord, it's worse than ever; I can't walk to a strange Rectory through seven miles of this."

In a distance he discerned a shed by the side of the road, broke into a run, and, reaching it, took shelter with a bound which landed him in a shallow puddle lying just within the dark entrance. "Oh, damn and blast!" he cried with a great voice. "Why was this bloody world created?"

"As a sewer for the stars," a voice in front of him said. "Alternatively, to know God and to glorify Him for ever."

Kenneth peered into the shed, and found that there was sitting on a heap of stones at the back a young man of about his own age, with a lean, long face, and a blob of white on his knee which turned out in a few minutes to be a writing-pad.

"Quite," Kenneth said. "The two answers are not, of course, necessarily alternative. They might be con—con— consanguineous? contemporaneous? consubstantial? What *is* the word I want?"

"Contemptible, concomitant, conditional, consequental, congruous, connectible, concupiscent, contaminable, considerable," the stranger offered him. "The last is, I admit, weak."

"The question was considerable," Kenneth answered. "You no doubt are considering it? You are even writing the answer down?"

"A commentary upon it," the other said. "But consanguineous was the word I wanted, or its brother." He wrote.

Kenneth sat down on the same heap of stones and watched till the writing was finished, then he said: "Circumstances almost suggest, don't you think, that I might hear the context—if it's what it looks?"

"Context—there's another," the stranger said. "Contextual—— 'And that contextual meaning flows Through all our manuscripts of rose.' Rose—Persia—Hafix—Ispahan. Perhaps rose is a little ordinary. 'And that contextual meaning streams Through all our manuscripts of dreams.'"

"Oh, no, no," Mornington broke in firmly. "That's far too minor. Perhaps something modern—'And that impotent contextual meaning stinks In all our manuscripts, of no matter what coloured inks.' Better be modern than minor."

"I agree," the other said. "But a man must fulfil his destiny, even to minority. Shall I 'think the complete universe must be Subject to such a rag of it as me?'"

He was interrupted by Kenneth kicking the earth with his heels and crying: "At last! at last! 'Terror of darkness! O thou king of flames!' I didn't think there was another living man who knew George Chapman."

The stranger caught his arm. "Can you?" he said, made a gesture with his free hand, and began, Mornington's voice joining in after the first few words:

> "*That with thy music-footed horse dost strike*
> *The clear light out of crystal on dark earth,*
> *And hurl'st instructive fire about the world.*"

The conversation for the next ten minutes became a duet, and it was only at the end that Kenneth said with a sigh: "'I have lived long enough, having seen one thing.' But before I die—the context of consanguineous?"

The stranger picked up his manuscript and read:

> "*How does thy single heart possess*
> *A double mode of happiness*
> *In quiet and in busyness!*

Fardles

Profundities of utter peace
Do their own vehemence release
Through rippling toils that never cease.

Yet of those ripples' changing mood,
Thou, ignorant at heart, dost brood
In a most solemn quietude.

Thus idleness and industry
Within that laden heart of thee
Find their rich consanguinity."

"Yes," Kenneth murmured, "yes. A little minor, but rather beautiful."

"The faults, or rather the follies, are sufficiently obvious," the stranger said. "Yet I flatter myself it reflects the lady."

"You have printed?" Kenneth asked seriously, for they were now discussing important things, and in answer the other jumped to his feet and stood before him. "I have printed," he said, "and you are the only man—besides the publisher—who knows about it."

"Really?" Mornington asked.

"Yes," said the stranger. "You will understand the horrible position I'm in if I tell you my name. I am Aubrey Duncan Peregrine Mary de Lisle D'Estrange, Duke of the North Ridings, Marquis of Craigmullen and Plessing, Earl and Viscount, Count of the Holy Roman Empire, Knight of the Sword and Cape, and several other ridiculous fantasies."

Mornington pinched his lip. "Yes, I see," he said. "That must make it difficult to do anything with poetry."

"Difficult," the other said, with almost a shout. "It makes it impossible."

"Oh well, come," Kenneth said; "impossible? You can publish, and the reviews at least won't flatter you."

"It isn't the *reviews*," the Duke said. "It's just chatting

D   97

with people and being the fellow who's written a book or two—not very good books, but *his* books, and being able to quote things, and so on. How can I quote things to the people who come to see *me*? How can I ask the Bishop what he thinks of my stuff or tell him what I think of his? What will the Earl my cousin say about the Sitwells?"

"No, quite," Mornington answered, and for a few minutes the two young men looked at one another. Then the Duke grinned. "It's so *silly*," he said. "I really do care about poetry, and I think some of my stuff might be almost possible. But I can never find it anywhere to live for more than a few days."

"Anonymity?" Kenneth asked. "But that wouldn't help."

"Look here," the Duke said suddenly, "are you going anywhere in particular? No? Why not come up to the house with me and stop a few days?"

Mornington shook his head regretfully. "I have promised to stop with the Archdeacon of Fardles over the week-end," he said.

"Well, after then?" the Duke urged. "Do, for God's sake come and talk Chapman and Blunden with me. Look here, come up now, and I'll run you over to Fardles in the car, and on Monday morning I'll come and fetch you."

Kenneth assented to this, though he refused to leave his shelter. But within some half an hour the Duke had brought his car to the front of the shed and they were on the way to Fardles. As they drew near the village, approaching it from the cottage side of Cully, they passed another car in a side turning, in which Mornington seemed to see, as he was carried past, the faces of Gregory Persimmons and Adrian Rackstraw. But he was in a long controversy with the Duke on the merits of the Laureate's new prosody, and though he wondered a little, the incident made hardly any impression on his mind.

The Archdeacon, it appeared, knew the Duke; the Duke

was rather detachedly acquainted with the Archdeacon. The detachment was perhaps due to the fact, which had emerged from the few minutes' conversation the three had together, that the Duke of the North Ridings was a Roman Catholic (hence the Sword and Cape), so far as his obsession with poetry and his own misfortunes left him leisure to be anything. But he promised to come to lunch on Monday, and disappeared.

"I forgot Batesby," the Archdeacon said suddenly to Mornington, as the car drove off. "Dear me! I'm afraid the Duke and he won't like one another. Batesby's dreadfully keen on Reunion; he has a scheme of his own for it—an admirable scheme, I'm certain, if only he could get other people to see it in the same way."

"I should have thought the same thing was—officially— true of the Duke," Mornington said as they entered the house.

"But only because he's part of an institution," the Archdeacon said, "and one can more easily believe that institutions are supernatural than that individuals are. And an institution can believe in itself and can wait, whereas an individual can't. Batesby can't afford to wait; he might die."

At lunch Mornington had Mr. Batesby's scheme of Reunion explained at length by its originator. It was highly complicated and, so far as Kenneth could understand, involved everyone believing that God was opposed to Communism and in favour of election as the only sound method of government. The Archdeacon remarked that discovering the constitution of the Catholic Church was a much pleasanter game than tennis, to which he had been invited that afternoon.

"Though they know I don't play," he added plaintively. "So I was glad you were coming, and I had an excuse."

"How do you get exercise?" Kenneth asked idly.

"Well, actually, I go in for fencing," the Archdeacon said, smiling. "I used to love it as a boy romantically, and since I have outgrown romance I keep it up prosaically."

Fardles

The constitution of the Catholic Church occupied the lunch so fully that not until Mr. Batesby had gone away to supervise the Lads' Christian Cricket Club in his own parish, some ten miles off, did Kenneth see an opportunity of talking to his host about *Christianity and the League of Nations.* And even then, when they were settled in the garden, he found that by the accident of conversation the priest was already chatting about the deleted paragraph of *Sacred Vessels in Folklore.*

"Who?" he asked suddenly, arrested by a name.

"Persimmons," the Archdeacon answered. "I wonder if he had anything to do with your firm. I seem to remember seeing him the day I called on you."

"But if it's the man who's taken a house near here called Mullins or Juggins or something, of *course* he's something to do with our firm," Mornington cried. "He's Stephen's father; he used to *be* the firm. Does he live at Buggins?"

"He lives at Cully," the Archdeacon said, "which may be what you mean."

"But how do you know he wanted the paragraph out?" Kenneth demanded.

"Because Sir Giles told me so—confirmed by the fact that he tried to cheat me out of the Graal, and the other fact that he eventually had me knocked on the head and took it," answered the Archdeacon.

Kenneth looked at him, looked at the garden, looked across at the church. "I am not mad," he murmured, " 'My pulse doth temperately keep time.' . . . Yes, it does. 'These are the thingummybobs, you are my what d'ye call it.' But that a retired publisher should knock an Archdeacon on the head . . ."

The Archdeacon flowed into the whole story, and ended with his exit from Cully. Mornington, listening, felt the story to be fantastic and ridiculous, and would have given himself up to incredulity, had it not been for the notion of the Graal itself. This, which to some would have been the extreme fantasy, was to him the easiest thing to believe. For he approached the idea of the sacred vessel, not as did Sir Giles, through antiquity and savage folklore, nor as did the Archdeacon, through a sense of religious depths in which the mere temporary use of a particular vessel seemed a small thing, but through exalted poetry and the high romantic tradition in literature. This living light had shone for so long in his mind upon the idea of the Graal that it was by now a familiar thing—Tennyson and Hawker and Malory and older writers still had made it familiar, and its familiarity created for it a kind of potentiality. To deny it would be to deny his own past. But this emotional testimony to the possibility of its existence had an intellectual support. Kenneth knew—his publicity work had made clear to him—the very high reputation Sir Giles had among the learned; a hundred humble reviews had shown him that. And if the thing were possible, and if the thing were likely. . . . But still, Gregory Persimmons. . . . He looked back at the Archdeacon.

"You're sure you saw it?" he asked. "Have you gone to the police?"

"No," the Archdeacon said. "If you don't think I saw it, would the police be likely to?"

"I do, I do," Kenneth said hastily. "But why should he want it?"

"I haven't any idea," the priest answered. "That's what baffles me too. Why should anyone want anything as much as that? And certainly why should anyone want the Graal —if it is the Graal? He talked to me about being a collector, which makes me pretty sure he isn't."

Kenneth got up and walked up and down. There was a silence for a few minutes, then the Archdeacon said: "However, we needn't worry over it. What about me and the League of Nations?"

"Yes," Kenneth said absently, sitting down again. "Oh, well, Stephen simply leapt at it. I read it, and I told him about it, and I suggested sending it to one of our tame experts—only

I couldn't decide between the political expert and the theological. At least, I was going to suggest it, but I didn't have time. 'By an Archdeacon? By an orthodox Archdeacon? Oh, take it, take it by all means, by all manner of means.' He positively tangoed at it."

"This is very gratifying," the Archdeacon answered, "and the haste is unexpected."

"Stephen", Kenneth went on, "has a weakness for clerical books; I've noticed it before. Fiction is our stand-by, of course; but he takes all the manuscripts by clergymen that he decently can. I think he's a little shy of some parts of our list, and likes to counterbalance them. We used to do a lot of occult stuff; a particular kind of occult. The standard work on the Black Mass and that sort of thing. That was before Stephen himself really got going, but he feels vaguely responsible, I've no doubt."

"Who ran it then?" the Archdeacon asked idly.

"Gregory," Mornington answered. He stopped suddenly, and the two looked at one another.

"Oh, it's all nonsense," Mornington broke out. "The Black Mass, indeed!"

"The Black Mass is all nonsense, of course," the Archdeacon said; "but nonsense, after all, does exist. And minds can get drunk with nonsense."

"Do you really mean", Mornington asked, "that a London publisher sold his soul to the devil and signed it away in his own blood and that sort of thing? Because I'm damned if I can see him doing it. Lots of people are interested in magic, without doing secret incantations under the new moon with the aid of dead men's grease."

"You keep harping on the London publisher," the other said. "If a London publisher has a soul—which you're bound to admit—he can sell it if he likes: not to the devil, but to himself. Why not?" He considered. "I think perhaps, after all, I ought to try and recover that chalice. There are decencies.

There is a way of behaving in these things. And the Graal, if it is the Graal," he went on, unusually moved, "was not meant for the greedy orgies of a delirious tomtit."

"Tomtit!" Mornington cried. "If it could be true, he wouldn't be a tomtit. He'd be a vulture."

"Well, never mind," the priest said. "The question is, can I do anything at once? I've half a mind to go and take it."

"Look here," said Mornington, "let me go and see him first. Stephen thought it would look well if I called, being down here. And let me talk to Lionel Rackstraw." He spoke almost crossly. "Once a silly idea like this gets into one's mind, one can't see anything else. I think you're wrong."

"I don't see, then, what good you're going to do," the Archdeacon said. "If I'm mad——"

"Wrong, I said," Kenneth put in.

"Wrong because being hit on the head has affected my mind and my eyes—which is almost the same thing as being mad. If I'm demented, anyhow—you won't be any more clear about it after a chat with Mr. Persimmons on whatever he does chat about. Nor with Mr. Rackstraw, whoever he may be."

Kenneth explained briefly. "So, you see, he's really been a very decent fellow over the cottage," he concluded.

"My dear man," the Archdeacon said, "if you had tea with him and he gave you the last crumpet, it wouldn't prove anything unless he badly wanted the crumpet, and not much even then. He might want something else more."

This, however, was a point of view to which Kenneth, when that evening he walked over to the cottage, found Lionel not very willing to agree. Gregory, so far as the Rackstraws were concerned, had been nothing but an advantage. He had lent them the cottage; he had sent a maid down from Cully to save Barbara trouble; he had occupied Adrian for hours together with the motor and other amusements, until the child was very willing for his parents to go off on more or less extensive walks while he played with his new friend. And Lionel saw no reason to associate himself actively—even in sympathy—with the archidiaconal crusade; more especially since Mornington himself was torn between scepticism and sympathy.

"In any case," he said, "I don't know what you want me to *do*. Anyone that will take Adrian off my hands for a little while can knock all the Archdeacons in the country on the head so far as I am concerned."

"I don't want you to do anything", Kenneth answered, "except discuss it."

"Well, we're going up to tea at Cully to-morrow," Lionel said. "I can talk about it there, if you like."

Kenneth arrived at Cully on the Sunday afternoon, after having heard the Archdeacon preach a sermon in the morning on "*Thou shalt not covet thy neighbour's house*," in which, having identified "thy neighbour" with God and touched lightly on the text "*Mine are the cattle upon a thousand hills*," he went off into a fantastic exhortation upon the thesis that the only thing left to covet was "thy neighbour" Himself. "Not His creation, not His manifestations, not even His qualities, but Him," the Archdeacon ended. "This should be our covetousness and our desire; for this only no greed is too great, as this only can satisfy the greatest greed. The whole universe is His house, the soul of thy mortal neighbour is His wife, thou thyself art His servant and thy body His maid—a myriad oxen, a myriad asses, subsist in the high inorganic creation. Him only thou shalt covet with all thy heart, with all thy mind, with all thy soul, and with all thy strength. And now to God Almighty, the Father, the Son, and the Holy Ghost, be ascribed, as is most justly due, all honour . . ." The congregation searched for six-pences.

Lionel, Barbara, and Adrian were with Persimmons and Sir Giles on the terrace behind the house when Kenneth arrived, and had already spoken of his probable visit. Gregory welcomed him pleasantly enough, as one of the staff who had originally worked under him. But Kenneth's mind was already in a slight daze, for, as he had been conducted by the maid through the hall, he had seen on a bracket about the height of his head from the ground, in a corner near the garden door, an antique cup which struck him forcibly as being very like the one the Archdeacon had described to him. It seemed impossible that, if the priest's absurd suspicions were right, Persimmons should so flaunt the theft before the world—unless, indeed, it were done merely to create the impression of impossibility. "There is no possible idea", Kenneth thought as he came on to the terrace, "to which the mind of man can't supply some damned alternative or other. Yet one must act. How are you, Mr. Persimmons? You'll excuse this call, I know."

The conversation rippled gently round the spring publishing season and books in general, with backwaters of attention in which Adrian immersed himself.

It approached, gently and unobserved by the two young men, the question of corrections in proof, and it was then that Sir Giles, who had until then preserved a sardonic and almost complete silence, said suddenly: "What I want to know is, whether proofs are or are not private?"

"I suppose they are, technically," Lionel said lazily, watching Adrian. "Subject to the discretion of the publisher."

"Subject to the discretion of the devil," Sir Giles said. "What do you say, Persimmons?"

"I should say yes," Gregory answered. "At least till they are passed for press."

"I ask," Sir Giles said pointedly, "because my last proofs were shown to an outsider before the book was published. And if one of these gentlemen was responsible I want to know why."

"My dear Tumulty, it doesn't matter," Gregory in a quiet, soothing tone put in. "I asked you not to mention it, you know."

"I know you did," Sir Giles answered, "and I said—that I felt I ought to. After all, a man has a right to know why a mad clergyman is allowed to read paragraphs of his book which he afterwards cancels. I tell you, Persimmons, we haven't seen the last of your . . . Archdeacon yet."

It was evident that Barbara's presence was causing Sir Giles acute difficulty in the expression of his feelings. But this was unknown to Kenneth, who, realizing suddenly what the other was talking about, said, leaning forward in his chair, "I'm afraid that's my fault, Sir Giles. It was I showed the Archdeacon your proofs. I'm extremely sorry if it's inconvenienced you, but I don't think I agree that proofs are so entirely private as you suggest. Something must be allowed to a publisher's need for publicity, and perhaps something for the mere accidents of a publishing house. There was no special stipulation about privacy for your book."

"I made no stipulation," Sir Giles answered, staring hostilely at Kenneth, "because I didn't for an instant suppose I should find it being read in convocation before my final corrections were made."

"Really, really, Tumulty," Gregory said. "It's unfortunate, as it's turned out, but I'm sure Mornington would be the first to deplore a slight excess of zeal, a slight error of judgement, shall we say?"

"Error of judgement?" Sir Giles snarled. "It's more like a breach of common honesty."

Kenneth came to his feet. "I admit no error in judgement," he said haughtily. "I was entirely within my rights. What is the misfortune you complain of, Mr. Persimmons?" He moved so as to turn his back on Sir Giles.

"I don't complain," Gregory answered hastily. "It's just one of those things that happen. But the Archdeacon, owing to your zeal, my dear Mornington, has been trying to saddle me with the responsibility for the loss of this chalice Sir Giles was writing about. I do wish he'd never seen the proofs. I think you must admit they ought to be treated as private."

"It's exactly like reading out a private letter from the steps of St. Paul's," Sir Giles added. "A man who does it ought to be flung into the gutter to starve."

"Now, now, Tumulty," Gregory put in, as the enraged Kenneth wheeled round, and Barbara and Lionel hastily stood up, "it's not as bad as that. I think perhaps strict commercial morality would mean strict privacy, but perhaps we take a rather austere view. The younger generation is looser, you know—less tied—less dogmatic, shall we say?"

"Less honest, you mean," Sir Giles said. "However, it's your affair more than mine, after all."

"Let's say no more about it," Gregory said handsomely.

"But I will say more about it," Kenneth cried out. "Do you expect me to be called a thief and a liar and I don't know what, because I did a perfectly right thing, and then be forgiven for it? I beg your pardon, Barbara, but I can't stand it, and I won't."

"You can't help it," Sir Giles said, grinning. "What will you do? We've both forgiven you, my fine fellow, and there it stops."

Kenneth stamped his foot in anger. "I'll have an apology," he said. "Sir Giles, what is the importance of this beastly book of yours?"

Barbara moved forward and slipped her arm in his. "Kenneth dear," she murmured; and then to Gregory, "Mr. Persimmons, I don't quite know what all this is about, but couldn't we do without forgiving one another?" She smiled at Sir Giles. "Sir Giles has had to forgive so many people, I expect, in different parts of the world, that he might spare us this time."

Lionel came to her help. "It's my fault more than Mornington's," he said. "I was supposed to be looking after the proofs, and I let an uncorrected set out of my keeping. It's me you must slang, Sir Giles."

"In the firm is one thing," Sir Giles said obstinately, "one

risks that. But an outsider, and a clergyman, and a mad
clergyman—no."

"Mad clergyman be——" Kenneth began, and was silenced
by Barbara's appealing, "But what *is* it all about? Can you tell
me, Mr. Persimmons?"

"I can even show you," Gregory said pleasantly. "As a
matter of fact, Adrian's seen it already. We had a game with
it this morning. It's a question of identifying an old chalice."
He led the way into the hall, and paused before the bracket.
"There you are," he said, "that's mine. I got it from a Greek,
who got it from one of his countrymen who fled before the
Turkish recovery in Asia Minor. It comes, through Smyrna,
from Ephesus. Old enough and interesting, but as for being the
Graal—— Unfortunately, after the Archdeacon had read this
paragraph about which we've all been behaving so badly,
three things happened. I did ask him if he had a chalice to
spare for a friend of mine who has a very poor parish; thieves
made an attempt on the church over there; and the Archdeacon was knocked on the head by a tramp. He seems to
think that this proves conclusively that I was the tramp and
that this is his missing chalice. At least, he says it's missing."

"How do you mean, sir—says it's missing?" Lionel asked.

"Well, honestly—I dare say it's mere pique—but we none
of us really *know* the Archdeacon, do we?" Gregory asked.
"And some of the clergy aren't above turning an honest penny
by supplying American millionaires with curios. But it looks
bad if it does happen to come out—so if the thing *can* disappear
by means of a tramp or an unknown neighbour . . ."

There was a moment's pause, then Kenneth said, "Really,
sir, if you *knew* the Archdeacon . . ."

"Quite right," Gregory answered. "Oh, my dear fellow,
I'm being unjust to him, no doubt. But a man doesn't expect
his parish priest practically to accuse him of highway robbery.
I shouldn't be surprised if I heard from the police next. Probably the best thing would be to offer him this one to replace

the one he says he's—I mean the one he's lost. But I don't think I'm quite Christian enough for that."

"And how did you play with it this morning?" Barbara asked, smiling at Adrian.

"Ah, that is a secret game, isn't it, Adrian?" Gregory answered merrily. "*Our* secret game. Isn't it, Adrian?"

"It's hidden," Adrian said seriously. "It's hidden pictures. But you mustn't know what, Mummie, must she?" He appealed to Gregory.

"Certainly not," Gregory said.

"Certainly not," Adrian repeated. "They're my hidden pictures."

"So they shall be, darling," Barbara said. "Please forgive me. Well, Mr. Persimmons, I suppose we ought to be going. Thank you for a charming afternoon. You're making this a very pleasant holiday."

Sir Giles had dropped away when they had entered the hall, and the farewells were thus robbed of their awkwardness; although Gregory detained Kenneth in order to say, "I think I can put it right with Tumulty, although he was very angry at first. Talked of appealing to my son and getting you dismissed, you know."

"Getting me what?" Kenneth cried.

"Well, you know what my son is," Gregory said confidentially. "Efficient and all that—but you've known him in business, Mornington, and you know what he is. Rather easily influenced, I'm afraid. And Sir Giles is a good name for his list."

"A very good name," Kenneth admitted, feeling less heated and more chilly than he had done. It was true—Stephen Persimmons was weak, and would be terrified of losing Sir Giles. And he had before now been guilty of dismissing people in a fit of hysterical anger.

"But I've no doubt it's all right," Gregory went on, watching the other closely, "no doubt at all. Let me know if anything goes wrong. I've a great regard for you, Mornington, and a word, perhaps . . . And keep the Archdeacon quiet, if you can. It would be worth your while."

He waved his hand and turned back into the house, and Kenneth, considerably more disturbed than before, walked slowly back to the Rectory.

Chapter Nine

THE FLIGHT OF THE DUKE OF THE NORTH RIDINGS

When the Duke's car arrived outside the Rectory about twelve on the Monday, its driver saw at the gates another car, at the wheel of which sat a policeman whom he recognized.

"Hallo, Puttenham," he said. "Is the Chief Constable here then?"

"Inside, your Grace," Constable Puttenham answered, saluting. "Making inquiries about the outrage, I believe."

The Duke, rather annoyed, looked at the Rectory. He disliked the Chief Constable, who had taken up the business of protecting people, developed it into a hobby, and was rapidly making it a mania and a nuisance—at least, so it appeared to the Duke. He remembered now that at a dinner at his own house some few days before the Chief Constable had held forth at great length on a lack of readiness in the public to assist the police, as exemplified by the failure of the Archdeacon of Fardles to report to them one case of sacrilege and one of personal assault. It had been objected that the Archdeacon had been confined to his bed for some time, but now that he had preached again the Chief Constable had obviously determined to see what his personal investigation and exhortation could do. The Duke hesitated for a moment, but it occurred to him that Mornington might welcome the opportunity of escaping, and he strolled slowly up to the door. Introduced into the study, he found the Chief Constable in a high state of argumentative irritation, Mornington irrationally scornful of everything, and the Archdeacon—for all he could see—much as usual.

The Flight of the Duke of the North Ridings

"How do, Ridings," the Chief Constable said, after the priest had greeted his visitor. "Perhaps you may help me to talk sense. The Archdeacon here says he's lost a chalice, and won't help the proper authorities to look for it."

"But I don't want them to look for it," the Archdeacon said, "if you mean the police. You asked me if I knew what the hypothetical tramp or tramps were looking for, and I said yes —the old chalice that used to be here. You asked me if it had disappeared, and I said yes. But I don't want you to look for it."

The Duke began to feel that there might be something satisfying about even an Anglican priest. There were few things he himself would like less than to have the Chief Constable looking for anything he had lost. But robbery was robbery, and though, of course, a priest who wasn't a priest could have no real use for a chalice, still, a chalice was a chalice, and, anyhow, the Chief Constable was sure to go on looking for it, so why not let him? But he didn't say this; he merely nodded and glanced at Mornington.

"I suppose you want to find it?" the Chief Constable said laboriously.

"I don't—you must excuse me, but you drive me to it," the Archdeacon answered. "I don't want the police to find it. First, because I don't care for the Church to make use of the secular arm; secondly, because it would make the whole thing undesirably public; thirdly, because I know where it is; and fourthly, because they couldn't prove it was there."

"Well, sir," Kenneth said sharply, "then, if it can't be proved, we oughtn't to throw accusations about."

"Precisely what I am *not* doing," the Archdeacon answered, crossing his legs. "I don't accuse anyone. I only say I know where it is."

"And where is it?" the Chief Constable asked. "And how do you know it is there?"

"First," the Archdeacon said, "in the possession of Mr.

Persimmons of Cully—probably on a bracket in his hall, but I'm not certain of that. Secondly, by a combination of directions arising out of the education of children, books of black magic, a cancelled paragraph in some proofs, an attempt to cheat me, the place where the Cup was kept, a motor-car, a reported threat, and a few other things."

The Chief Constable was still blinking over the sudden introduction of Mr. Persimmons of Cully, and it was the Duke who asked, "But if you have all these clues, what's the uncertainty—in your own mind?" he added suddenly, as he also became aware of the improbability of a country householder knocking an Archdeacon on the head in order to steal his chalice.

"There is no uncertainty in my own mind," the priest answered. "But the police would not be able to find a motive."

"We of course can," Kenneth said scornfully.

"We—if you say we—can," the Archdeacon said, "for we know what it was, and we know that many kinds of religion are possible to men."

"You are sure now that it was—it?" Kenneth answered.

"No," the priest answered, "but I have decided in my own mind that I will believe that. No-one can possibly do more than decide what to believe."

"Do I understand, Mr. Archdeacon," the Chief Constable asked, "that you accuse Mr. Persimmons of stealing this chalice? And why should he want to steal a chalice? And if he did, would he be likely to keep it in his hall?"

"There is always the *Purloined Letter*," the Duke murmured thoughtfully. "But even there the letter wasn't pinned up openly on a notice-board. Couldn't we go and see?"

"That is what I was going to suggest," said the Chief Constable. He stood up cheerfully. "I quite understand about your anxiety over the loss of this chalice"—Kenneth cackled suddenly and walked to the window. "Anyone would be anxious about a chalice of, I understand, great antiquarian interest. But I feel so certain you're mistaken in this . . . idea about Mr. Persimmons that I can't help feeling that a meeting perhaps, and a little study of his chalice, and so on. . . . And then you must give us a free hand." He looked almost hopefully at the priest. "If you could spare us half an hour now, say?"

"I can't possibly move from here," the Archdeacon said, "without a clear understanding that I don't accuse Mr. Persimmons in any legal or official sense at all. I will come with you if you like, because I can't refuse a not-immoral call from the Chief Magistrate"—the Chief Constable looked gratified— "and, as I have no reason to consider Mr. Persimmons's feelings— I really haven't," he added aside to Kenneth, who had turned to face the room again—"I should like, as a matter of curiosity, to see if it's another chalice or if it's mine. But that's all."

"I quite understand," the Chief Constable said sunnily. "Ridings, are you coming? Mr.——?" He hesitated uncertainly. The Duke looked at Kenneth, who said: "I think I ought to go; it won't take long. Would you mind waiting a few minutes?"

"I'll take you to the gate," the Duke said, "and wait for you there—then we'll go straight on."

Between the Archdeacon and the Chief Constable in their car the only conversation was a brief one upon the weather; in that which preceded them, Mornington, in answer to the Duke's inquiries, sketched the situation as he understood it.

"And what do you think yourself?" the Duke asked.

Mornington grimaced. "Certum quia impossibile," he said. "If I must come down on one side or the other, I fall on the Archdeacon's. Especially since yesterday," he said resentfully. "But it's all insane. Persimmons's explanation is perfectly satisfactory—and yet it just isn't. The paragraph and the Cup were both there—and now they both aren't."

"Well," the Duke said, "if I can help annoy the Chief

Constable, tell me. He once told me that poetry wasn't practical."

At the gates of Cully the cars stopped. "Will you come in, Ridings?" the Chief Constable asked.

"No," the Duke said; "what have I to do with these things? Don't be longer than you can help catechizing and analysing and the rest of it." He watched them out of sight, took a writing-pad from his pocket, and settled down to work on a drama in the Greek style upon the Great War and the fall of the German Empire. The classic form appeared to him capable at once of squeezing the last drop of intensity out of the action and of presenting at once the broadest and most minute effects. The scene was an open space behind the German lines in France; the time was in March 1918; the chorus consisted of French women from the occupied territory; and the *deus ex machina* was represented by a highly formalized St. Denis, whom the Duke was engaged in making as much like Phœbus Apollo as he could. He turned to the god's opening monologue.

> *Out of those habitable fields which are*
> *Nor swept by fire nor venomous with war,*
> *But, being disposed by . . .*

He brooded over whether to say Zeus or God.

Meanwhile, Gregory received his guests with cold politeness, to which a much warmer courtesy was opposed by the Archdeacon. "It isn't my fault that we're here," the priest said, when he had introduced the Chief Constable. "Colonel Conyers insisted on coming. He's looking for the chalice that was stolen."

"It certainly isn't my wish," the irritated Colonel said, finding himself already in a false position. "The Archdeacon gave me to understand that he believed the chalice had somehow got into Cully, and I thought if that was cleared up we should all know better where we were."

The Flight of the Duke of the North Ridings

"I suppose," Gregory said, "that it was Mr. Mornington who told you I had a chalice here."

"You remember I saw it myself," the Archdeacon said. "It was the position then that made me feel sure it was the . . . it was an important one. You people are so humorous." He shook his head, and hummed under his breath: "Oh, give thanks to the God of all gods . . ."

Colonel Conyers looked from one to the other. "I don't quite follow all this," he said a trifle impatiently.

" 'For his'—it doesn't at all matter—'mercy endureth for ever,' " the Archdeacon concluded, with a genial smile. He seemed to be rising moment by moment into a kind of delirious delight. His eyes moved from one to the other, changing from mere laughter as he looked at the Colonel into an impish and teasing mischief for Persimmons, and showing a feeling of real affection as they rested on Kenneth, between whom and himself there had appeared the beginnings of a definite attraction and friendship. Gregory looked at him with a certain perplexity. He understood Sir Giles's insolent rudeness, though he despised it as Giles despised his own affectation of smoothness. But he saw no reason in the Archdeacon's amusement, and began to wonder seriously whether Ludding's blow had affected his mind. He glanced over at Mornington— there at least he had power, and understood his power. Then he looked at the Chief Constable and waited. So for a minute or two they all stood in silence, which the Colonel at last broke.

"I thought," he began, rather pointedly addressing himself to Persimmons, "that if you would show us this chalice of yours it would convince the Archdeacon that it wasn't his."

"With pleasure," Gregory answered, going towards the bracket and followed by the others. "Here it is. Do you want to know the full history? I had it——" he began, repeating what Kenneth had heard the previous day.

Colonel Conyers looked at the priest. "Well?" he said.

116

The Flight of the Duke of the North Ridings

The Archdeacon looked, and grew serious. His spirit felt its own unreasonable gaiety opening into a wider joy; its dance became a more vital but therefore a vaster thing. Faintly again he heard the sound of music, but now not from without, or indeed from within, from some non-spatial, non-temporal, non-personal existence. It was music, but not yet music, or if music, then the music of movement itself—sound produced, not by things, but in the nature of things. He looked, and looked again, and felt himself part of a moving river flowing towards some narrow channel on a ripple of which the Graal was as a gleam of supernatural light. "Yes," he said softly, "it is the Cup."

Gregory shrugged, and looked at the Chief Constable. "I will give you the address of the man from whom I bought it," he said, "and you can make what inquiries you like—if you think it necessary."

The Colonel pursed his lips, and said in a lowered voice, "I will tell you if it's necessary. But I'm not sure the identification is sufficiently valuable. I understand the Archdeacon had an accident to his head some time ago."

"Unfortunately, it was I who found him lying in the road and brought him home, and I think that's confused the idea of robbery *with* me," Gregory continued, also in a subdued voice. "It's very unfortunate, and rather embarrassing for me. I don't want to appear un-neighbourly, and if it goes on I shall have to think about selling the house. He's an old resident, and I'm a new one, and, of course, people would rather believe him. If I gave him this chalice—but I should be sorry to part with it. I like old things, but I don't like them enough to half kill a clergyman to get them. I'm in your hands, Colonel. What do you advise?"

The Colonel considered. Kenneth had walked a little distance away, so as not to appear to overhear their talk; the Archdeacon was still gazing at the chalice as if in a trance. But now he was conscious of some slight movement on his own part towards which he was impelled; he knew the signs of that approaching direction, and awaited it serenely. By long practice he had accustomed himself in any circumstances—in company or alone, at work or at rest, in speech or in silence—to withdraw into that place where action is created. The cause of all action there disposed itself according to that Will which was its nature, and, so disposing itself, moved him easily as a part of its own accommodation to the changing wills of men, so that at any time and at all times its own perfection was maintained, now known in endurance, now in beauty, now in wisdom, now in joy. There was no smallest hesitation which it would not solve, nor greatest anxiety which it did not make lucid. In that light other things took on a new aspect, and the form of Gregory, where he stood a few steps away, seemed to swell into larger dimensions. But this enlargement was as unreal as it was huge; the sentences which he had altered a few days back on denying and defying Destiny boomed like unmeaning echoes across creation. Nothing but Destiny could defy Destiny; all else which sought to do so was pomposity so extreme as to become merely silly. It was a useless attempt at usurpation, useless and yet slightly displeasing, as pomposity always is. In the universe, as in Fardles, pomposity was bad manners; from its bracket the Graal shuddered forward in a movement of innocent distaste. The same motion that seemed to touch it touched the Archdeacon also; they came together and were familiarly one. And the Archdeacon, realizing with his whole mind what had happened, turned with unexpected fleetness and ran for the hall door.

Everyone else ran also. The Colonel, having made up his mind, had drawn Gregory a few steps away, and was telling him what he advised. Neither of them had seen, as Kenneth did, the unexpected yet gentle movement with which the Archdeacon seemed suddenly to reach up, take hold of the Cup, and begin to run. But they heard the first step, and rushed. Kenneth, who was nearer the door, was passed by the priest before he could move; then he also took to his heels. The Archdeacon, practised on his feet in many fencing bouts, flew out of the door and down the drive, and Gregory and the Colonel both lost breath—the first yelling for Ludding, the second shouting after the priest. Kenneth only, in as good condition, younger and with longer legs, overtook the fugitive half-way to the gates. Up to that moment he had still been sceptical and undetermined in his mind; but he knew, as he came level, that, right or wrong, it was impossible for him to lay a detaining hand upon his friend, and as he felt the decision taken his own gaiety returned. He ran on in advance, reached the gate and threw it open, reached the Duke's car in three strides, and opened that door also.

The Duke had been writing poetry; Constable Puttenham had been asleep in the August sun. But the Duke, hesitating over a word, had been staring at the gate, and saw the returning guests before the distant shouts had done more than pleasantly mingle with the constable's dreams.

"Drive like hell," Kenneth said to the Duke as the Archdeacon reached the car, and himself jumped up by the driver's side. The constable, awaking to cries of " Puttenham" from the Colonel rushing round the curve of the drive, sat bolt upright. "Stop him, Puttenham," the Colonel yelled. But the bewildered policeman saw no-one to stop. He saw the Archdeacon settling down in the car, and Mornington by the Duke's side. He saw the other car begin to move, but who it was he was to stop was by no means clear—it couldn't be the Duke. Nevertheless, the ducal car was the only thing in sight —unless it was Gregory Persimmons; he by now had reached the gate in advance of the shouting Colonel. The constable ran for him, and met him. "Not me, you everlasting ape!" Gregory howled at him. "The car, you baboon, the car!" "The Archdeacon," the Colonel bellowed. "Stop the Archdeacon!" The constable left Gregory and began to run after the car, which by now had got fairly started. "Stop, God blast you!'' the Colonel yelled again. "Come back, you fool!'' The constable, in one entire maze, stopped and came back, to find Gregory and the Colonel scrambling into their own car. "Drive like hell,'' the Colonel said; "we may catch him."

"After the Duke, sir?'' the bewildered constable asked.

"After that damned black-coated hypocrite,'' the Colonel shouted, still in a stentorian voice, so that the Archdeacon, a quarter of a mile away, unconsciously turned to protest. "I'll unfrock him—I'll have him in the dock!"

"*Drive*," Gregory said, looking unpleasantly at the constable, and the constable drove.

So through the English roads the Graal was borne away in the care of a Duke, an Archdeacon, and a publisher's clerk, pursued by a country householder, the Chief Constable of a county, and a perplexed policeman. And these things also perhaps the angels desired to look into.

At least the Duke of the North Ridings did. After a few moments he said to Mornington, "I suppose you know what we're doing?"

"We're carrying the San Graal," Mornington said. "Lancelot and Pelleas and Pellinore—no, that's not right— Bors and Percivale and Galahad. The Archdeacon's Galahad, and you can be Percivale: you're not married, are you? And I'm Bors—but I'm not married either, and Bors was. It doesn't matter; you must be Percivale, because you're a poet. And Bors was an ordinary workaday fellow like me. On, on to Sarras!" He looked back over his shoulder. "Sarras!" he cried to the car behind. "We shall meet at Carbonek!"

"What in God's name are you singing about?" the Duke asked.

Mornington was about to reply when the Archdeacon, leaning forward, said with a slight formality: "I couldn't take advantage of your kindness, my lord, unless you knew the circumstances. I don't want to rush you . . ."

The Flight of the Duke of the North Ridings

"Really?" the Duke said, manipulating a corner. "Oh, really? Well, I'm not objecting, but—damn that dog!—there seems to be a slight rush somewhere. Perhaps it's the people behind. Mornington, stop laughing and tell me where I'm to drive to."

"But, indeed," the Archdeacon protested, "I'd rather you put me down than——"

"No, look here," Kenneth said, pulling himself together, "it's all right really. Honestly, Ridings. The Archdeacon *has* got the Graal there."

"The Graal?" the Duke said, and again, in a voice that rejected the idea still more strongly, "The Graal?"

"The Graal," Kenneth assured him. "Malory—Tennyson—Chrétien de Troyes—Miss Jessie Weston. *From Romance to Reality*, or whatever she called it. That's what's happening, anyhow. I give you my word, Ridings, that it's really serious."

The Duke spared him a glance. An hour's conversation on literature between two ardent minds with a common devotion to a neglected poet is a miraculous road to intimacy. Mornington went on explaining as quietly and as clearly as was possible, and at last the Duke said, shrugging his shoulders, "Well, if you say so. . . . But where are we going?"

Kenneth looked back at the Archdeacon, then changed his mind and said, "Where *are* we going now, anyhow?"

"London as straight as we can," the Duke answered.

"Humph!" said Kenneth. "I suppose you've got a house there?"

"Of sorts," the Duke answered.

"Well, let's go there, and we can tell you the whole thing in full. Unless they telephone to the police on the way?" Over his shoulder he offered the Archdeacon the question.

"I don't think he'll do that," the priest said. "He wants it kept quiet too."

"They can't stop us without arresting us," the Duke said thoughtfully, "if I refuse to stop."

The Flight of the Duke of the North Ridings

"Arrest of the Duke of the North Ridings and the Arch-deacon of Fardles. Strange story. Is the Holy Graal in England? Evidence by a retired publisher. By God, Ridings, they daren't stop us!" Kenneth cried, as the magnitude of the possibilities of publicity became clear to him.

"London, then," the Duke said, and gave himself up to his destiny.

Kenneth glanced back at the pursuing car. "The Arch-deacon's lost his Rectory," he thought, "and I've lost my job, and the Duke's near losing his reputation. But poor old Gregory's lost the Graal—and Giles Tumulty will lose his nerve if I ever get a chance at him," he added, remembering the previous afternoon.

In the pursuing car the same thought of publicity entered the minds of its occupants, and first of Gregory. He was therefore in time to check the impulse of Colonel Conyers towards the station telephone by pointing out to him the dimensions of the scandal which might result. "In the courts it's bound at best to be a drawn battle; I may recover the chalice, but a lot of people will believe the Archdeacon—all the clerical party. Whereas, if we can only get hold of the Duke and explain matters, it's quite likely he'll see how strong my case is. Is he a great friend of the Archdeacon's?"

"I didn't know they even knew each other," the Chief Constable said. "The Duke's a Roman Catholic; all his family are. He's in with the Norfolks, too; his mother was a Howard. It makes this freak of his all the more surprising. That damned clergyman must have bamboozled him somehow."

As they rushed on, however, Gregory began to recover his poise; the Duke was the only unknown quantity in the allied opposition, and he found it impossible to believe that the Duke was unpersuadable. He had other resources after all; there was Sir Giles, who had a good deal of curious knowledge of hidden circles, for it was at his advice that a visit had been paid on the Saturday to the Greek in the chemist's shop. Sir

The Flight of the Duke of the North Ridings

Giles had insisted that a pedigree could be more easily and more certainly created there than by a reliance on the less effective Stephen. With this, and the police if necessary behind him, he smiled at the car in front, which maintained a steady space between them. It escaped, as a white hart of heaven, before the pursuing hounds—escaped for a while, but hardly, and with little hope. The teeth were gnashing behind at it; already the blood showed here and there on the white coat; already the pursuer felt the taste in his mouth. Mornington should suffer; that was clear; and the Archdeacon—but how was not yet clear. And the Graal should be withdrawn again into the seclusion of a frozen sanctuary.

They approached London, still with the distance varyingly, but on the whole steadily, maintained; they entered it, and ran down towards the West End. The Duke kept the car at as great a speed as possible, and stopped it at a house in Grosvenor Square. Mornington sprang out and opened the door for the Archdeacon, who got out, still holding the Graal, and the three ran to the front door, which opened before them. The Duke pushed the other two in, and, with his arms in theirs, led them on through the hall, saying over his shoulder as he did so, "If anyone calls, Thwaites, I am not at home."

"Very good, your Grace," the footman said, and went calmly to the door as footsteps sounded before it.

"Ridings, Ridings!" the Colonel called, and found his way blocked as the Duke and his friends disappeared in the indistinct shadows.

"His Grace is not at home, sir," the footman said.

"Damn it, man, I saw him!" the Colonel cried.

"I am sorry, sir, but his Grace is not at home."

"I am the Chief Constable of Hertfordshire," Colonel Conyers raged. "I represent the police."

"I am sorry, sir, but his Grace is not at home."

Gregory touched the Colonel's arm. "It's no use," he said. "We must write, or I must call presently."

The Flight of the Duke of the North Ridings

"It's perfectly monstrous," the Colonel cursed. "The whole thing's insane and ridiculous. Look here, my man, I want to see the Duke on important business."

"I am sorry, sir, but his Grace is not at home."

"Come with me," Gregory said. "Let's make sure of my right first and enforce it afterwards."

"You'll hear more of this," the Colonel said threateningly. "It's no use standing there and telling me these lies. Tell Ridings I'm going to have an explanation, and the sooner he lets me hear from him the better. I've never been treated like this before in my whole life."

"I'm sorry, sir, but his Grace——"

The Colonel flung away, and Gregory went with him. The footman closed the door, and, hearing the bell, went to the library.

"Have they gone?" the Duke asked.

"Yes, your Grace. One of the gentlemen seemed rather annoyed. He asked you to write to him explaining."

The three looked at one another. "Very well, Thwaites," the Duke said. "I'm not at home to anyone till after lunch, and see that we have something to eat as soon as possible." Then, as the servant left the room, he sat down and turned to the priest. "And now," he said, "let's hear about this Graal."

Chapter Ten

THE SECOND ATTEMPT ON THE GRAAL

Inspector Colquhoun, summing up the situation of the Persimmons investigations, found himself inclining towards three trails, though he was conscious of only one, and that the remnants of the Wesleyan mission bill. The prospects of this fragment producing anything were of the slightest, but he would have done what could be done sooner had he not been engaged in checking and investigating the movements of the staff of Persimmons. His particular attention was by now unconsciously fixed on two subjects—Lionel Rackstraw and Stephen Persimmons. For the first Sir Giles was responsible; for the second, absurdly enough, the adequacy of the alibi. Where few had anything like a sufficient testimony to their occupation during the whole of one particular hour, it was inevitable that the inspector should regard, first with satisfaction but later almost with hostility, the one man whose time was sufficiently vouched for by almost an excess of evidence. His training forbade this lurking hostility to enter his active mind; consciously he ruled out Stephen, unconsciously he lay in ambushed expectation. The alibi, in spite of himself, annoyed him by its perfection, and clamoured, as a mere work of art, to be demolished. He regarded Stephen as the notorious Athenian di Aristides.

Unconscious, however, of this impassioned frenzy, the inspector spent an hour or more going through the files of the *Methodist Recorder* and investigating the archives of the Methodist Bookroom. He found that during the few weeks preceding the murder three missions had been held in London at Wesleyan churches—at Ealing, at East Ham, and near

Victoria. He achieved also a list of some seven churches in the country which fitted his demands—ranging from Manchester to Canterbury. He expected no result from this investigation, which, indeed, he undertook merely to satisfy a restless conscience; it might be worth while asking the various ministers whether they had heard of any unexpected disappearance in their districts, but the chance was small. The inspector thought it more than likely that the disappearance had been explained and arranged for, and his mind returned slowly to a sullen hatred of Sir Giles and a sullen satisfaction with Stephen Persimmons as he rode back on a bus to his home.

The two emotions working with him led, however, to an unexpected if apparently unprofitable piece of news. For they drove him to a third interview with Stephen, ostensibly to collect a few more details about the staff and the premises, actually to mortify his heart again by the sight of the one man who could not have committed the murder. The conversation turned at last on Sir Giles, and Stephen happened to say, while explaining which of his books the firm had published and why, "But of course he knows my father better than me. Indeed, he's staying with him now."

At the moment the inspector thought nothing of this; but that night, as he lay half asleep and half awake, the two names which had haunted him arose like a double star in his sky. He felt them like a taunt; he bore them like a martyrdom; he considered them like a defiance. A remote thought, as from the departed day of common sense, insisted still: "Fool, it's his father, his father, his father." A nearer fantasy of dream answered: "He and his father—the name's the same. Substitution—disguise—family life—vendettas—vengeance—ventriloquism . . ." It lost itself in sleep.

The next evening he spent in writing a report on the case, and part of the afternoon in being examined upon it by an Assistant Commissioner, who appeared to be a little irritated by the hopelessness of the investigation up to that date.

The Second Attempt on the Graal

"You haven't any ideas about it, inspector?" he asked.

"Very few, sir," the inspector answered. "There must obviously be a personal motive; and I think it must have been premeditated by someone who knew this Rackstraw wasn't going to be there at the time. But till I know who or what the man was, I can't get my hands on the murderer. I'm having inquiries made in the Wesleyan districts—one of them's near where I live, out by Victoria, and I've told my wife to keep her ears open. She goes to church. But the man's just as likely as not to have been a stranger to the district, just passing or lodging there for a week or so."

The Assistant Commissioner grunted. "Well," he said, "let me know what happens. It's a bad thing, these undiscovered murders. Yes, I know, but they oughtn't to happen. All right."

The inspector saluted and went out, passing on his way Colonel Conyers, who, having been landed in London, was making use of the afternoon to dispose of certain official business. Having settled this, he lingered to ask whether the Duke of the North Ridings was known to Scotland Yard, but discovered that, with the exception of one summons for having ridden a bicycle without a light and one for assault on Boat Race Night, nothing evil was to be discovered. Nor of the Archdeacon of Fardles. Nor of Mr. Gregory Persimmons. Nor of Dmitri Lavrodopoulos, chemist.

"This is all very curious, Colonel," the Assistant Commissioner said. "What's the idea?"

"Nothing official," Conyers answered. "I won't go into it all now. But if ever you hear anything about any of those names, you might let me know. Good-bye."

"Stop a moment, Colonel," said the other. "I think I ought to know why you want to know about this Gregory Persimmons. Nothing against him, but we've come across his name in another connection."

"Well . . ." the Colonel hesitated. He had included Gregory's name in his inquiries from habit and nothing else;

if you were investigating, even in the most casual way, you included everybody and everything in your investigations; and if a case had arisen in which his own wife had played some unimportant part, the Colonel would have been capable of putting her name down on the list for inquiries to be made regarding her life and circumstances. He had paid a visit with Gregory to the shop in Lord Mayor Street, where the Greek, as weary and motionless as ever, had confirmed Persimmons's statement. Yes, he had sold the chalice; he had had it from another Greek, a friend of his who was now living in Athens but had visited London two or three months before; yes, he had a receipt for the money he had himself paid; yes, he had given Mr. Persimmons a receipt; the chalice had come from near Ephesus, and had been brought to Smyrna in the flight before the Turkish advance.

It all seemed quite right. The Colonel felt that Mr. Persimmons was being very harshly dealt with, and he looked now at the Assistant Commissioner with a slight indignation.

"A very nice fellow," he said. "I don't want to go into the story, because at present we want it kept quiet. I think the Archdeacon has gone mad, and if the Duke hadn't behaved in the most unjustifiable manner the whole thing would have been settled by now."

"It all sounds very thrilling," the Assistant Commissioner said. "Do tell me. We don't usually get cases with Dukes and Archdeacons in. The Dukes are usually in the divorce court and the Archdeacons in the ecclesiastical."

He was nevertheless slightly disappointed with the story. There seemed to be no remotest connection between the loss of the chalice and the murder in the publishing office except the name of Persimmons. Still, he wondered what Persimmons had been doing while the murder was going on. But that was a month or more ago; it would be very difficult to find out. The Assistant Commissioner had never ceased to wonder at the way in which many people always seemed to be quite

certain what they were doing at four in the afternoon of the
ninth of December when they were being examined at half-
past eleven on the morning of the twenty-fifth of January.
He turned the page of the reports in the file before him.

"You didn't meet Sir Giles Tumulty by any chance?" he
asked. "Or Mr. Lionel Rackstraw?"

"I did not," the Colonel said.

"Or Mr. Kenneth Mornington?"

"There was a Mr. Mornington—or some name like it—with
the Archdeacon," the Chief Constable said. "But I didn't
really catch his name when he was introduced, so I didn't
mention it. It may have been Mornington. He ran away
with the Duke."

"Very funny," the other murmured. "A chalice, too—
such a funny thing to run away with. Ephesus, you say?
I wonder if any particular chalice came from Ephesus."
He made a note. "All right, Colonel; we'll remember the
names."

About the same time the allies in Grosvenor Square
separated. There had been some discussion after lunch what
the next move should be. The Duke inclined to ask Sir Giles
definitely whether he identified this chalice with the Graal.
But he had not met the antiquarian, and neither the Archdeacon nor Mornington thought it likely that Sir Giles would
do more than cause them as much embarrassment as possible.
The Archdeacon was inclined to put the Graal in safe keeping
in the bank; the Duke, half convinced of its authenticity, felt
that this would be improper. He, like Kenneth, attached a
good deal more importance than the Archdeacon to the actual
vessel. "It will be quite safe here," he said; "I'll put it in a
private safe upstairs and get Thwaites to keep an eye on it.
And you'd better stop here too for the present." This, however,
the Archdeacon was reluctant to do; his place, he felt, was in
his parish, which Mr. Batesby would soon be compelled to
leave for his own. He consented, however, to stop for a couple

of nights, in case any further move should be made by their opponents.

Kenneth's plan for that afternoon was definite. He intended to go down to the publishing offices on two errands; first, to forestall Gregory Persimmons if that power behind the throne should attempt to influence the throne in the matter of the proofs; and secondly, to obtain a set of the uncorrected proofs containing the paragraph that had caused the trouble, and, if possible, Sir Giles's postcard. He felt that it might be useful in the future to have both these in his possession. For Kenneth, not being more or less above the law like the Duke, or outside it like the Archdeacon, had a distinct feeling that, though it might be good fun to steal your own property under the nose of the police, the police were still likely to maintain an interest in it. Besides, he had never read the paragraph itself, and he very much wanted to.

On arrival at the offices, therefore, he slipped in by the side entrance, reached Lionel's office without passing anyone of sufficient eminence to inquire what had caused this visit, and searched for and found the proofs he desired. Then, going on to his own room, he rang up the central filing office. "I want," he said, "the file of Tumulty's *Sacred Vessels* at once. Will you send it down?" In a few minutes it arrived; he stopped the boy who brought it. "Is Mr. Persimmons in?" he asked. "Find out, will you?"

While the boy was gone on this errand, Kenneth looked through the correspondence. But it consisted wholly of business-like letters, a little violent on Sir Giles's part, a little stiff on Lionel's. There was no special reference to the article on the Graal as far as he could see, beyond the question of illustrations; certainly no reference to black magic. He abstracted the last postcard, took a copy of the book itself from his shelves, and by the time the boy had returned was ready for Stephen.

Mr. Persimmons was in. Mornington went along the

corridor, tapped, and entered. Stephen looked up in surprise. "What brings you here?" he asked. "I thought you'd be away till to-morrow week."

"So I am, sir," Mornington said. "But I wanted to see you rather particularly. I called on Mr. Gregory Persimmons yesterday, and I'm not altogether easy about our interview."

Stephen stood up hurriedly and came nearer. "What happened?" he said anxiously. "What's the trouble?"

Kenneth explained, with a certain tact. He didn't blame Gregory at all, but he made it clear that Sir Giles and Gregory between them wanted blood, and that after the morning's chase Gregory was likely to want it more than ever; and he hinted as well as he could that he expected Stephen to stand up for the staff. Unfortunately, the prospect seemed to cause Stephen a good deal of uneasiness. With a directness unusual in him he pressed the central question.

"Do you mean," he said, "that my father will want me to get rid of you?"

"I think it is possible," Kenneth answered. "If ever a man wanted the tongue of his dog to be red with my blood it was Giles Tumulty. That's the kind of fellow he is."

"Oh, Giles Tumulty!" Stephen said. "I don't dismiss my people to please Giles Tumulty."

"He's a source of revenue," Kenneth pointed out. "And Mr. Gregory Persimmons will probably be rather annoyed himself."

"My dear Mornington," Stephen said, looking at the papers on his table, "my father wouldn't dream of interfering . . . either with me or with the staff—especially any of his old staff." He heard his own voice so unconvincingly that he walked over to the window and looked out. He felt his possession— his business and occupation and security—beginning to quiver around him as he considered the foreboded threat. He knew that he was incapable of standing up against his father's determination, but he knew also that the determination would not have to be called into play; the easier method of threatening his financial stability would be used. His father, Stephen had long felt, never put forward more power than was sufficient to achieve his object; it was the vaster force in reserve which helped to create that sense of laziness emanating from the elder Persimmons, as a man who pushes a book across with a finger seems more indolent than one who picks it up and lays it down in a new place. But an attack on Mornington roused alarm in Stephen on every side. His subordinate was as far indispensable to the business as anyone ever is; he was personally sympathetic, and Stephen was very unwilling to undergo the contempt which he felt the other would show for him if he yielded. Of the more obvious disadvantages of dismissal to Kenneth, Stephen in this bird's-eye view of the situation took little heed; "I can always get him another job," he thought, and returned to his own troubles.

Kenneth in these few minutes' silence realized that he would have to fight for his own hand, with the Graal (figuratively) in it.

"Well," he said, "I've told you about it, sir, so that if anything is said you may know our point of view."

"Our," said Gregory's voice behind him, "meaning the Archdeacon and your other friend, I suppose?"

Stephen jumped round. Kenneth looked over his shoulder. "Hallo," the publisher said, "I . . . I didn't expect you."

Gregory looked disappointed. "Tut, tut!" he said. "Now I hoped you always did. I hoped you were always listening for my step. And I think you are. I think you expect me every moment of the day. A pleasant thought, that. However, I only came down now to put a private telephone call through." He laid his hat and gloves on the table. Kenneth was unable to resist the impulse.

"A new hat, I'm afraid, Mr. Persimmons," he said. "And new gloves. The Chief Constable, of course, had them."

Gregory, sitting down, looked sideways at him. "Yes," he

said, "we shall have to economize somehow. Expenses are dreadfully heavy. I want to go through the salary list with you in a few minutes, Stephen."

"I'll send for it," Stephen said, with a nervous smile.

"Oh, I don't think you need," Gregory answered. "Only a few items; perhaps only one to-day. In fact, we could settle it now—I mean Mr. Kenneth Mornington's item. Don't you thing we pay him too much?"

"Ha, ha!" Stephen said, with a twisted grin. "What do you say, Mornington?"

Kenneth said nothing, and Gregory in a moment or two went on, "That is immaterial; in fact, the salary itself is immaterial. He is to be dismissed as a dishonest employee."

"Really——" Stephen said. "Father, you can't talk like that, especially when he's here."

"On the contrary," Kenneth said, "he can quite easily talk like that. It's a little like Sir Giles certainly, but your father, if I may say so, sir, never had much originality. Charming, no doubt, as a man, but as a publisher—third rate. And as for dishonesty . . ."

Gregory allowed himself to smile. "That," he said, "is vulgar abuse. Stephen, pay him if you'd rather and get rid of him."

"There is such a thing as wrongful dismissal," Kenneth remarked.

"My dear fellow," Gregory said, "we're reducing our staff in consequence of my returning to an active business life . . . did you speak, Stephen? . . . and you suffer. And your present employer and I between us can make it precious difficult for you to get another job. However, you can always sponge on the Duke or your clerical friend. Stephen . . ."

"I won't," Stephen said; "the thing's ridiculous. Just because you two have quarrelled . . ."

"Mr. Stephen Persimmons featuring the bluff employer," his father murmured. He got up, went over to the publisher, and began whispering in his ear, following him as he took a few steps and halted again. Kenneth had an impulse to say that he resigned, and another to knock Gregory down and trample on him. He stared at him, and felt a new anger rising above the personal indignation he had felt before. He wanted to smash; he wanted to strangle Gregory and push him also underneath Lionel's desk; for the sake of destroying he desired to destroy. The contempt he had always felt leapt fierce and raging in him; till now it had always dwelt in a secret house of his own; if anything, calming his momentary irritations. But now it and anger were one. He took a blind step forward, heard Stephen exclaim, and Gregory loose a high cackle of delight. "God, he likes it!" he thought to himself, and pulled madly at his emotions. "Sweet Jesus," he began, and found that he was speaking aloud.

Gregory was in front of him. "Sweet Jesus," his voice said jeeringly. "Sweet filth, sweet nothing!" Kenneth struck out, missed, felt himself struck in turn, heard a high voice laughing at him, was caught and freed himself, then was caught by half a dozen hands, and recovered at last to find himself held by two or three clerks, Stephen shuddering against the wall, and Gregory opposite him, sitting in his son's chair.

"Take him away and throw him down the steps," Gregory said; and, though it was not done literally, it was effectively. Still clutching the proofs of *Sacred Vessels*, Kenneth came dazedly into the street and walked slowly back to Grosvenor Square.

When he reached it, he found the Duke and the Archdeacon were both out, and Thwaites on guard in the Duke's private room. The Duke returned to dinner, at which he found Kenneth a poor companion. The Archdeacon returned considerably later, having been detained on ecclesiastical business first ("I had to come up anyhow," he explained, "this afternoon, so Mr. Persimmons didn't really disarrange me"), and secondly by a vain search for the Bishop.

The Second Attempt on the Graal

The three went to the Duke's room for coffee, which however, was neglected while Kenneth repeated the incidents of the afternoon. The removal of the proofs, which was a mild satisfaction, led to the employment question, on which both his hearers, more moved, began to babble of secretaries, and from that to an account of the riot. When Kenneth came to repeat, apologetically, Gregory's cries, the Duke was startled into a horrified disgust; the Archdeacon smiled a little.

"I'm sorry you let yourself go so," he said. "We *must* be careful not to get like him."

"Sorry?" the Duke cried. "After that vile blasphemy? I wish I could have got near enough to have torn his throat out."

"Oh, really, really," the Archdeacon protested. "Let us leave that kind of thing to Mr. Persimmons."

"To insult God——" the Duke began.

"How can you insult God?" the Archdeacon asked. "About as much as you can pull His nose. For Kenneth to have knocked Mr. Persimmons down for calling him dishonest would have been natural—a venial sin, at most; for him to have done it in order to avenge God would have been silly; but for him to have got into a blurred state of furious madness is a great deal too like Mr. Persimmons's passions to please me. And I am not at all clear that Mr. Persimmons doesn't know it. We *must* keep calm. *His* mind's calm enough."

"At least," Mornington said, "we're pretty certain now." And with the word they all turned and looked at the Graal which the Duke, when they entered, had withdrawn from the safe. In a minute the Duke, crossing himself, knelt down before it. Kenneth followed his example. The Archdeacon stood up.

Under the concentrated attention the vessel itself seemed to shine and expand. In each of them differently the spirit was moved and exalted—most perhaps in the Duke. He was aware of a sense of the adoration of kings—the great tradition of his house stirred within him. The memories of proscribed and martyred priests awoke; masses said swiftly and in the midst of the fearful breathing of a small group of the faithful; the ninth Duke who had served the Roman Pontiff at his private mass; the Roman Order he himself wore; the fidelity of his family to the Faith under the anger of Henry and the cold suspicion of Elizabeth; the duels fought in Richmond Park by the thirteenth Duke in defence of the honour of our Lady, when he met and killed three antagonists consecutively—all these things, not so formulated but certainly there, drew his mind into a vivid consciousness of all the royal and sacerdotal figures of the world adoring before this consecrated shrine. "Jhesu, Rex et Sacerdos," he prayed. . . .

Kenneth trembled in a more fantastic vision. This, then, was the thing from which the awful romances sprang, and the symbolism of a thousand tales. He saw the chivalry of England riding on its quest—but not a historical chivalry; and, though it was this they sought, it was some less material vision that they found. But this had rested in dreadful and holy hands; the Prince Immanuel had so held it, and the Apostolic chivalry had banded themselves about him. Half in dream, half in vision, he saw a grave young God communicating to a rapt companionship the mysterious symbol of unity. They took oaths beyond human consciousness; they accepted vows plighted for them at the beginning of time. Liturgical and romantic names melted into one cycle—Lancelot, Peter, Joseph, Percivale, Judas, Mordred, Arthur, John Bar-Zebedee, Galahad—and into these were caught up the names of their makers—Hawker and Tennyson, John, Malory and the mediævals. They rose, they gleamed and flamed about the Divine hero, and their readers too—he also, least of all these. He was caught in the dream of Tennyson; together they rose on the throbbing verse.

> And down the long beam stole the Holy Graal,
> Rose-red with beatings in it.

The Second Attempt on the Graal

He heard Malory's words—"the history of the Sangreal, the whiche is a story cronycled for one of the truest and the holyest that is in thys world"—"the deadly flesh began to behold the spiritual things"—"fair lord, commend me to Sir Lancelot my father." The single tidings came to him across romantic hills; he answered with the devotion of a romantic and abandoned heart.

The Archdeacon found no such help in the remembrances of kings or poets. He looked at the rapt faces of the young men; he looked at the vessel before him. "Neither is this Thou," he breathed; and answered, "Yet this also is Thou." He considered, in this, the chalice offered at every altar, and was aware again of a general movement of all things towards a narrow channel. Of all material things still discoverable in the world the Graal had been nearest to the Divine and Universal Heart. Sky and sea and land were moving, 'not towards that vessel, but towards all it symbolized and had held. The consecration at the Mysteries was for him no miraculous change; he had never dreamed of the heavenly courts attending Christ upon the altar. But in accord with the desire of the Church expressed in the ritual of the Church the Sacred Elements seemed to him to open upon the Divine Nature, upon Bethlehem and Calvary and Olivet, as that itself opened upon the Centre of all. And through that gate, upon those tides of retirement, creation moved. Never so clearly as now had he felt that movement proceeding, but his mind nevertheless knew no other vision than that of a thousand dutifully celebrated Mysteries in his priestly life; so and not otherwise all things return to God.

When their separate devotions ceased, they looked at one another gravely. "There's one thing," the Duke said. "It must never be left unwatched. We must have an arranged order—people whom we can trust."

"*Intelligent* people whom we can trust," the Archdeacon said.

"In fact, an Order," Kenneth murmured. "A new Table."

"A new Table!" the Duke cried. "And a Mass every morning." He stopped short and looked at the Archdeacon.

"Quite so," the priest said, not in answer to the remark.

The Duke hesitated a moment, then he said politely, "I don't want to seem rude, sir, but you see that since, quite by chance, it has come into my charge, I must preserve it for . . . for . . ."

"But, Ridings," Kenneth said in a slightly alert voice, "it isn't in your charge. It belongs to the Archdeacon."

"My dear fellow," the Duke impatiently answered, "the sacred and glorious Graal can't *belong*. And obviously it is in my charge. I don't want to press my rights and those of my Church, but equally I don't want them abused or overlooked."

"Rights?" Kenneth asked. "It is in the hands of a priest."

"That," the Duke answered, "is for the Holy See to say. As it has done."

The two young men looked at one another hostilely. The Archdeacon broke in.

"Oh, children, children," he said. "Did either of you ever hear of Cully or Mr. Gregory Persimmons? It being (legally, my dear Duke) my property, I should like Mr. Persimmons not to get hold of it until I know a little more about him. But, on the other hand, I will promise not to hurt anyone's feeling by using it prematurely for schismatic Mysteries. A liqueur glass would do as well." Kenneth grinned; the Duke acknowledged the promise with a bow, and rather obviously ignored the last remark.

It was already very late; midnight had been passed by almost an hour. The Archdeacon looked at his watch and at his host. But the Duke had returned to his earlier idea.

"If we three can share the watch till morning," he said, "I will bring Thwaites in; he is one of our people. And there are certain others. It is one o'clock now—say, one to seven; six hours. Archdeacon, which watch will you take?"

The Second Attempt on the Graal

The Archdeacon felt that a passion for relics had its inconveniences, but he hadn't the heart to check its ardour. "I will take the middle, if you like," he said, normally accepting the least pleasant; "that will be three to five."

"Mornington?"

"Whichever you like," Kenneth answered. "The morning?"

"Very well," the Duke said. "Then I will watch now."

They were at the door of the room, and, as they exchanged temporary good nights, the Archdeacon glanced back at the sacred vessel. He seemed to blink at it for a moment, then he took a step or two back into the room, and gazed at it attentively. The two young men looked at him, at it, at each other. Suddenly the priest made a sudden run across the room and took the Graal up in his hands.

It seemed to move in them like something alive. He felt as if a continuous slight shifting of all the particles that composed it were proceeding, and that blurring of its edges which had first caught his eyes was now even more marked. Close as he held it, he felt strangely uncertain exactly where the edge was, exactly how deep the cup was, how long the stem. He touched the edge, and it seemed to have a curious softness, to give under his finger. The shape did not yield to his grasp, but it suggested that it was about to do so. It quivered, it trembled; now here, now there, its thickness accumulated or faded; now it seemed to take the shape of his fingers, now to harden and resist them. The Archdeacon gripped it more firmly, and, keeping his eyes on it, turned to face the others.

"Something is going on," he said, almost harshly. "I do not know what. It may be that God is dissolving it but I think there is devilry. Make yourselves paths for the Will of God."

"But what is it?" the Duke said amazedly. "What harm can come to it here? What can they do to its hurt?"

"Pray," the Archdeacon cried out, "pray, in the name of God. They are praying against Him to-night."

It crossed Kenneth's mind, as he sank to his knees, that if

God could not be insulted, neither could He be defied, nor in
that case the procession and retrogression of the universe disturbed by the subject motion of its atoms. But he saw, running
out like avenues, a thousand metaphysical questions, and they
disappeared in the excitement of his spirit.

"Against what shall we pray?" the Duke cried.

"Against nothing," the Archdeacon said. "Pray that He
who made the universe may sustain the universe, that in all
things there may be delight in the justice of His will."

A profound silence followed, out of the heart of which there
arose presently a common consciousness of effort. The interior
energy of the priest laid hold on the less trained powers of his
companions and directed them to its own intense concentration. Fumbling in the dark for something to oppose, they were,
each in secrecy, subdued from that realm of opposition and
translated to a place where their business was only to repose.
They existed knit together, as it were, in a living tower built
up round the sacred vessel, and through all the stones of that
tower its common life flowed. Yet to all their apprehensions,
and especially to the priest's, which was the most vivid and
east distracted, this life received and resisted an impact from
without. The tower was indeed a tower of defence, though it
offered no aggression, and resisted whatever there was to be
resisted merely by its own immovable calm. Once or twice it
seemed to the Duke as if he heard a soft footprint behind him
just within the room, but he was held too firmly still even to
turn his head. Once or twice on Kenneth there intruded a
sudden vision of something other than this passivity; a taunt,
unspoken but mocking, moved just beyond his consciousness,
a taunt which was not his, but arose somehow out of him.
Sudden phrases he had used in the past attacked him—"the
world can't judge"; "man chooses between mania and folly";
"what a fool Stephen is." In the midst of these the memory of
the saying about every idle word obtruded itself; he began to
justify them to himself, and to argue in his own mind. Little by

little he became more and more conscious of his past casual contempt, and more disposed to direct a certain regretful attention to it. The priest felt the defence weaken; he did not know the cause, but the result was there; the Graal shook in his hands. He plunged deeper into the abysmal darkness of divinity, and as he did so heard, far above, his own voice crying "Pray!" Kenneth heard, and knew his weakness; he abolished his memories, and, so far as was possible, surrendered himself to be only what he was meant to be. Yet the attack went on: to one a footstep, a whisper, a slight faint touch; to another a gentle laugh, a mockery, a reminder; to the third a spiritual pressure which not he but that which was he resisted. The Graal vibrated still to that pressure, more strongly when it was accentuated, less and less as the stillness within and amidst the three was perfected. Dimly he knew at what end the attack aimed; some disintegrating force was being loosed at the vessel—not conquest, but destruction, was the purpose, and chaos the eventual hope. Dimly he saw that, though the spirit of Gregory formed the apex of that attack, the attack itself came from regions behind Gregory. He saw, uncertainly but sufficiently defined, the radiations that encompassed the Graal and the fine arrows of energy that were expended against it. Unimportant as the vessel in itself might be, it was yet an accidental storehouse of power that could be used, and to dissipate this material centre was the purpose of the war. But through the three concentrated souls flowed reserves of the power which the vessel itself retained; and gradually to the priest it seemed, as in so many celebrations, as if the Graal itself was the centre—yet no longer the Graal, but a greater than the Graal. Silence and knowledge were communicated to him as if from an invisible celebrant; he held the Cup no longer as a priest, but as if he set his hands on that which was itself at once the Mystery and the Master of the Mystery. But this consciousness faded almost before it was realized; his supernatural mind returned into his natural, leaving only the certainty that for the time at least the attack was ended. Rigid and hard in his hands, the Graal reflected only the lights of the Duke's study; he sighed and relaxed his hold, glancing at his two companions. The Duke stood up suddenly and glanced round him. Kenneth rose more slowly, his face covered with a certain brooding melancholy. The Archdeacon set the Graal down on the table.

"It is done," he said. "Whatever it was has exhausted itself for the time. Let us go and rest."

"I thought I heard someone here," the Duke said, still looking round him. "Is it safe to leave it?"

"I think it is quite safe," the Archdeacon said.

"But what has happened?" the Duke asked again.

"Let us talk to-morrow," the priest said very wearily. "The Graal will guard itself to-night."

Chapter Eleven

THE OINTMENT

The afternoon which had preceded the supernatural effort to destroy the Graal had been made use of by Mr. Gregory Persimmons to pay two visits. The first had been with the Chief Constable of Hertfordshire to the shop in Lord Mayor Street. But after the visit was made and the information acquired Colonel Conyers and he had parted in the Finchley Road, the Colonel to go to Scotland Yard in a chance taxi, he ostensibly for the Tube at Golder's Green. Once the Colonel had disappeared, however, Gregory returned as swiftly as possible to the shop.

The Greek had resumed his everlasting immobility, but, though he said nothing, his eyes lightened a little as he saw the other again come in.

"Do you know what has happened?" Gregory asked in that subdued tone to which the place seemed to compel its visitors.

"It seems they have recovered it," the Greek said and looked askew at a much older man who had just come into the shop from a small back room. The new-comer was smaller than the Greek, and much smaller than Gregory; his movements were swift and his repose alert. His bearded face was that of a Jew.

"You heard?" the Greek said.

"I heard," the stranger answered. He looked angrily at Gregory. "How long have you known this?" he asked, with a note of fierceness.

"Known—known what?" Gregory said, involuntarily falling back a step. "Known that they had it? Why, he only took it this morning."

"Known that it was—that," the other said. "What time we have wasted!" He stepped up to the Greek and seized him by the arm. "But it isn't too late," he said. "We can do it to-night."

The Greek turned his head a little. "We can do it if you like," he acquiesced. "If it is worth while."

"Worth while!" the Jew snapped at him. "Of course it is worth while. It is a stronghold of power, and we can tear it to less than dust. I do not understand you, Dmitri."

"It doesn't matter," Dmitri answered. "You will understand one day. There will be nothing else to understand."

The other began to speak, but Gregory, whom his last words had brought suddenly back to the dirty discoloured counter, said suddenly, but still with that subdued voice, "What do you mean? Tear it to dust? Do you mean *that*? What are you going to do?"

The others looked over at him, the Jew scornfully, the other with a faint amusement. The Greek said, "Manasseh and I are going to destroy the Cup."

"Destroy it!" Gregory mouthed at them. "*Destroy* it! But there are a hundred things to do with it. It can be used and used again. I have made the child see visions in it; it has power."

"Because it has power," the Jew answered, leaning over the counter and whispering fiercely, "it must be destroyed. Don't you understand that yet? They build and we destroy. That's what levels us; that's what stops them. One day we shall destroy the world. What can you do with it that is so good as that? Are we babies to look to see what will happen to-morrow or where a lost treasure is or whether a man has a gluttonous heart? To destroy this is to ruin another of their houses, and another step towards the hour when we shall breathe against the heavens and they shall fall. The only use in anything for us is that it may be destroyed."

Before the passion in his tones Gregory again fell back. But he made another effort.

"But can't we use it to destroy *them*?" he asked. "See, I have called up a child's soul by it and it answered me. Let me keep it a little while to do a work with it."

"That's the treachery," the Jew answered. "Keep it for this, keep it for that. Destroy it, I tell you; while you keep anything for a reason you are not wholly ours. It shall tremble and fade and vanish into nothingness to-night."

Gregory looked at the Greek, who looked back impassively. The Jew went on muttering. At last Dmitri, putting out a slow hand, touched him, and the other with a little angry tremor fell silent. Then the Greek said, looking past them, "It is all one; in the end it is all one. You do not believe each other and neither of you will believe me. But in the end there is nothing at all but you and that which goes by. You will be sick at heart because there is nothing, nothing but a passing, and in the midst of the passing a weariness that is you. All things shall grow fainter, all desire cease in that sickness and the void that is about it. And this, even for me, is when I have only looked into the bottomless pit. For my spirit is still held in a place of material things. But when the body is drawn into the spirit, and at last they fall, then you shall know what the end of desire and destruction is. I will do what you will while you will, for the time comes when no man shall work."

Manasseh sneered at him. "When I knew you first," he said, "you did great things in the house of our God. Will you go and kneel before the Cup and weep for what you have done?"

"I have no tears and no desire," the Greek said. "I am weary beyond all mortal weariness and my heart is sick and my eyes blind with the sight of the nothing through which we fall. Say what you will do and I will do it, for even now I have power that is not yours."

"I will bring this thing into atoms and less than atoms," Manasseh answered. "I will cause it to be as if it had never been. I will send power against it and it shall pass from all knowledge and be nothing but a memory."

"So," the Greek said. "And you?" he asked Gregory.

"I will help you, then," Gregory answered, a little sullenly, "if it must be done."

"No, you shall not help us," Manasseh said sharply, "for in your heart you desire it still."

"Let him that desires to possess seek to possess," the Greek commanded, "and him that desires to destroy seek to destroy. Let each of you work in his own way, until an end comes; and I who will help the one to possess will help the other to destroy, for possession and destruction are both evil and are one. But alas for the day when none shall possess your souls and they only of all things that you have known cannot be destroyed for ever."

He stood upright. "Go," he said to Gregory, "and set your traps. Come," to Manasseh, "and we will think of these things."

But Manasseh delayed a moment. "Tell me," he said to Gregory, "of what size and shape is the Cup?"

Gregory nodded towards the Greek. "I brought the book up last Saturday with the drawing in," he said. "You can see it there. But why should I try to recover it if you are going to destroy it?"

The Greek answered him. "Because no one knows what the future may bring to your trap; because till you prepare yourself to possess you cannot possess. Because destruction is not yet accomplished."

Gregory brooding doubtfully, turned, and went slowly out of the shop.

He went on to his son's office, and there, inflamed with a certain impotent rage at the destruction threatened to that which he had spent some pains to procure, eased it by doing all he could to destroy Kenneth's security. After which he banished Stephen from the room, and talked for some time on the telephone to Ludding at Cully.

It was in pursuance of the instructions then received that Ludding the next morning strolled down to the Rectory. In a neat chauffeur's uniform, clean-shaved and alert, he presented so different an appearance from that of the bearded tramp who had called on the Archdeacon a month earlier that Mrs. Lucksparrow, even had the time been shorter, would not have recognized him. He had come down, it appeared, on a message from Mr. Persimmons to the Archdeacon.

"The Archdeacon isn't at home," Mrs. Lucksparrow said. "I'm sure I'm sorry you've had your trouble for nothing."

"No trouble, ma'am," Ludding answered; "indeed, as things have turned out, it's given me more pleasure than if he had been." His bow pointed the remark.

"Well," said Mrs..Lucksparrow, "I won't deny but what it's a pleasure to see someone to speak to, we being rather out of the way here—except for clergymen and tramps; and naturally the clergy don't come and talk to me, not but what some of them are nice enough in their way. Why, we've had the Bishop here before now, and a straightforward, pleasant-speaking gentleman too, though a bit on the hurried side, always wanting to get on somewhere else and do the next thing. I don't hold with it myself, not so much of it. What's done too quick has to be done twice my mother used to say, and she had eleven children and two husbands, though most of them was before I was born, being the youngest. Many's the time she's said to me, 'Lucy, my girl, you've never dusted that room yet, I'll be bound.'"

She stopped abruptly, a habit arising from a natural fear which possessed her when in attendance on the Archdeacon and his clerical visitors that she might be talking too much. But the sudden silence substituted for a gentle flow of words was apt to disconcert strangers, who found themselves expected to answer before they had any idea they had finished listening. Ludding was caught so now, and had to say in some haste, "Well,. I'd rather trust you than a Bishop, Mrs. Lucksparrow."

"Oh, no," the housekeeper answered, "I don't think you

should say that, Mr. Ludding, for they're meant to teach us, though there, again, my schoolmistress used to say, 'Take your time, girls, take your time,' though mostly over maps."

"Yes," Ludding said, prepared this time. "And I suppose you don't know when the Archdeacon will be back. I expect he takes *his* time." He laughed gently. "If he was married I expect he'd have to be back sooner."

"If he was married," Mrs. Lucksparrow said, "he wouldn't do a lot he does now. He's brought women home before now —well, it's not right to talk of it, Mr. Ludding, for fear of giving him a bad name, though he meant them nothing but good, little as they deserved it; and sometimes he never goes to bed at all, up in the church all night, when he thinks I'm asleep. If it wasn't that he can't eat pork I'd think he wasn't human, for I like a bit of pork, and it comes hard never being able to have it, for, of course, two joints is what I couldn't think of, and it's bad enough never daring to mention it or I believe it'd slip out, and then he'd go and buy a pig and have it sent home, all for a chop or two, but as for coming back, that I couldn't say, with only a telegram to say detained to-night, meaning yesterday—though, if it was anyone dying or anything, there's Mr. Batesby here."

"It wasn't really important," Ludding said, "only that Mr. Persimmons thought he'd like some fruit and flowers for the Harvest Festival, and wanted to know when it was likely to be."

"Second Sunday in September," Mrs. Lucksparrow said, "at least it was last year. But there *is* Mr. Batesby, and he'd know if anyone did, outside the Archdeacon."

Ludding looked over his shoulder to see Mr. Batesby emerging from the churchyard gate in the company of a stranger, a young man in a light grey suit and soft hat who was strolling carelessly by the priest's side. Mrs. Lucksparrow looked also, and said suddenly: "Why, it's a Chinaman; he's got those squinting eyes the Chinaman had when he stopped with the Archdeacon two years ago," rather as if there was only one

Chinaman in the world. Ludding, however, as the two came nearer, doubted Mrs. Lucksparrow's accuracy; there seemed nothing Chinese about this stranger's full face—it was perhaps a little dark, a kind of Indian, the chauffeur thought vaguely.

"Shrines," Mr. Batesby was saying, "shrines of rest and peace, that's what our country churches ought to be, and are, most of them. Steeped in quiet, church and churchyard—all asleep, beautifully asleep. And all round them the gentle village life, simple, homely souls. Some people want incense and lights and all that—but I say it's out of tune, it's the wrong atmosphere. True religion is an inward thing. It's so true, isn't it? 'the Kingdom of God is *within* you.' Just to remember that—*within you.*"

"It cometh not by observation," the stranger said gravely.

"True, true," Mr. Batesby assented. "So what do we want with candles?"

They reached the door, and he looked inquiringly at Ludding, who explained his errand, and added that he was sorry the Archdeacon wasn't at home and was it known when he would be back?

Mr. Batesby shook his head. "Not to a day or two," he said. "Gone on good works, no doubt. 'Make hay while the sun shineth, for the night cometh,'" and then, feeling dimly uncertain of this quotation, went on hastily, "We must all do what we can, mustn't we? Each in our small corner. Little enough, no doubt, just a car"—he looked at Ludding—"or a kitchen"—he looked at Mrs. Lucksparrow—"or—something," he ended, looking at the stranger, who nodded seriously, but offered no enlightenment for a moment. Then, as if in pity at Mr. Batesby's slightly obvious disappointment, he said, "I have been a traveller."

"Ah, yes, to be sure," the priest answered. "A broadening life, no doubt. Well, well, I venture to think you have seen nothing better than this in all your travels." He indicated church and garden and fields. "Not, of course, that the serpent isn't here too. The old serpent. But we crush his head."

"And your heels?" the stranger asked. Mr. Batesby took a moment to grasp this, and then said, gently smiling. "Yes, yes, not always unstung, I fear. Why, the Archdeacon here was assaulted only a few weeks ago in broad daylight. Scandalous. If it hadn't been for a good neighbour of ours, I don't know what might have happened. Why, you were there too, Ludding, weren't you?"

"Were you?" the stranger asked, looking him in the face.

"I was," Ludding said, almost sullenly, "if it's any business of yours."

"I think perhaps it may be," the stranger said softly. "I have come a long journey because I think it may be." He turned to Mr. Batesby. "Good day. I am obliged to you," he said, and turned back to Ludding. "Walk with me," he went on casually. "I have a question to ask you."

"Look here," the chauffeur said, moving after him, "who the hell do you think you are, asking me questions? If you want——"

"It is a very simple question," the stranger said. "Where does your master live?"

"Anyone will tell you," Ludding answered reluctantly and almost as if explaining to himself why he spoke. "At Cully over there. But he isn't there now."

"He is perhaps in London with the Archdeacon?" the stranger asked. "No, don't lie; it doesn't matter. I will go up to the house."

"He isn't there, I tell you," Ludding said, standing still as if he had been dismissed. "What the devil's the good of going to the house? We don't want Chinks hanging round up there, or any other kind of nigger. D'ye hear me? Leave it alone, can't you? Here, I'm talking to you, God blind you! You let Mr. Persimmons alone!" As the stranger drew farther away his voice became louder and his words more violent, so that

The Ointment

Inspector Colquhoun, who was allowing himself a few days in the village, partly out of his holiday, partly in a kind of desperate wonder whether Cully would yield any suggestions, came round a turn in the road on his way from the station to see a man standing still and shouting after an already remote figure.

"Anything wrong?" he asked involuntarily.

Ludding turned round furiously. "Yes," he said, "you're wrong. Who asked you to blink your fat eyes at me, you flat-nosed, fat-bellied louse?"

The inspector considered the uniform. "You take care, my man," he said.

"Christ Almighty!" Ludding yelled at him, "if you don't get off I'll smash your——"

Colquhoun stepped nearer. "Say another word to me," he said, "you jumping beer-barrel, and I'll knock you into the middle of Gehenna!" The prospect of being able to repay someone connected with a Persimmons for all that he had gone through was almost delightful. Nevertheless, he hardly expected the chauffeur to make such an immediate rush for him as he did. He defended himself with strength enough to make aggression an imperceptible sequence, and succeeded in drawing Ludding to one side of the road, until he unexpectedly crashed into the ditch behind him. Colquhoun stepped back a pace. "Come out if you like," he said, "and let me knock you into it again."

It was upon the chauffeur scrambling furiously out of the ditch that Mr. Gregory Persimmons looked when he in turn, a little later than the inspector, being a slower walker, came along the road from the station. He had paid his visit to Lord Mayor Street that morning, to find Manasseh almost beside himself with enraged disappointment, and only too anxious to take any steps for recovering the Graal. The Greek had taken little part in their discussion; the effort of the night had left him so exhausted physically that he was lying back in a chair with closed eyes, and only now and then threw a suggestion to the others. Gregory's chief difficulty was to insist on maintaining the friendly relations with the Rackstraws that were essential to his designs on Adrian, and might, he recognized, already have been endangered by the break with Mornington. This, however, he hoped to arrange; judicious explanations and promises might do much, and Adrian's own liking for him was a strong card to play. At last he had compelled Manasseh to see his aim, and then a fresh proposal had been made. Manasseh with the Greek would concern themselves with securing the Graal, and Gregory was to get hold of Adrian within the next few days. "Then," Manasseh said, "we can take the hidden road to the East."

"The hidden road?" Gregory asked.

Manasseh smiled knowingly. "Ah," he said, "you've a lot to learn yet. Ask your friend Sir Giles; he knows about it, I expect. Ask him if he's ever been to the furniture shop in Amsterdam or the picture dealer in Zurich. Ask him if he knows the boat-builder in Constantinople and the Armenian ferry. You are only on the edge of things here in London. The vortex of destruction is in the East. I have seen a house fall to fragments before a thought and men die in agony because the Will overcame them. Bring the child and come, and we will go into the high places of our god."

In the subtle companionship that existed between them Gregory felt the hope in his heart expand. "In three days from now I will be with you," he said. "By Friday night I will bring the child here."

With this purpose and a plan formed in his mind, he had returned to Fardles, to find his chauffeur struggling out of the ditch in the face of a contemptuous enemy.

When Ludding saw his employer he came to the road with a final effort and paused rather ridiculously. The inspector saw the hesitation, and looked round at Gregory, realizing that the odds were in favour of its being Gregory. He took the initiative.

"Mr. Persimmons?" he asked.

The Ointment

"I am Mr. Persimmons," Gregory answered mildly.

"I suspect this man is your chauffeur," the inspector said, and, as Gregory nodded, went on, "I'm sorry to have been obliged to knock him down. I found him shouting out in the roadway, and when I asked if anything was wrong he was first grossly rude and then attacked me. But I don't think he's hurt."

"Hurt," Ludding broke out, and was checked by Gregory's lifted hand. "I'm sorry," Persimmons said. "If by any chance it should happen again, pray knock him down again."

"No offence intended to you, sir," the inspector said. He thought for a moment whether he would make an attempt to enter into conversation with the other, but decided against it; he wanted, so far as he had a clear wish, to pick up opinion in the village first. So, with a casual inclination of the head, he started off down the road.

Persimmons looked at Ludding. "And now perhaps you will explain," he said. "Dear me, Ludding, you are letting this temper grow on you. You must try and control it. Why, you might be attacking *me* next; mightn't you?" He moved a little nearer. "Answer me, you swine, mightn't you?"

"I don't know why I hit him, sir," Ludding said unhappily. "It was the other man who irritated me."

"The other man: what other man?" Persimmons asked. "Are you blind or drunk, you fool?"

Ludding made an effort to pull himself together. "It was a young man, sir, in a grey suit. Asked after you and where you lived, and went off up to Cully. He made me see red, sir, and I was shouting after him when this fellow came up."

"A young man," Gregory said, "wanting to see *me*? This is very curious. And you didn't know him, Ludding?"

"Never seen him before, sir," Ludding answered. "He looked rather like an Indian, I thought."

Gregory's mind flew to what Manasseh had said of the hidden way to the East; was this anything to do with it? What possibilities, what vistas, might be opened! Whatever throne existed there, an end to that path he had followed so long and so painfully, would it not welcome him, coming with the Graal in one hand and the child for initiation in the other? He quickened his steps. "Let us see this young man," he said, and hastened on to Cully.

Followed by Ludding, he came to the gates and up the drive, down which he had rushed twenty-four hours before. As he rounded the turn from which Colonel Conyers had shouted at the constable, he met the stranger face to face, and all three of them stood still.

Gregory's first impression was that Ludding had been merely romancing when he spoke of the stranger being an Indian; the face that confronted him was surely as European as his own. There was something strange about it, but it was a strangeness rather of expression than of race, a high, contained glance that observed an unimportant world. The eyes took him in and neglected him at once, and together with him took in the whole of the surroundings and dismissed them also as of small worth. One hand carried gloves and walking-stick; the other, raised to the level of the face, moved lazily forward now and then as if to wave away some sort of slight unpleasantness, and every now and then also nostrils were wrinkled a little as if at some remote but objectionable smell that floated in the air. He had the appearance of being engaged upon a tiresome but necessary business, and this was enhanced as he paused on the drive and allowed his glance to dwell on Gregory.

"You want me?" Persimmons said, and the instant that he spoke became conscious that he actively disliked the stranger, with a hostility that surprised him with its own virulence. It stood out in his inner world as distinctly as the stranger himself in the full sunlight of the outer; and he knew for almost the first time what Manasseh felt in his rage for utter destruction. His fingers twitched to tear the clothes off his enemy and to break and pound him into a mass of flesh and bone, but he knew nothing of that external sign, for his being was absorbed in a more profound lust. It aimed itself in a thrust of passion which should wholly blot the other out of existence, and again its young opponent's upraised and open hand moved gently forward and downward, as if, like the Angel by the walls of Dis, he put aside the thick and noisome atmosphere of his surroundings.

"No," he said coldly, "I do not think I want you."

"What are you doing here, then?" Gregory asked thickly. "Why are you wandering about my house?"

"I am studying the map," the stranger said, "and I find this a centre marked on it."

"My servants shall throw you out," Gregory cried. "I do not allow trespassers."

"You have no servants," the other said; "you have only slaves and shadows. And only slaves can trespass, and they only among shadows."

"You are mad," Gregory cried again. "Why have you come to my house?"

"I have not entered your house," the stranger answered, "for the time is not yet. But it is not that which you should fear—it is the day when you shall enter mine."

Ludding, encouraged by his master's presence, took a step forward. The stranger threw him a glance and he stopped. His anger was so intense, however, that it drove him into speech.

"Who are you—coming here and talking like this?" he said. "Who the hell are you?"

"Yes," Gregory said, "tell us your name. You have damaged my property—you shall pay for it."

The other moved his hand outward again and smiled. "My name is John," he said, "and you know some, I think, that know me."

Gregory thought of his enemies. "That pestilent priest, perhaps?" he sneered, "or the popinjay of a Duke? Are these your

friends? Or is the Duke too vulgar for you? What kings have
you in the house of which you brag?"

"Seventy kings have eaten at my table," the stranger said.
"You say well, for I myself am king and priest and sib to all
priests and kings."

He dropped his hand and moved leisurely forward. Gregory
inevitably stepped out of his direct path. As he passed Ludding
the chauffeur put a hand out towards his shoulder. But he
didn't somehow lay hold, and with an equal serenity of gait
the stranger went on and at length passed out of the gates.
Gregory, pulsating with anger too bitter for words, turned
sharply and went on to the house. And the chauffeur, cursing
himself, drifted slowly to the garage.

By the afternoon, however, Gregory had recovered his
balance, or, rather, his intention. Whether the stranger was a
wandering lunatic or whether he had some real link with the
three fools who had carried off the Graal he did not know;
and, anyhow, it did not matter. His immediate business was
with the Rackstraws, and an hour before tea he went down
towards the cottage to find them.

They were a little distance from it among some trees.
Barbara was reading Mr. Wodehouse's latest Jeeves book, and
Lionel, stretched on the ground, was telling Adrian the adventures of Odysseus the wise, the far-travelled. The story
broke off when Gregory appeared.

"Have you been to London?" Adrian asked.

"Darling——" Barbara murmured.

"Well, Jessie said he had, Mummie," Adrian protested.
Jessie was the maid from Cully.

"Jessie was perfectly right," Gregory answered. "I have been
to London, and I have come back. In London, Adrian, they
have large trains and many soldiers." He paused.

"I have a large train in London," Adrian soliloquised. "It
has a guard's van with luggage in."

"I saw a train," Gregory said, "which belongs to your

London train. It asked to be taken to Adrian because it belonged to him."

"What, another train? A train I haven't seen?" Adrian asked, large-eyed.

"A train you haven't seen, but it belongs to you," Gregory answered seriously. "Everything belongs to you, Adrian. You are the Lord of the World—if you like. One day, if you like, I will give you the world."

"After this week I could almost believe that, Mr. Persimmons," Barbara said. "What would you do with the world, Adrian?"

Adrian considered. "I would put it in my train," he said. "Where is the train I haven't seen?" he asked Gregory.

"Up at the big house," Gregory answered. "Let's all go up there to tea, shall we? And after tea you shall see the train. It's gone to sleep now, and it won't be awake till after tea," he explained gravely.

Adrian took his hand. "Shall we go?" he said, and pulled anxiously to lead the way.

"Let us go," Gregory assented, and looked back laughing over his shoulder. "Will you come?" he cried.

Barbara stretched out her hands, and Lionel pulled her to her feet. "I just want to shimmer up, like Jeeves, not walk," she said. "Do you like Jeeves, Mr. Persimmons?"

"Jeeves?" Gregory asked. "I don't think I know it or him or them."

"Oh, you must," Barbara cried. "When I get back to London I'll send you a set."

"It's a book, or a man in a book," Lionel interrupted. "Barbara adores it."

"Well, so do you," Barbara said. "You always snigger when you read him."

"That is the weakness of the flesh," Lionel said. "One shouldn't snigger over Jeeves any more than one should snivel over *Othello*. Perfect art is beyond these easy emotions. I think

Jeeves—the whole book, preferably with the illustrations—one of the final classic perfections of our time. It attains absolute being. Jeeves and his employer are one and yet diverse. It is the Don Quixote of the twentieth century."

"I must certainly read it," Gregory said, laughing. "Tell me more about it while we have tea."

After the meal the four of them climbed to the gallery and Mr. Persimmons's room, where the train was marvellously arrayed and arranged. Adrian gave himself up to it, with Barbara assisting. Gregory took Lionel over to the bookcases. Presently, however, they were recalled by calls from the train, and found that somewhere in the complicated mechanism a hitch had occurred. Gregory examined it, turning the engine over in his hands; then he said: "I think I see what the fault is." He fiddled with it for a minute or two, then he looked at Barbara with a smile. "Would you mind holding it, Mrs. Rackstraw?" he asked. "I just can't get the right bit past the screw with one hand."

Barbara took it willingly, and Gregory pushed and thrust at the mechanism for a minute or two. Then he altered the position of his left hand so that it lay lightly over Barbara's fingers and thrust again with his right. There was a slip, a jangle, an oath from Gregory, a light shriek from Barbara, an exclamation from Lionel; then the engine had dropped to the floor, while the men stared at a long scratch on the inside of Barbara's wrist and lower arm from which the blood was already oozing.

"My dear Mrs. Rackstraw, I am so sorry," Gregory exclaimed. "Do please forgive me. Does it hurt you much?"

"Heavens, no!" Barbara said. "Lend me your handkerchief, Lionel, mine isn't big enough. Don't worry, Mr. Persimmons, it'll be all right in a few minutes if I just do it up."

"Oh, but you must put something on it," Gregory said. "Look here, I've got some ointment here—only a patent medicine, I admit; I forget what they call it—not Zam-buk, but something like it. Anyhow, it works rather well." He had gone

The Ointment

across to a drawer, and now produced a small round wooden box, which he held out to Barbara. "And there's some rag somewhere; ah, here it is."

Barbara wrinkled her nose as she took the box. "What a funny smell!" she said. "Thank you so much. But I've got vaseline at home."

"Don't wait," Gregory said, "put some on now and do it up." He turned to Adrian. "Still," he said, "I put the engine right. But it oughtn't to have had a sharp edge like that. I must take it back next time I'm in town."

Half an hour slipped away. Then Lionel, turning by accident to put a book down on the table, saw his wife's face.

"Barbara," he said suddenly, "do you feel ill?"

She was lying back in her chair, and as he spoke she looked across at him, at first unrecognizingly. Then she said, speaking dizzily: "Lionel, Lionel, is that you? I'm fainting or something; I don't know where I am! Lionel!"

Lionel was across the room and by her side, even as Gregory, who was sitting on the floor by Adrian, rose to his feet. Persimmons glanced at his guest, went across and pressed the bell, and returned. Rackstraw was speaking as quietly as he could, to soothe her. But she sat up suddenly and began to scream, her eyes blind to everything round her, her hands thrusting away from her. "Lionel! Lionel! Oh, God! Oh, God! Lionel!"

Lionel threw a look towards Gregory. "Adrian!" he said. Gregory turned to the child, who, startled and horrified, was beginning to cry, picked him up with murmured consolations and encouragements, and went quickly to meet Ludding at the door.

"Mrs. Rackstraw is ill," he said. "Telephone to the doctor; and then come back. I may want you. He'll be here as quickly if you telephone as if you go down in the car, won't he? Hurry!"

Ludding vanished, and Gregory, going with Adrian into the next room, produced a parcel of curious shape, which he presented to the child. But Adrian heard, even through the

The Ointment

closed doors, the spasmodic shrieks that came from the next room, and clung despairingly to Gregory. Then amid the cries they heard movements and footsteps, a chair falling, and Lionel's voice on a quick note of command. Adrian began to scream in alarm, and Ludding, on his return from the telephone, was sent to find the maid Jessie, between whom and Adrian a pleasant friendship had ripened. She carried him off to her own quarters, and Gregory ran into the next room.

There Barbara had collapsed again into a seat, in which she was writhing and twisting, at intervals crying out still for Lionel.

"But, my darling, I'm here," he said, tortured beyond any of his own visionary fears. "Can't you see me? Can't you feel me?" He took her hands.

By the long alliance of their bodies, knit by innumerable light touches of impatience or of delight, some kind of bridge seemed to be established. Barbara's hands closed on his, and her voice grew into a frenzy of appeal. "Save me, Lionel, save me! I can't see you. Come to me, Lionel!"

Lionel looked back at Gregory. "What on earth's happened?" he said in a low voice. "Can't we do anything?"

"I've sent for the doctor," Gregory answered in equally subdued tones. "We can't do anything but hang on till he comes. Adrian's with Jessie. Try her with the child's name."

Barbara had relapsed again into comparative silence, though her frame was shuddering and trembling in the moment's exhaustion. Gregory, from behind Lionel, considered her thoughtfully. The operation of the ointment would have, he supposed, some sort of parallel to his own experience. But where in him, it had released and excited his directing purpose to a fuller consummation, in Barbara Rackstraw, who probably drifted through the world like most people, "neither for God nor for his enemies," it was more likely simply to define and energize the one side, without giving it entire separation and control. All with which he had felt himself one would be to Barbara an invader, a conqueror, perhaps even an infernal lover; she would feel it in her body, her blood, her mind, her soul. Unless indeed she also *became* that, though since without her definite intention, so without her definite control. Then, instead of calling for Lionel, would she shriek at him? How funny! He picked up the box of ointment and dropped it into his pocket; there was another more harmless box in the drawer, if inquiries were made.

Almost another quarter of an hour had passed since the crisis had begun. Gregory saw no necessity for it ever to end. In himself the ointment had been a means to a certain progress and return, but Barbara had no will to either, and might, it seemed to him, exist for ever in this divided anguish of war. He wondered very much what the doctor would say.

Suddenly Barbara moved and stood up. Her voice began again its despairing appeals to God and Lionel, but her limbs began to dispose themselves in the preliminary motions of a dance. Gently at first, then more and more swiftly, her feet leapt upon the carpet; her arms tossed themselves in time to unheard music. Lionel made an effort to stop her, throwing one arm round her waist and catching her hands with the other; before his movement was complete she broke his hold and sent him staggering across the room. Gregory's heart beat high; this then was the outer sign of the inner dance he had himself known: the ointment had helped him to seal his body while his soul entered ecstasy. But here the ointment gave the body helpless to the driving energy of the Adversary, and only through the screaming mouth a memory that was not conquered cried out to her lover and to her God.

Gregory heard a movement outside the door; there was a tap. But he was too absorbed to speak. Then the door opened and the village doctor stood in the opening. At the same moment, as if she had waited for it, Barbara, still moving in that wild dance, threw up her hand and, carelessly and unconsciously tore open her light frock and underwear from the breast downwards. It hung, a moment, ripped and rent, from the girdle that caught it together; then it fell lower, and she shook her legs free without checking the movement of the dance.

Even Gregory was not very clear afterwards what had then happened. It had needed the three of them to bring her into some sort of subordination, and to bind her with such material as could be obtained. The doctor's next act was to inject morphia, a proceeding which Gregory watched with considerable pleasure, having his own views on what result this was likely to bring about. She was carried into one of the spare rooms at Cully, and Lionel took up his station there also. "They'll put another bed in presently," Gregory told him. "And my man Ludding will sleep in the next room, so if you want anything ask him. Good heavens, it's not seven yet! Now, about Adrian. . . . He shall sleep in my room if he likes, that will distract him, and he'll feel important. Hush, hush, my dear fellow, we must all do what we can. The doctor's coming in again later."

The doctor indeed, after asking a few questions, and looking at the box of harmless ointment, had been glad to get away and think over this unusual patient. Gregory, having made inquiries, found that Adrian was out in the gardens with Jessie, and strolled out to find them, just preventing himself from whistling cheerfully in case Lionel should hear. It occurred to him that it would be pleasant before the child went to bed to see if anything could be discovered about the stranger who had disturbed him earlier, but whom, warm with his present satisfaction, he was inclined to neglect. Still . . .

He suggested, therefore, to Adrian—who had allowed himself to be persuaded how delightful it would be to sleep in his uncle's own room, and that his mother had better be left alone that evening—that another game at hidden pictures would be pleasant. The cup they had used before was not, it seemed, possible, but there were other means.

Installed therefore on a chair in front of a table bearing a shining black disc arranged in a sloping position, Adrian said anxiously:

"Now ask me what I can see."

Gregory leant back in his chair opposite, fixed his eyes on Adrian, made an image of the stranger in his mind, and said slowly: "Can you see a tall man, with a grey suit on, and a soft hat?" He imposed the image on the child's mind.

With hardly any hesitation Adrian answered: "Oh, yes, I can see him. He's on a horse, and ever so many other people are all round him on horses, with long, long sticks. They're all riding along. Oh, it's gone."

Gregory frowned a little. A cavalry regiment? Was his visitor merely a lieutenant in the Lancers? He concentrated more than ever. "What is he doing now?" he asked.

"He's sitting on cushions," Adrian poured out raptly. "And there's a man in red and a man in brown. They're both kneeling down. Oh, they're giving him a piece of paper. Now he's smiling, now they're going. It's gone again," he ended in a tone of high delight.

Gregory brooded over this for some minutes. "Where does he come from?" he asked. "Can you see water or trains?"

"No," said Adrian immediately, "but I can see a lot of funny houses and a lot of churches too. He's coming out of one of the churches. He's got a beautiful, beautiful coat on! And a crown! and there are a lot of people coming out with him, and they've all got crowns and swords! and flags! Now he's on a horse and there are candles all round him and funny things going round in the air and smoke. Oh, it's gone."

Gregory, as delicately and as soon as possible, broke off the proceedings. There was something here he didn't understand. He sent Adrian off to bed with promises of pleasant amusements the next day, and himself, after a short visit to Lionel, went out again into the grounds to await the doctor's second call. Barbara, it seemed, was lying still; he wondered what exactly was happening. If the morphia was controlling her limbs, what about the energy that had wrung them? If it couldn't work outward, was it working inward? Was the inner being that was Barbara being driven deeper and deeper into that flow of desire which was the unity and compulsion of man? What an unusual experience for a charming young housewife of the twentieth century! And perhaps she also would not be able to return.

Chapter Twelve

THE THIRD ATTEMPT ON THE GRAAL

Lionel Rackstraw leant by the open window and looked out over the garden. Behind him Barbara lay, in stillness and apparent sleep; below him at some distance Mr. Gregory Persimmons contemplated the moon. In an ordinary state of mind Lionel might have contemplated it too, as a fantasy less terrible than the sun, which appeared to him often as an ironical heat drawing out of the earth the noxious phantoms it bred therein. But the phantoms of his mind were lost in the horrible, and yet phantasmal, evil that had befallen him; his worst dreams were, if not truer than they had always been —that they could not be—at least more effectual and more omnipotent. The last barricade which material things offered had fallen; the beloved was destroyed, and the home of his repose broken open by the malice of invisible powers. Had she been false, had she left him for another—that would have been tolerable; probably, when he considered himself, he had always felt it. What was there about him to hold, in the calm of intense passion, that impetuous and adorable nature? But this unpredictable madness, without, so far as could be known, cause or explanation, this was the overwhelming of humanity by the spectral forces that mocked humanity. He gathered himself together in a persistent and hopeless patience.

He took out his case and lit a cigarette mechanically. She, he supposed, would never smoke cigarettes again, or, if she did, it would never be the same. At the same time, that question of ways and means which is never far from the minds of the vast majority of the English at any moment, which

poisons their sorrows and modifies their joys, which insists on
being settled before any experience can be properly tasted, and,
if unsatisfactorily settled (as it most frequently is), turns love
and death into dancing parodies of themselves, which ruins
personal relationship and abstract thought and pleasant hours
—this question presented itself also to him. What about money?
what about Adrian? what about their home? what about the
future? He couldn't look after Adrian; he couldn't afford to
keep Barbara *and* a housekeeper; besides, he couldn't, he supposed, have a housekeeper to live in the same house with
Adrian and himself—unless she were old enough. And how did
you get old housekeepers, and what did you pay them? Barbara might get better, but obviously after such an attack she
couldn't for a long time be left alone with Adrian; and if she
didn't get better? She had an aunt somewhere in Scotland—
a strong Calvinistic Methodist; Lionel cursed as he thought of
Adrian growing up in a Calvinistic household. Not, his irony
reminded him, that he wasn't something of a Calvinist himself,
with his feeling about the universe; but his kind of Calvinism
wouldn't want to proselytize Adrian, and the aunt's would.
He himself had no available relations—and his friends? Well,
friends were all very well, but you couldn't dump a child on
your friends indefinitely. Besides, his best friends—Kenneth,
for instance—hadn't the conveniences. What a world!

Mr. Persimmons, turning from the moon, looked up at the
house, saw him, waved a hand, and walked towards the door.
It crossed Lionel's mind that it would be very satisfactory if
Adrian could stop at Cully. It was no use his saying that he
had no right to think of it; his fancy insisted on thinking of it,
and was still doing so when Gregory, entering softly, joined
him at the window.

"All quiet?" he asked in a low voice.

"All quiet," Lionel answered bitterly.

"It occurred to me," Gregory said—"I don't know, of course
—but it occurred to me that you might be worrying over the

boy. You won't, will you? There's no need. He can stop with me, here or in London, as long as ever you like. He likes me and I like him."

"It's very kind of you," Lionel said, feeling at once that this would solve a problem, and yet that the solving it would leave him with nothing but the horror of things to deal with. Even such a worrying question as what to do with Adrian was a slight change of torment. But that, he reflected sombrely, was selfish. Selfish, good heavens, selfish! And, after a long pause he said again, "It's very kind of you."

"Not a bit," Gregory answered. "I should even—in a sense —like it. And you must be free. It's most unfortunate. It seems sometimes as if there was an adverse fate in things—lying in ambush."

"Ambush?" Lionel asked, relieved yet irritated at being made to talk. What did people like Gregory know of adverse fate? "Not much ambush, I think. It's pretty obvious, once one's had a glimpse of the world."

Religion normally has a mildly stupefying effect on the minds of its disciples, and this Gregory had not altogether escaped. He had thought it would give him half an hour's pleasant relaxation to worry Lionel, and he had not realized that Lionel was, even in his usual state, beyond this. He went on accordingly: "There seems a hitch in the way things work. Happiness is always just round the corner."

"No hitch, surely," Lionel said. "The whole scheme of things is malign and omnipotent. That *is* the way they work. 'There is none that doeth good—no, not one.'"

"It depends perhaps on one's definition of good," Gregory answered. "There is at least satisfaction and delight."

"There is no satisfaction and no delight that has not treachery within it," Lionel said. "There is always Judas; the name of the world that none has dared to speak is Judas."

Gregory turned his head to see better the young face

167

from which this summary of life issued. He felt perplexed and uncertain; he had expected a door and found an iron barrier.

"But," he said doubtfully, "had Judas himself no delight? There is an old story that there is rapture in the worship of treachery and malice and cruelty and sin."

"Pooh," Lionel said contemptuously; "it is the ordinary religion disguised; it is the church-going clerk's religion. Satanism is the clerk at the brothel. Audacious little middle-class cock-sparrow!"

"You are talking wildly," Gregory said a little angrily. "I have met people who have made me sure that there is a rapture of iniquity."

"There is a rapture of anything, if you come to that," Lionel answered; "drink or gambling or poetry or love or (I suppose) satanism. But the one certainty is that the traitor is always and everywhere present in evil and good alike, and all is horrible in the end."

"There is a way to delight in horror," Gregory said.

"There is no way to delight in the horrible," Lionel answered. "Let us pray only that immortality is a dream. But I don't suppose it is," he added coldly.

A silence fell upon them, and Gregory was suddenly conscious that he felt a trifle sick. He felt dizzy; he shut his eyes and leant against the wall to save himself lurching. Lionel's face, as it looked out over the garden, frightened him; it was like a rock seen very far off. He opened his eyes and studied it again, then he glanced back over his shoulder at Barbara lying on the bed. This was Cully; Adrian was asleep in *his* room; *he* had overthrown Barbara's mind. And now he was driven against something else, something immovable, something that affected him as if he had found himself suddenly in a deep pit of smooth rock. Lionel, who had been pursuing his own thoughts, began to speak suddenly, in the high voice of incantation with which he was given to quoting poetry,

The Third Attempt on the Graal

"Which way I fly is hell, myself am hell,
And in the lowest deep a lower deep
Still gaping to devour me opens wide,
To which the hell I suffer seems a heaven."

Gregory stamped his foot, and managed to change it into a mere shifting of position. After all, he wasn't going to quarrel with Lionel just now, though if he had time he would smash him into splinters. A clerk at a brothel!

"Well," he said, "there's just one thing I should like to say. If the doctor doesn't seem much good when he comes, I have been thinking that I know an old man in London who's seen some curious things and has funny bits of knowledge. I'll get him on the telephone to-morrow and ask him to come down. He mayn't be any good, but he may."

"It's really very kind of you," Lionel said. "But how can anyone do anything?"

"Well, we shall see," Gregory answered cheerfully. "Hallo, there *is* the doctor. And Sir Giles. Shall we go and meet them?"

Sir Giles, who had been out all day on an antiquarian visit, had run into the doctor at the gates. They walked up the drive a little distance apart, and at the door he made to annex Persimmons, who, however, put him aside till he had spoken with the doctor. A new examination of the patient brought no new light. The doctor, who refused to stay for the night, but promised to call again in the morning, went off. Lionel returned to his vigil, and Gregory, having patted him on the shoulder, and said cheerfully, "Well, well, don't despair. We'll ring up old Manasseh first thing," went off with Sir Giles to his own room.

"What's the idea?" Tumulty asked. "And who is old Manasseh, anyhow?"

"Ah, you don't know everyone yet," Gregory answered in high glee. "Pity you weren't here; you'd have liked to see how

Mrs. Rackstraw went on. Quite unusual, for an English lady. Unusual for an English doctor, too. Did you think he was a bit bewildered, Tumulty? But you'll meet Manasseh in the morning."

"Coming down, is he?" Sir Giles asked. "Well, there's someone else down here too."

"Yes," Gregory said. "The masquerading fellow in grey? Now, if you can tell me who *he* is——"

"I knew you'd go mad," Sir Giles said, with satisfaction. "What fellow in grey? I don't know what hell's clothes he was wearing, something from his own suburban tape-twister, I expect."

"Why suburban?" Gregory asked. "He didn't look to me like the suburbs. And what did he mean by his name being John?"

"His name may be Beelzebub," Sir Giles answered, "but the man is that lump-cheeked inspector who's trying to find out who committed the murder. *He's* down here."

Gregory stared. "What, *that*?" he said. "Why, I thought they'd dropped all that. There's absolutely nothing to show——What does he want here?"

"Probably either me or you," Sir Giles answered. "Well, I told you at the beginning, Persimmons, I'm going to damn well see to it he doesn't have *me*. I don't care what insane May dance you get up to, but I'm not going to be dragged in. If the police are after you, they can have you for all I care. I'm leaving to-morrow, and I'm off to Baghdad next week. And, if he asks me anything, I shall tell him."

"Tell him that you told me you were going to ask Rackstraw to have lunch with you, so that the room——" Gregory began.

"Tell him you've been waking up in the night shrieking 'blood, blood,' if it's necessary," Sir Giles said. "The English police are corrupt enough, of course, but the trouble is one doesn't know *where* they're corrupt, and you may hit on the wrong man. Besides, I'll see that lurching sewer-rat in Hinnom before I spend good money on him."

"You're making a ridiculous fuss," Gregory said. "You don't really think he's got evidence?"

"I don't care a curse," Sir Giles answered. "You're not interesting enough to run any risks for, Persimmons; you're merely an overgrown hobbledehoy stealing beer—the drainings in other people's pots. And I'm not going to have to poison myself for you. And now who's this reptile in grey you're bleating about?"

Gregory had grown used to neglecting half of Sir Giles's conversation, but for a moment he remembered Lionel's remark earlier in the evening, and looked nastily across at the other. However, he pulled himself in, and said carelessly, "Oh, a mad fellow we met in the drive. Talked like a clergyman and said he knew seventy kings."

"Only seventy?" Sir Giles asked. "No other introduction?"

"I didn't like him," Gregory admitted, "and he made Ludding foam at the mouth. But he wasn't doing anything except wander about the drive. He mentioned he was a priest and king himself." He dropped his voice and came a little nearer. "I wondered at first whether he was anything to do with—the shop. You know what I mean. But somehow he didn't fit in."

Sir Giles sat erect. "Priest and king," he said, half sceptically. "You're sure you're not mad, Persimmons?" He stood up sharply. "And his name was John?" he asked intently.

"He said so," Gregory answered. "But John what?"

Sir Giles walked to the window and looked out, then he came back and looked with increasing doubt at Gregory. "Look here," he said, "you take my advice and leave that damned bit of silver gilt trumpery alone. Ludding told me about your all going off after it. You may be up against something funnier than you think, Master Gregory."

The Third Attempt on the Graal

"But who *is* he?" Gregory asked impatiently yet anxiously. "What's he got to do with the—the Graal?"

"I'm not going to tell you," Sir Giles said flatly. "I never knew any good come of trying to pretend things mightn't be when they might. I've heard tales—lies, very likely—but tales. Out about Samarcand I heard them and down in Delhi too —and it wasn't the Dalai Lama either that made the richest man in Bengal give all he had to the temples and become a fakir. I don't believe in God yet, but I wonder sometimes whether men haven't got the idea of God from that fellow —if it's the same one."

"What have I to do with God?" Gregory said.

"I don't know whether the Graal belongs to him or he belongs to the Graal," Sir Giles went on, unheeding. "But you can trace it up to a certain point and you can trace it back from a certain point, and someone had it in between. And if it was he, you'd better go and ask the Archdeacon to pray for you—if he will."

"Will you tell me who he is?" Gregory asked.

"No, I won't," Sir Giles said. "I've seen too much to chatter about him. You drop it, while there's time."

"I suppose it's Jesus Christ come to look for His own property?" Gregory sneered.

"Jesus Christ is dead or in heaven or owned by the clergy," Sir Giles answered. "But they say this man is what he told you—he is king and priest and his name is John. They say so. I don't know, and I tell you I funk it." He looked at the open window again.

"Well, run then," Gregory said. "But I and my great lord will know him and meet him."

"So you may, for me," Sir Giles answered, and with no more words disappeared to his own room.

The child Adrian slept long and peacefully, and only his angel, in another state of the created universe, knew what his dreams were. But, except for him and the servants, the night was, for those in Cully, empty of sleep. Lionel lay on the couch that had been hastily made up, watching and listening for any movement from his wife. How far she slept none could tell. She lay motionless, but Lionel doubted, when he was near her, whether it were more than a superimposed and compulsory immobility. Her eyes were shut, but her breath trembled as if some interior haste shook it, and every now and then there issued from her lips a faint and barely perceptible moan, faint but profound. Lionel brooded over this companion of his way, torn apart into the depths of some jungle whose terror he could not begin to conceive. He himself would have been, to however small an extent, prepared; but that Barbara, with her innocent concentration on window-curtains and the novels of Mr. Wodehouse and Adrian's meals, should be plunged into it, was a fatality against which even his pessimism felt the temptation to rebel.

Not far from his room Sir Giles also lay wakeful, considering episodes and adventures of his past. Brutal with himself no less than with others, he did not attempt to hide from himself that the new arrivals in the village caused him some anxiety. He had known, in his exploration of that zone of madness which encloses humanity, certain events which had been referred by those who had spoken of them to a mysterious power whose habitation was unknown and whose interference was deadly. Once indeed, in a midnight assembly in Beyrout, he had, he thought, dimly seen him; there had been panic and death, and in the midst of the shrinking and alarmed magicians a half-visible presence, clouded and angry and destructive. At the time he had thought that he also had been affected by a general hallucination, but he knew that hallucination was a word which, in these things, meant no more than that certain things seemed to be. Whether they were or not . . . He promised himself again to leave England as soon as possible, and to leave Cully certainly to-morrow.

Gregory, after some consideration, had dismissed Sir Giles's warnings as, on the whole, silly. Things were going very well; by the next night he hoped that both the Graal and Adrian would be, for a while, in his hands or those of his friends. Of all those who lay awake under those midnight stars he was the only one who had a naturally religious spirit; to him only the unknown beyond man's life presented itself as alive with hierarchical presences arrayed in rising orders to the central throne. To him alone sacraments were living realities; the ointment and the Black Mass, the ritual and order of worship. He beyond any of them demanded a response from the darkness; a rush of ardent faith believed that it came; and in full dependence on that faith acted and influenced his circumstances. Prayer was natural to him as it was not to Sir Giles or Lionel, or, indeed, to Barbara, and to the mind of the devotee the god graciously assented. Conversion was natural to him, and propaganda, and the sacrifice both of himself and others, if that god demanded it. He adored as he lay in vigil, and from that adoration issued the calm strength of a supernatural union. As the morning broke he smiled happily on the serene world around him.

Sir Giles took himself off after breakfast, leaving his small amount of luggage to be sent on. Gregory and Lionel left Ludding to call them if Barbara moved—a nurse was to arrive later—and went to the telephone in the hall. There, after some trouble, Gregory got through to his desired number and, Lionel gathered, to the unknown Manasseh. He explained the circumstances briefly, urging the other to take the next train to Fardles.

"What?" he asked in a moment. "Yes, Cully—near Fardles. . . . Well, anything in reason, anything, indeed. . . . What? I don't understand. . . . Yes, I know you did, but . . . No, but the point is, that I haven't . . . Yes, though I don't know how you knew. . . . But I can't. . . . Oh, nonsense! . . . No, but look here, Manasseh, this is serious; the patient's had some sort of fit or something. . . . But you can't mean it.

. . . Oh, well, I suppose so. . . . But, Manasseh. . . . But you
wouldn't . . . No, stop . . ."

He put the receiver back slowly and turned very gravely
to Lionel. "This is terrible," he said. "You know that chalice
I had? Well, I knew Manasseh wanted it. He thinks he can
cure Mrs. Rackstraw, and he offers to try, *if* I'll give him the
chalice."

"Oh, well," Lionel said insincerely, "if he wants that—I
suppose it's very valuable? Too valuable for me to buy, I
mean?"

"My dear fellow," Gregory said, "you should have it without a second thought. Do you suppose I should set a miserable
chalice against your wife's health? I like and admire her far
too much. But I haven't got it. Don't you remember I told
you yesterday—but we've been through a good deal since
then—the Archdeacon's bolted with it. He insists that it is
his, though Colonel Conyers is quite satisfied that it isn't,
and I really think the police might be allowed to judge.
He and Kenneth Mornington and a neighbour of mine bolted
with it—out of my own house, if you please! And now, when
I'd give anything for it, I can't get hold of it." He stamped
his foot in the apparent anger of frustrated desire.

The little violence seemed to break Lionel's calm. He
caught Gregory's arm. "But must your friend have that?" he
cried. "Won't anything else in heaven or hell please him?
Will he let Babs die in agony because he wants a damned
wine-cup? Try him again, try him again!"

Gregory shook his head. "He'll ring us up in an hour,"
he said, "in case we can promise it to him. That'll give him
time to catch the best morning train to Fardles. But what
can I do? I know the Archdeacon and Mornington have
taken it to the Duke's house. But they're all very angry with
me, and how can I ask them for it?" He looked up suddenly.
"But what about you?" he said, almost with excitement.
"You know Mornington well enough—I daren't even speak

to him; there was a row about that book yesterday at the office, and he misunderstood something I said. He's rather —well, quick to take offence, you know. But he knows your wife, and he might be able to influence that Archdeacon; they're very thick. Get on the 'phone to him and try. Try, try anything to save her now."

He wheeled round to the telephone and explained what he wanted to the local Exchange; then the two of them waited together. "Manasseh's a hard man," Gregory went on. "I've known him cure people in a marvellous way for nothing at all, but if he's asked for anything he never makes any compromise. And he doesn't always succeed, of course, but he does almost always. He works through the mind largely— though he knows about certain healing drugs he brought from the East. No English doctor would look at them or him, naturally, but I've never known an English doctor succeed where he failed. Understand, Rackstraw, if you can get the Archdeacon to see that he's wrong, or to give up the chalice *without* seeing that he's wrong, it's yours absolutely. But don't waste time arguing. I know it's no good my arguing with Manasseh, and I don't think it's much good your arguing with the Archdeacon. Tell Mornington the whole thing, and get him to see it's life or death—or worse than life or death. Beg him to bring it down here at once and we'll have it for Manasseh when he comes. There you are; thank God they've been quick."

In a torrent of passionate appeal Lionel poured out his agony through the absurd little instrument. At the other end Kenneth stood listening and horrified in the Duke's study; the Duke himself and the Archdeacon waited a little distance "But what's the matter with Babs?" Kenneth asked. "I don't understand."

"Nobody understands," Lionel answered desperately. "She seems to have gone mad—shrieking, dancing—I can't tell you. Can you do it? Kenneth, for the sake of your Christ!

After all, it's only a chalice—your friend can't want it all that much!"

"*Your* friend seems to want it all that much," Kenneth said, and bit his lips with annoyance. "No, sorry, Lionel, sorry. Look here, hold on—no, of course, you can't hold on. But I must find the Archdeacon and tell him." He held up a hand to stop the priest's movement. "Tell me, what's Babs doing now?"

"Lying down with morphia in her to keep her quiet," Lionel answered. "But she's *not* quiet, I know she's not quiet, she's in hell. Oh, hurry, Kenneth, hurry."

Considerably shaken, Mornington turned from the telephone to the others. "It's Barbara Rackstraw," he said, paused a moment to explain to the Duke, and went on. "Gregory's been doing something to her, I expect; Lionel doesn't know what's the matter, but she seems to have gone mad. And that—creature has got a doctor up his sleeve who can put her right, he thinks, but he wants *that*——" He nodded at the Graal, which stood exposed in their midst, and went over the situation again at more length to make the problem clear.

Even the Archdeacon looked serious. The Duke was horrified, yet perplexed. "But what can we do?" he asked, quite innocently.

"Well," Kenneth said restrainedly, "Lionel's notion seemed to be that we might give him the Graal."

"Good God!" the Duke said. "Give him the Graal! Give him *that*—when we know that's what he's after!"

Kenneth did not answer at once, then he said slowly: "Barbara's a nice thing; I don't like to think of Barbara being hurt."

"But what's a woman's life—what are any of our lives—compared to *this*?" the Duke cried.

"No," Kenneth said, unsatisfied, "no. . . . But Barbara. . . . Besides, it isn't her life, it's her reason."

"I am the more sorry," the Duke answered. "But this thing is more than the whole world."

Kenneth looked at the Archdeacon. "Well, it's yours to decide," he said.

During the previous day it had become evident in Grosvenor Square that a common spiritual concern does not mean a common intellectual agreement. The Duke had risen, the morning after the attack on the Graal, with quite a number of ideas in his mind. The immediate and chief of these had been the removal of the Graal itself to Rome, and its safe custody there. He urged these on his allies at breakfast, and by sheer force of simple confidence in his proposal had very nearly succeeded. The Archdeacon was perfectly ready to admit that Rome, both as a City and a Church, had advantages. It had the habit of relics, the higher way of mind and the lower business organization to deal with them. Rome was as convenient as Westminster, and the Apostolic See more traditional than Canterbury. But he felt that even this relic was not perhaps so important as Rome would inevitably tend to make it. And he felt his own manners concerned. "It would rather feel like stealing my grandmother's lustres from my mother to give to my aunt," he explained diffidently, noted the Duke's sudden stiffening, and went on hastily: "Besides, I am a man under authority. It isn't for me to settle. The Bishop or the Archbishop, I suppose."

"The Judicial Committee of the Privy Council is the final voice of authority still, isn't it?" the Duke pointedly asked. "I know Southend is a Jew and one or two others are notorious polygamists—unofficially."

"The Privy Council, as everybody knows, has no jurisdiction . . ." Mornington began.

"There we go again," the Archdeacon complained. "But, anyhow, so far as the suggestion is concerned, mere movement in space and time isn't likely to achieve much. It couldn't solve the problem, though it might delay it."

The Third Attempt on the Graal

"Well, what do you propose to do?" the Duke asked.

"I don't know that I really thought of doing anything," the Archdeacon answered. "It would be quite safe here wouldn't it? Or we might simply put it in a dispatch-case and take it to the Left Luggage office at Paddington or somewhere. No," he added hastily, "that's not quite true. But you staunch churchpeople always make me feel like an atheist. Frankly, I think the Bishop ought to know—but he's away till next week. So's the Archbishop. And then there are the police. It's all very difficult."

There certainly were the police. Colonel Conyers made a call that morning; the Assistant Commissioner made a point of having tea with the Duchess, who was the Duke's aunt, that afternoon. The Duke was at his most regal (ducal is too insignificant a word) with both. Neither of them were in a position to give wings to a colossal scandal by taking action unless forced to it by Mr. Persimmons, and Mr. Persimmons had returned to Cully, after reiterating to the Colonel his wish that public action should not be taken. To the Assistant Commissioner the Duke intimated that further attacks on the vessel had taken place.

"What, burglars?" the other said.

"Not burglars," the Duke answered darkly. "More like black magic."

"Really?" the Assistant Commissioner said, slightly bewildered. "Oh, quite, quite. Er—did anything *happen?*"

"They tried to destroy It by *willing* against It," the Duke said. "But by the grace of God they didn't succeed."

"Ah . . . willing," the other said vaguely. "Yes, I know a lot can be done that way. Though Baudouin is rather against it, I believe. You—you didn't *see* anything?"

"I thought I heard someone," the Duke answered. "And the Archdeacon felt It soften in his hands."

"Oh, the Archdeacon!" the Assistant Commissioner said, and left it at that.

The Third Attempt on the Graal

The whole day, in short, had been exceedingly unsatisfactory to the allies. The Duke and Mornington, in their respective hours of vigil before the sacred vessel, had endeavoured unconsciously to recapture some of their previous emotion. But the Graal stood like any other chalice, as dull as the furniture about it. Only the Archdeacon, and he much more faintly, was conscious of that steady movement of creation flowing towards and through the narrow channel of its destiny. And now when, on the next morning, he found himself confronted with this need for an unexpected decision he felt that he had not really any doubt what he would do. Still—" 'Wise as serpents '," he said, "Let us be serpentine. Let us go to Cully and see Mrs. Rackstraw, and perhaps meet this very obstinate doctor."

The Duke looked very troubled. "But can you even hesitate?" he asked. "Is anything worth such a sacrifice? Isn't it sacrilege and apostasy even to think of it?"

"I do not think of it," the Archdeacon said. "There is no use in thinking of it and weighing one thing against another. When the time comes He shall dispose as He will, or rather He shall be as He will, as He is."

"Does He will Gregory Persimmons?" Kenneth said wryly.

"Certainly He wills him," the Archdeacon said, "since He wills that Persimmons shall be whatever he seems to choose. That is not technically correct perhaps, but it is that which I believe and feel and know."

"He wills evil, then?" Kenneth said.

" 'Shall there be evil in the City and I the Lord have not done it?' " the Archdeacon quoted. "But I feel certain He wills us to get down to Fardles. And of the rest we will talk later."

Neither Kenneth nor the Duke accused the priest of evading the issue, for both of them felt he was speaking from a world of experience into which they had hardly entered. They fell back on the simpler idea that agony and evil were displeasing to God, but that He permitted them, and indeed Kenneth, at any rate, found it necessary, while he telephoned to Lionel their decision to come to Cully, and even on the way there, to keep this firmly in his mind as a counterbalance to the anxiety that he felt. For never before had he been confronted with the fact that certain strong and effective minds were ready and willing to inflict pain with or without a cause. He was becoming frightened of Gregory, and he naturally and inevitably therefore decided that Gregory was displeasing to God. It was his only defence; in such a crisis "if God did not exist it would be necessary to invent Him."

Yet this, even up to the moment when they all met in the hall at Cully, Lionel had refrained from doing. That the universe was displeasing to him did not prove that a god existed who could save him from the universe. But the universe seemed sometimes to relax a little, to permit a little grace to be wrung from it; and he thought it barely possible that such small grace might be granted now. It was undignified to be so greedy, but it was for Barbara—he excused himself to his own scornful mind.

Manasseh had arrived before the other three, and had spent the interval chatting with Gregory in the hall. Persimmons had begged Lionel so earnestly not to make any attempt to moderate his terms, and had seemed to have such a belief in and such a respect for his skill and obstinacy, that Lionel had easily fallen in with the suggestion. Cully had been placed so entirely at his disposal; the chalice itself had been —or was to be—his to yield to Manasseh; his anxiety about Adrian had been reduced; lastly, the possibility of a cure for Barbara had been so wholly Gregory's idea that prudence as well as gratitude demanded so much. He remained therefore, rather to the annoyance of the nurse, who had come by the same train as Manasseh, in Barbara's room, wondering whether the occasional flicker of movement he seemed to discern in her was real or only the suggestion of his own hope or fear.

Manasseh chatted with Gregory, and as the two paced the hall their sympathy with Lionel and Barbara seemed considerably lightened. "It only needs two things," Gregory said. "You must be firm when the other people come, and you ought to be able to do something to make Rackstraw think his wife is getting over it."

"Trust me to be firm," Manasseh answered. "As for the other—I think I can do that too. I've got some stuff that will send her into the heaviest sleep she's ever known; morphia's nothing to it. And it'll last for forty-eight hours or so. By then we can be away."

"I wonder if we've done wisely, after all," Gregory said. "But I don't altogether trust the way things are shaping here. They carry heavy guns, with the Duke—and Tumulty tells me the police haven't dropped that killing yet."

"What—Pattison?" Manasseh asked in surprise. "But Dmitri told me that he thought you'd managed that very well. He was sent to you, wasn't he?"

"He was sent from within," Gregory said. "It was made clear to me that I must kill, and he happened to be getting difficult. He did a pretty little piece of forgery for me once and played up well. But a few months ago he came across a Wesleyan mission-preacher and began to get troublesome. I was going to send him to Canada—but the other chance seemed too good to lose. So it was that."

Manasseh looked at him approvingly. "You will find soon," he said, "that possession is nothing besides destruction. We will go together to the East, and take the child and the Cup with us. And we will leave this madness behind us—and perhaps something else. We will talk with Dmitri. I should like to leave a memory of us with that priest."

There was a ring at the front door. Ludding, who had been told to be in attendance, came through to open it. At the other end of the hall Gregory and Manasseh turned to meet their guests, and Ludding, almost achieving irony, cried out in the voice of a herald: "The Duke of the North Ridings, the Archdeacon of Fardles, Mr. Mornington."

They entered, the Archdeacon carrying a small case, from which Persimmons carefully kept his eyes averted. They entered, and he said to Ludding: "Ask Mr. Rackstraw to come down." Then, as the man went away, he went on: "It is better that Mr. Rackstraw, and Dr. Manasseh here, and you should settle what is to be done. I have given over to Mr. Rackstraw all my interest in the chalice."

The Archdeacon bowed formally and looked at Manasseh. Immediately afterwards Lionel came down the stairs to join them, nodded to Kenneth, and was introduced by Gregory to Manasseh. Then Persimmons went on: "I'll leave you to discuss it for a few minutes. But one way or another the thing should be settled at once." He turned away up the stairs and along the corridor from which Lionel had come.

He went, indeed, straight to the room where Barbara lay, chatted for a moment or two with the nurse, who was about to dress the wound, and then went over to the bed, where he paused to look down on her.

"Poor dear," he said thoughtfully, "and on her holiday, and in such glorious weather!"

"It seems to make it worse somehow, doesn't it, sir?" the nurse said, Mr. Persimmons of Cully being obviously an important personage. Gregory shook his head and sighed. "Yes," he said, "it's very sad, very. And we have fine country here, too. You know it—no? Oh, you must. In your breaks you'll use my car as much as you want, won't you? Now, over there," he went on, drowning the nurse's hesitating thanks, "they say you can almost see the top of the spire of Norwich Cathedral."

"Norwich!" the nurse said, surprised and turning to look out of the window.

The Third Attempt on the Graal

"They say!" Gregory said, half-laughing, and running his finger down the long, unhealed wound twice and again. "But I admit I've never seen it. However, I mustn't delay you now. Perhaps you'll let me take you for a run one afternoon."

He smiled, nodded, left the room, and strolled back along the corridor to the top of the stairs.

" . . . moral decency demands it," the Duke was saying. "I am not concerned with all that," Manasseh answered, more truthfully than any but Gregory knew. "I have told you that from what Mr. Persimmons has told me I am sure I can heal Mrs. Rackstraw. But I must have my price. Unless I have it I will not act."

"There are English doctors," the Duke said coldly.

"Yes," Manasseh said, "you have tried one. Well, as you like . . ."

Gregory frowned. It was the Duke again, he supposed. But he himself dared not interfere; that would probably make matters worse, for he was suspect to all save Lionel. Well, he would have Adrian, anyhow; the other must be tried for again. But another five minutes might make a difference; he hoped Manasseh wouldn't rush things. Lionel and Kenneth were speaking together; the Archdeacon was imperceptibly drawn in, and the other two awaited their decision.

"I cannot buy it," Lionel broke out; "I have no possible excuse for asking for it. I ought not to have told you even. But I have told you, and there is an end to it."

"No, but, Lionel——" Kenneth began.

"Mr. Rackstraw," the Archdeacon interrupted, "the end to it is very simple. For myself, I would not have delayed so long. I would give up any relic, however wonderful, to save anyone an hour's neuralgia—man depends too much on these things. But, having friends, I felt only——"

He stopped. For from above the shrieks that had shaken Cully the previous night had suddenly begun again. The

nurse came flying to the stairs, crying, "She's up, and I can't
hold her. Help! help!" But almost at the same instant Barbara
was there too, her face wild with an appalling fear, her arms
wide and clutching, her voice shrieking incomprehènsible
things, of which the group in the hall caught only the wild
words: "The edge! the edge!" and then again, "I can't stop!
The edge, the edge!" Gregory sprang as if to check her;
she was past him and rushing down the stairs. Lionel and
Kenneth met her as she came, and were flung aside by the
irresistible energy that held her. The Duke, horrified, took
an unintentional step back and crashed into the Archdeacon,
so that Manasseh ran forward alone towards the foot of the
stairs. The voice now was beyond description terrible, and
still she cried, "The edge, the edge!" and still was hurled
blindly forward. And then, at the very height of the agonizing
moment, when it seemed that some immediate destruction
must rend her whole being, of a sudden the voice faltered
and stopped. As Manasseh closed upon her she paused,
stumbled, and in one long gentle movement seemed to collapse
towards the floor. He had her before she reached it, but,
as his eyes momentarily met Gregory's, there appeared in
them a great perplexity. In a second or two they were all
around her; Lionel and Kenneth moved with her to one of
the long seats scattered about the hall and laid her gently
down, and Manasseh bent over her. She seemed, as she lay
there, almost as if asleep; asleep in that half-repose, half-
collapse, which follows prolonged strain. A few tears crept
from her closed eyes; her body shook a little, but as if from
the mere after-effects of agony, not in the stiff spasms of
agony itself. Manasseh straightened himself, and looked round
at the others. "I think it is over," he said. "It will need time
and patience, but the will is caught and brought back. Her
mind will now be safe—now or presently, I cannot tell to
a few days. Thère may be another slighter outbreak, but I
do not think so." He drew a small bottle from his pocket.

"Give her two drops of this—not more—in a wineglass of water when she wakes, and once every twelve hours afterwards. I will come down again the day after to-morrow."

Kenneth giggled hysterically. Manasseh's speech had an insane likeness to any doctor concluding a visit. Of course, doctors *were* all the same, but the Archdeacon's black case, the anguish they had seen in Barbara's face, seemed to demand a more exalted conclusion. His giggle passed unnoticed, however, for the Archdeacon was holding the case out to Manasseh. "This is what you wanted, I think," he said, paused a moment, and added as he turned to the door, "But no bargain yet brought anyone near to the Graal or to the heart of its Lord." He bowed slightly to Manasseh and slightly to Persimmons and walked out.

On the steps he waited for his friends. They followed him at once, the Duke taking no notice of anyone, Kenneth with a murmur to Lionel; and the three looked at each other. "Well," the Archdeacon said, "I shall go back to the Rectory. Will you come with me or what?"

"No," the Duke said. "Our trust has been ended. I go back to the Castle. Will you come with me for a night or two, Mornington, as you meant to?"

Kenneth considered. He would have to see about getting a job, but a day or two first could do no harm. And if by any wild chance the Duke should really want a secretary . . . But he tried to suppress the idea. "I think I will," he said. "I should like to hang round till I knew Barbara was well again."

"I don't see that we can do anything if she isn't," the Duke said. "We've lost all our assets."

"Assets?" the Archdeacon asked. " 'The sacred and glorious Graal'? Oh, really, my dear Duke!"

The Duke looked a little embarrassed; his remark had been really irritable, not judicial. But he said stubbornly: "We could have pretended to bargain, at least."

The Third Attempt on the Graal

They had begun walking down the drive, and the Archdeacon made no answer for a minute or two. Then he said, "I will not bargain any more for anything, if I can help it. How can one bargain for anything that is worth while? And what else is worth bargaining for?"

"If one bargained for nothing, would everything be worth while?" Kenneth said, but more as a dream than a question.

They came to the gates and paused; then the Archdeacon said cheerfully to Kenneth, "Well, if you run over to see Mrs. Rackstraw in the next day or two, you'll look in on me? I must relieve Batesby—and the parish," he added as an afterthought.

"Certainly I will," Kenneth said, shaking hands. The Duke followed suit, saying a little sadly, "I suppose this is the end."

"I wouldn't be too sure of that," the Archdeacon answered. "If I were Manasseh, I shouldn't trust the Graal too far. But he probably thinks it important."

By the way he was clutching the case, he probably did. Gregory and Lionel, not wanting to disturb Barbara's profound sleep, inserted pillows and cushions under and round her, and then, while Lionel sat down close at hand, Gregory walked over to Manasseh.

"You did that very well," he said softly. "Or—didn't you do it?"

Manasseh hesitated; then, his face a little troubled, he answered, "No; and that's what makes me wonder. I thought I could do it one way or another, but she stopped first. I could have drowned her knowledge, and instead she seemed to know something else. It was as if she found everything all right, even on the very edge of the pit."

"'He shall give His angels charge over her,'" Gregory said. "Perhaps He managed it in time. They've usually been rather late. My wife, and Stephen, and even poor dear Pattison. But it doesn't matter."

"No," Manasseh said, and then suddenly, "But I don't like her getting away. She was on the very edge of destruction; she might have been torn to bits *there*—and she wasn't. Is she really safe? Can we try the ointment again?"

"No, we can't," Gregory said. "Don't be a fool. You've got the Cup, take it with you, and, unless something hinders me, I'll be with you to-night. To-morrow certainly, but I think to-night. You won't do anything till I come?"

"No," Manasseh answered. "You shall bring the child and we will talk with Dmitri. We win."

"Praise to our lord," Gregory said. But Manasseh smiled and shook his head. "He is the last mystery," he murmured, "and all destruction is his own destroying of himself."

Chapter Thirteen

CONVERSATIONS OF THE YOUNG
MAN IN GREY

When Sir Giles reached the station that morning he met a young man in grey just issuing from the booking-office. He stopped on the pavement and surveyed him. The stranger returned his gaze with a look of considerable interest.

"Are you running away, Sir Giles?" he said rather loudly.

"No," Sir Giles said at once. "Are you Persimmons's bugbear?"

"No," the stranger answered; "yours, much more truly. I like to watch you running."

"I am *not* running," Sir Giles almost shouted. "I was going to-day anyhow, and I have told Persimmons a thousand times I won't be dragged into his Boxing Day glee parties. And, anyhow, he's getting a bore. . . . Haven't I met you before?"

"Once or twice," the stranger said. "We shall meet again, no doubt. I like to watch your mind working. So long as you don't make yourself too much of a nuisance."

Sir Giles's overpowering curiosity, freed from other desires, thrust him forward. "And who are you?"

"I will tell you, if you like," the stranger said, smiling, "for at least you are really curious. I am Prester John, I am the Graal and the Keeper of the Graal. All enchantment has been stolen from me, and to me the Vessel itself shall return."

Sir Giles stepped back. "Nonsense!" he said. "Prester John, indeed! However, it's not my affair. You don't seem to have kept the Graal very well." He stepped towards the station, but paused as he heard the stranger's voice behind him.

Conversations of the Young Man in Grey

"This is the second time we have met, Giles Tumulty," it said. "I warn you that one day when you meet me you shall find me too like yourself to please you. It is a joyous thing to study the movements of men as you study insects under a stone, but you shall run a weary race when I and the heavens watch you and laugh at you and tease you to go a way that you would not. Then you shall scrabble in the universe as an ant against the smoothness of the inner side of the Graal, and none shall pick you out or deliver you for ever. There is a place in the pit where I shall be found, but there is no place for you who do not enter the pit, though you thrust others in."

During the high tones that had been used at the beginning of their conversation Sir Giles had glanced once or twice at a porter who was lounging near. But the porter had not seemed to take any notice, and even now, while this warning sounded through the bright morning air, he still leant idly against the station wall. Sir Giles, while the stranger was still speaking, went up to him. "What platform for the London train?" he said sharply, and the porter answered at once, "Over the bridge, sir." Sir Giles looked at him hard, but there was no suggestion of anything unusual on the man's face, though the stern voice still rang on. Tumulty shivered a little, and thought to himself, "I must be imagining it; Persimmons is wrecking my nerve." An ant scrabbling in an empty chalice—a foul idea! He looked back as he entered the booking-office; the stranger was strolling away down the station entrance.

Prester John, if it was he indeed, passed on down the country roads till he came near the Rectory, having timed himself so well that he met Mr. Batesby emerging. The clergyman recognized at once his companion of the day before, and greeted him amiably. "Still staying here?" he said. "Well, you couldn't do better. 'Through pleasures and palaces though we may roam, there's no place like home.' Though, strictly speaking, I expect Fardles isn't your home. But a church is our home everywhere—in England, of course I mean. I suppose you don't find the churches abroad really *homely.*"

"It depends," the young man said, "on one's idea of a home. Not like an English home perhaps."

"No," Mr. Batesby said, "they haven't, I gather, a proper sense of the family. Didn't one of the poets say that Heaven lies about us in our family? And where else, indeed?"

"What then," the stranger asked, "do you mean by the Kingdom of Heaven?"

"Well, we have to *understand,*" Mr. Batesby said. As Ludding had increased in brutality, and Gregory in hatred, so, in conversation with the stranger, Mr. Batesby's superior protectiveness seemed to increase; he became more than ever a guide and guard to his fellows, and the Teaching Church seemed to walk, a little nervously and dragging its feet, in the dust behind him. "We have to *understand.* Of course, some take it to mean the Church—but that's very narrow. I tell my young people in confirmation classes the Kingdom of Heaven is all good men—and women, of course . . . and women. Just that. Simple perhaps, but helpful."

"And good men," the other said, "are——?"

"Oh, well, good men, one knows good men," Mr. Batesby said. "By their fruits, you know. They do not kill. They do not commit adultery. They are just kind and honest and thrifty and hard-working, and so on. Good—after all, one feels goodness."

"The Kingdom of Heaven is to be felt among the honest and industrious?" the stranger asked. "And yet it's true. The Church is indeed marvellously protected from error."

"Yes," Mr. Batesby agreed. "The Faith once delivered. We can't go wrong if we stick to the old paths. What was good enough for St. Paul is good enough for me."

191

"When he fell to the ground beyond Damascus and was blinded?" the stranger asked. "Or when he persecuted the Christians in Jerusalem? Or when he taught them in Macedonia?"

"Ah, it was the same Paul all the time," Mr. Batesby rather triumphantly answered. "Just as it's the same me. I can grow older, but I don't change."

"So that when the Son of Man cometh He shall find faith upon the earth? It was beyond His expectation," the stranger said.

"The five righteous in Sodom," Mr. Batesby reminded him.

"There were not five righteous in Sodom," the young man said. "O Jerusalem, Jerusalem! . . ."

"Well, not strictly perhaps," Mr. Batesby allowed, a little hurt, but recovering himself. "But a parable has to be *applied*, hasn't it? We mustn't take it too literally, too much in the foot of the letter, as the French so wittily say. More witty than moral the French, I'm afraid."

So conversing, they walked on till they came to the village, where, at the inn door, Inspector Colquhoun was regarding it pensively. He looked unrecognizingly at them as they approached. But the stranger stopped and smiled at him in greeting.

"Why, inspector," he said, "what are you doing down here?"

The inspector looked at him critically. "I've no doubt it's your business," he said, "but I'm quite sure it's mine. I don't seem to remember your face."

"Oh, many a time!" the stranger said lightly; "but I won't ask you any questions. Mr. Batesby . . . do you know Inspector Colquhoun? Inspector, this is Mr. Batesby, who is looking after the parish for the time being."

The two others murmured inaudibly, and the stranger went on, "You ought to have a kindness for one another, for on you two the universe reposes. Movement and stability, aspiration and order . . ."

"Yes," Mr. Batesby broke in, "I've often thought something like that. In fact, I remember once in one of my sermons I said that the police were as necessary for the Ten Commandments as the Church was. More so nowadays, when there's so little respect for the law."

"There never was much that I could ever hear of," the inspector said, willing to spend a quarter of an hour chatting to the local clergyman. "No, I don't think things are much worse."

"No, not in one way," Mr. Batesby said. "Man had fallen just as far twenty or thirty years ago as he has to-day. But the war made a great difference. Men nowadays don't seem so willing to be *taught*."

"Ah, there you have me, sir," the inspector answered. "I don't have much to do with teaching them, only with those who won't be taught. And I've seen some of them look pretty white," he added viciously.

"Ah, a guilty conscience," Mr. Batesby said. "Yes—guilt makes the heavy head to bend, the saddened heart to sob, and happy they who ere their end can feel remorseful throb. Love castest out perfect fear. Nothing is sadder, I think, than to see a man or woman *afraid*."

"It doesn't do to trust to it." The inspector shook his head. "It may drive them almost silly any moment, and make them dangerous. I've known a little whipper-snapper fairly gouge a policeman's eyes out."

"Really?" Mr. Batesby said. "Dear me, how sad! I don't think I know what fear is—temperamentally. Of course, an accident . . ."

"You have never been afraid of anyone?" the stranger said, his voice floating through the air as if issuing from it.

"Yes," the inspector said, "and pretty often."

G   193

Conversations of the Young Man in Grey

"Not, I think, afraid *of* anyone," Mr. Batesby said, mysteriously accentuating the preposition. "Of course, every priest has unpleasant experiences. Once, I remember, I was making a call on a farmer and a pig got into the room, and we couldn't get it to go away. And there are callers."

"Callers are the devil—I mean, the devil of a nuisance," the inspector remarked.

"You see, *you* can get rid of them," the clergyman said. "But *we* have to be patient. 'Offend not one of these little ones, lest a millstone is hanged about his neck.' Patience, sympathy, help. A word in season bringeth forth his fruit gladly."

The air stirred about him to the question. "And do these cause you fear?"

"Oh, not fear! by no means fear!" Mr. Batesby said. "Though, of course, sometimes one has to be firm. To pull them together. To try and give them a backbone. I have known some poor specimens. I remember meeting one not far from here. He looked almost sick and yellow, and I did what I could to hearten him up."

"Why was he looking so bad?" the inspector asked.

"Well, it was a funny story," Mr. Batesby said, looking meditatively through the stranger, who was leaning against the inn wall, "and I didn't quite understand it all. Of course, I saw what was wrong with him at once. Hysteria. I was very firm with him. I said, 'Get a hold on yourself.' He'd been talking to a Wesleyan."

Mr. Batesby paused long enough for the inspector to say, with a slight frown, "I'm almost a Wesleyan myself," gave him a pleasant smile as if he had been waiting for this, and went on: "Quite, quite, and very fine preachers many of them are. But a little unbalanced sometimes—emotional, you know. Too much emotion doesn't do, does it? Like poetry and all that, not stern enough. Thought, intelligence, brain —that's what helps. Well, this man had been saved—he called it saved, and there he was as nervous as could be."

Conversations of the Young Man in Grey

"What was he nervous about if he'd been saved?" the inspector asked idly.

Mr. Batesby smiled again. "It seems funny to say it in cold blood," he said, "but, do you know, he was quite sure he was going to be killed? He didn't know how, he didn't know who, he didn't know when. He'd just been saved at a Wesleyan mission hall and he was going to be killed by the devil. So I heartened him up."

The inspector had come together with a jerk; the young stranger was less energetic and less observable than the flowers in the inn garden behind him.

"Who was this man?" the inspector said. "Did you hear any more of him?"

"Nothing much," Mr. Batesby said. "I rather gathered that he'd been employed somewhere near here and was going to Canada, but he wasn't very clear. It was over in my own church that I actually met him, not at Fardles. So I lent him a little book—two, as a matter of fact. One was called *Present Helps* and one was *The Sand and the Rock*. I must have given away hundreds of them. He sent them back to me a week or two after from London."

"Did he write a letter with them?" the inspector asked.

"Well, he did, in fact," Mr. Batesby said. "A touching little note—very touching. It shows how ideas get hold of people. I believe I've got it somewhere." He felt in his pocket, and from a number of papers extracted a folded letter. "Here we are," he said.

REVEREND SIR,—I return you your books, which you very kindly lent me. I've no doubt they're quite right, but they don't seem to mean the precious Blood. They don't help me when the devil comes. He'll kill me one day, but my blessed Saviour will have me then, I know, but I daren't think of it. I hope he won't hurt me much. It's quite right, I'm not grumbling. I've asked for it all. And Jesus will save me at last.

Thank you for the books, which I return herewith. I've not read them both all as I'm rather worried.

I am,

Reverend sir,

Yours faithfully,

JAMES MONTGOMERY PATTISON.

"A nice letter," Mr. Batesby said. "But of course, the devil——!"

"Excuse me, sir," the inspector said, "but is there any address on that letter?"

"Yes," said Mr. Batesby, slightly surprised; "227 Thobblehurst Road, Victoria, S.W."

"Thank you, sir; and the date?"

"May 27th," Mr. Batesby said, staring.

"Humph," the inspector said. "And to think it's within two doors of my own house! A small man, you said, sir?"

"Rather small," Mr. Batesby said. "Oh, decidedly rather small. Rather unintelligent-looking, you know. But did you know him, then?"

"I think I met him once or twice," the inspector said. "If I should want to ask you any more questions, shall you be here?"

"I shall be at my own parish, over there: Ridings, at the Vicarage. The Duke's house is in it you know, in the parish —Ridings Castle. I'm sorry he's a Papist, though in a sense he was born blind."

"Humph," the inspector said again. "Well, I must get off. Good-bye, sir." He fled into the inn.

Against the grey wall Mr. Batesby saw the young stranger's grey figure. "How silent you are," he said. "Thinking, yes, thinking no doubt."

Conversations of the Young Man in Grey

"I was thinking that even a sparrow has its ghost," the other said, "and that all things work together."

"For good," Mr. Batesby concluded.

"For God," the other substituted, and moved away.

In Ridings Castle that afternoon the Duke and Kenneth endeavoured to talk poetry. But both of them were distracted —the Duke by the memory of the Graal and Kenneth by the thought of Barbara; and conversation after conversation either dropped or led them wanderingly back to these subjects. Never, Kenneth thought, had he supposed that so much of English literature was occupied either with the Graal or with madness. Before them at every turn moved the Arthurian chivalry or Tom o' Bedlam. And at last, about tea-time, they both seemed to give up the attempt and fell into a silence, which lasted until Kenneth said rather hesitatingly, "I should like to know how Barbara's getting along."

The Duke shrugged. "Naturally," he said, "but I don't see how you can. You can hardly call at Cully and ask Persimmons."

"What I should like to do would be to run across Rackstraw privately," Kenneth answered. "I've half a mind just to go and hang round a little while on the chance. He might come out for a walk, mightn't he?"

"He might," the Duke said. "I shouldn't, myself, leave my wife, if I had one, alone with Mr. Gregory. But your friend seems to like him."

"I think you're a little unfair," Mornington said. "After all, Lionel hasn't known what we have. He doesn't even know that I've been kicked out of the office."

The Duke, with an effort, said, "I expect I am. But when I think of his getting his foul paws on the Cup, I—I could murder your Archdeacon."

There was another silence, then he went on: "And even now I'm not satisfied. After all, what exactly did this doctor *do*? From what I could see, he hadn't reached her when she fainted."

Kenneth looked up swiftly. "That's what I've been wondering about," he said. "Only it's easy to be deceived. But I was on the stairs above her, and he seemed to be a couple of yards off when she—— she didn't exactly faint, at least it was more like sinking down quite quietly *first*. I suppose she fainted afterwards."

"Well, then," the Duke cried, "will you tell me why we let the Archdeacon give them the Graal?"

"I suppose we'd promised it to him if he would take on the case," Kenneth said doubtfully, "and he'd agreed to."

"But that is exactly what we hadn't," the Duke cried again, knocking a pile of Elizabethan dramatists off the table as he turned, "exactly. I remember perfectly well. The Archdeacon was just going to when we heard her screaming. But he wasn't speaking to the doctor, he was talking to your friend. And even so, he hadn't said more than that he wouldn't have delayed so long *if*—something or other."

"By God, that's right," Kenneth said staring. "But, if it hadn't been promised him and if he didn't help Barbara, what——?"

"Precisely," the Duke said. "What's he doing with it?"

There was another short pause.

"In another sense," Kenneth said, "what's he doing with it? Is he with Persimmons? Is it all a put-up job? Or will Persimmons and he fight for it? No, that's not likely. Then it must have been all arranged."

"Well, what about getting it back?" the Duke asked.

"Yes," Kenneth said doubtfully. "More easily said than done, don't you think? We don't even know where this doctor comes from or went to. Unless——" He hesitated.

"Unless?" the Duke asked.

"Unless—when the Chief Constable was talking to Persimmons on Monday—the day before yesterday, by heaven! —I couldn't help hearing something of what they said, and

Gregory gave him an address. I remembered it because it was so absurd—3 Lord Mayor's Street, in London somewhere. But I don't quite know what we can do about it. We can't go there and just ask for it."

"Can't we?" the Duke said. "Can't we, indeed? We can go and see what sort of place it is, and whether this Doctor Manasseh hangs out there. And, if he does, we can tell him It belongs to us, and if he makes any objection we can take It. We—at least the Archdeacon—did it before."

"He'll bring the police in," Kenneth demurred. "He must —this time."

"And if he does?" the Duke asked. "Let me get the Graal in my hands for time enough to get it over to Thwaites or someone, and It shall be in Rome before the police can guess what's happening. And there are no extradition treaties yet with the Vatican."

"I suppose there aren't," Kenneth said, arrested by this idea. "What a frightful joke! But what about us?"

"We should be sent to prison for burglary perhaps—'first offenders' and all that sort of thing. And the Bishops ought to rally—and yours too. I should leave a statement for the Cardinal-Archbishop of Westminster. My father is supposed to have had something to do—indirectly—with getting him the Hat."

"But it probably won't be there!" Kenneth objected again.

"Then we're no worse off; they won't distrust us more, and they certainly won't call in the police," the Duke answered. "Of course, if it's still at Cully . . . Perhaps your friend might know. Look here, Mornington, let's go over and see if we can drop across him." He jumped up and went to the door.

Rather to relieve their irritation than because they wanted to, they set out to walk, after the Duke had flung abroad a general warning that he might have to go to London that night, and came at last to where a private road entered the grounds of Cully and, a little farther on, passed near the cottage of the Rackstraws. Nothing, as the Duke pointed out, was more natural than that Kenneth should wish to see his friend or should hesitate to call at the front doors of Cully. But, as they passed the private road, they saw Lionel and Barbara in the lane before them.

"Hallo," Kenneth said, "this is surprising and delightful. I didn't expect you to be rambling round like this. Is all well again?"

"I'm rather tired and rather lazy," Barbara said happily. "But otherwise I'm very comfortable, thank you."

"The devil you are!" Kenneth said, staring at her, with a smile. "I expected you to be in bed at least."

"I seem to have slept on cushions in Mr. Persimmons's hall till about four, but I woke up feeling quite normal," Barbara answered. "But what a business!" She spoke lightly, but her face grew whiter as she referred to it.

"It's all over, anyhow," Lionel said hastily. "I shall screw another's week's holiday out of Stephen, Kenneth, and we'll go to the seaside or something for a few days—without Adrian."

"What's going to happen to Adrian?" Kenneth asked.

"He's going to stop here," Lionel answered. "He's got very fond of one of the maids here, and he adores Gregory, and his motors and telephones and Chinese masks and things."

"And Gregory's willing to have him?" Kenneth asked.

"Loves him, he says," Lionel answered. "Good luck to them both. I don't want another twenty-four hours like the last. Of course, we must see this doctor fellow again first; that will be the day after to-morrow."

"Do you really think it was he that helped you, Babs?" Kenneth said.

Lionel looked at his wife. "Well, Babs doesn't know," he said, "not being in a state then to notice such things. And *I* don't know. If it wasn't him, what was it? And yet he was some way off and didn't seem to have a chance to do anything."

"I can't tell you anything," Barbara said gravely, "for I don't know. There was nothing but a darkness of the most dreadful pressure—and the edge of the pit I was falling towards. Nothing could stop me and just as I fell—no, it's all right, Lionel; I don't mind this part—just as I fell I was entirely all right. I fell into safety. I was just quite happy. I can't tell you—it was just being swallowed up by peace. And like—I don't know—like recognizing someone; when one says, "Oh, joy! there's—someone or other. I knew him at once."

The three young men considered her gravely. After a minute she went on: "So that now to look back on it's like having had a tooth out, unpleasant but small. I don't mind talking of it. But when I was there it seemed as if things so wicked I could never have thought of them had got their claws into me."

"*You* could never have thought of them!" Lionel scoffed tenderly.

She smiled at him, and then, as she leaned against the gate of the Cully grounds she unconsciously stretched her arms out along the top bar on either side. So, her feet close together, her palms turned upward, her face towards the evening sky, she seemed to hang remote, till Kenneth said sharply, "Don't, Babs; you look as if you were crucified."

She brought her eyes down to meet his without otherwise moving, then, looking past him, she came together suddenly, took a step forward, and cried out: "Oh, joy! it's——" and stopped, laughing and embarrassed.

Her companions looked round in surprise. Behind them, as they stood clustered by the gate, stood an ordinary looking young man smiling recognition at Barbara. She blushed as she shook hands, but, with her usual swiftness, raced into an apology. "It's extraordinarily silly, but I *can't* remember your name. But I'm so pleased you're here. Do forgive me and tell me."

"My name is John," the other said, "though I don't think you ever heard it. But we've certainly met several times."

"I know, I know," Barbara said. "Stop a moment and I shall remember. It was . . . it was just before I was married, surely. . . . No, since then, too. Somewhere only the other day. How stupid! Lionel, can't you help?" She turned a face crimson with surprise, delight, and shame to her husband.

But Lionel shook his head firmly. "I do seem to have seen you before," he said to the stranger, "but I haven't the ghost of a notion where."

"It really doesn't matter," the other said. "To be remembered is the chief thing. I think I have met these other gentlemen too."

"It's too absurd," Kenneth said, laughing outright, "but for a minute when I saw you I thought you were a priest I'd seen somewhere. But I couldn't at all fix where, so I suppose I haven't."

"It was certainly in church somewhere," the stranger said, and glanced at the Duke.

"At Oriel," the Duke said, "—in—whose rooms was it? But not lately, I think."

"Not so very much lately," answered the other. "But you haven't quite forgotten me, I'm glad to see."

"I don't understand it at all," Barbara, still flushed and excited, answered. "I feel as if it were only to-day. You weren't at . . . the house, were you?" she asked doubtfully.

The stranger smiled back. "I know Mr. Persimmons, and he will know me better soon. But don't worry. How's Adrian?"

"Very well, thank you," Lionel said; and rather hesitatingly looked at Barbara. "Babs, don't you think you ought to get back? My wife's not been very well," he added to the stranger, "and I don't want her to get at all excited. You understand, I'm certain."

The young man smiled again. "I understand very well indeed," he answered. "But there is no more danger for her here. Believe certainly that this universe also carries its salvation in its heart." He looked at Barbara. "We have met in places that shall not easily be forgotten," he said, "before you were married, and since, and to-day also. Sleep securely to-night, the gates of hell have no more power over you. And you, my lord Duke, because you have loved the thing that is mine, this also shall save you in the end. Only remember that in your heart as well as your house you shall keep vigil and prayer till the Master of the Graal shall come." He came a step nearer to Kenneth. "But for you I have no message," he said, "except the message of the Graal— '*Surely I come quickly.* To-night thou shalt be with Me in Paradise.'"

He moved backward, and, as they involuntarily glanced at each other, seemed to step aside, so that no one was quite certain which way he had gone. Or, rather, Lionel and the Duke were not certain. Barbara was gazing at Kenneth with rapt eyes. "It was he that was at the edge of the pit to-day," she breathed. "To-night! O Kenneth!"

Kenneth stood silent for a minute or two, then he said only: "Well, good night, Babs," as she gave him both her hands. "Good night, Lionel: I should certainly screw an extra week out of Stephen." He laid his hand on the Duke's arm. "Shall we go straight on to London?" he asked.

The evening had grown darker before the Archdeacon, wandering alone in his garden, saw at the gate the figure of the priest-king. He had been standing still for a moment looking out towards the road, and to his absent eyes it seemed almost as if the form had shaped itself from the sky and the fields and road about it. He came down to it and paused, and words sounded in his mind, but whether from without or from within he no more knew than whether this presence had moved along the road or come forth from the universe which it expressed. " 'The time is at hand,' " it said; " 'I will keep the passover with my disciples.' "

"Ah, fair sweet lord, Thou knowest," he answered aloud.

"I am a messenger only," the voice, if voice it were, uttered, "but I am the precursor of the things that are to be. I am John and I am Galahad and I am Mary; I am the Bearer of the Holy One, the Graal, and the keeper of the Graal. I have kept it always, whether I dwelt in the remote places of the world and kings rode after me or whether I removed to the farther parts of man's mind. All magic and all holiness is through me, and though men stole the Graal from me ages since I have been with it for ever. Brother and friend, the night of His coming is at hand."

"I have watched many nights," the Archdeacon answered, "and behold His mercy endureth for ever."

"Also I have watched with you," the voice said, "yet not I, but He that sent me. You shall watch yet through a deeper night, and after that I will come to this place on the second morning from now, and I will begin the mysteries of my Lord, and thereafter He shall do what He will, and you shall see the end of these things. Only be strong and of a good courage."

The form was gone. The Archdeacon looked out over the countryside, and his lips moved in their accustomed psalm.

Chapter Fourteen

THE BIBLE OF MRS. HIPPY

As the inspector was carried back to London in the first available train, he found himself slipping from side to side on the smooth ice of his uncertain mind. Impartially he considered that this sudden return was likely to be as futile as any other attempt he had made at solving the problem of the murder. But, on the other hand, there could not be many rather undersized men in the neighbourhood of London who within the last two months had been intimately connected with Wesleyan Methodism and with death. When Mr. Batesby had spoken that morning it had seemed as if two streams of things—actual events and his own meditations— had flowed gently together; as if not he, but Life were solving the problem in the natural process of the world. He reminded himself now that such a simplicity was unlikely; explanations did not lucidly arise from mere accidents and present themselves as all but an ordered whole. He dimly remembered Mrs. Hippy, the occupant of the house next but two to his own; he remembered that she was an acquaintance of his wife, who had gone with her to certain bazaars, sales of work, and even church services. If she had had a lodger who had disappeared, why hadn't his wife mentioned it before? It was such a failure on the part of his intimates that the inspector always expected, he told himself, and always found.

His wife was staying with her mother, so the inspector lunched near King's Cross, and then went on to 227 Thobblehurst Road. Mrs. Hippy came to the door, and appeared delighted to see him. "Why, come in, inspector," she said. "I thought Mrs. Colquhoun said you were going away."

The Bible of Mrs. Hippy

"So I did," the inspector said, following her to the drawing-room, as it was solemnly called, which looked on to the street. "But I had some inquiries to make which brought me back."

"Really?" Mrs. Hippy said, rather absently. "Inspector, can you think of a fish in two syllables?"

"A fish?" the inspector said vaguely. "Walrus? salmon? mackerel? No, that's three."

"It might *count* as two perhaps," Mrs. Hippy answered. "Why did the por-poise? Because it saw the mack-reel."

"Eh?" the inspector said. "What's the idea exactly?"

Mrs. Hippy, plunging at a number of papers on the chesterfield, produced an effort in bright green and gold, entitled in red *Puzzles and Riddles: a Magazine for All.* "They're offering a prize," she said, "for the best ten questions and answers of that sort. They say it's one of the best ways, but rather out of date. But I think they're splendid. Look, I've done four. Why does the shoe-lace?"

She paused, got no answer, and said delightedly, "Because the button-holes. The next——"

"Good! Splendid!" the inspector cried. "Splendid, Mrs. Hippy. I suppose they'll print them all if you win. And you're sure to. You'd be good at cross-word puzzles. But I won't disturb you long. I only came to ask if you could tell me anything about a fellow named Pattison you had stopping here."

"Mr. Pattison?" Mrs. Hippy said, opening her eyes. "Why, do you want to arrest him? I don't know where he is; he left me a month ago."

"Where did he go to? Can you tell me that?" Colquhoun asked.

"Canada," Mrs. Hippy answered. "At least, he said he was going to. But he was a funny creature altogether. Not sociable, if you understand. Dull, heavy, so to speak. I lent him all the old numbers of this"—she waved *Puzzles and Riddles,* "but he didn't work out a single one, though I told him the easiest. And he spoilt my Bible, scribbling all over it. My mother's

The Bible of Mrs. Hippy

Bible too—not the one I take to church. But there, it always seems to be like that when you try and help. People don't deserve it, and that's a fact."

"Perhaps you won't mind helping *me*, all the same," the inspector said. "Could I see the Bible? And did you *know* that he was going to Canada?"

"Not to say *know*," Mrs. Hippy said, looking longingly at the competition. "He *said* he was going; and one morning he wished me good-bye and said he'd send me a postcard. But he never has done."

Further interrogation made it clear that her knowledge was of the slightest. She sometimes let two rooms, furnished, to a single gentleman, and the late Mr. Pattison, arriving at Victoria one day and seeing the card in her window, had taken them, with solemn assurances of respectability and a month's rent in advance. He had seemed to be rather worried, though what about Mrs. Hippy had never understood. He had come to the Wesleyan Church she herself attended several times, but it had not seemed to calm his distress. He had borrowed a Bible from her, and had scribbled everywhere in it. Finally he had told her that he would be leaving for Canada shortly, and had departed one morning, carrying a suitcase and bidding her a final farewell.

As the rooms had been thoroughly "done out" and were now empty, awaiting the arrival of Mrs. Hippy's married sister, the inspector went through them with care and without success. He then withdrew with the Bible to his own deserted house and gave himself up to its study.

The scribbling seemed entirely haphazard. It was everywhere—on the fly-leaves, in the margins, and here and there right across the pages themselves. It consisted largely of fragmentary prayers, ejaculations, and even texts. A phrase which occurred on the printed page would be rewritten and underscored in the margin; and this seemed to have been done especially with such phrases as record or assert the Mercy and

Compassion of God. Sometimes this repetition would be varied by a wild "I believe, I believe" scrawled against a verse, by an "He saves," or a "God is love." On the other hand, certain verses were marked by a line and a question-mark. "Depart from me, ye cursed," was heavily lined; so was "he that is filthy, let him be filthy still"; so was "I have delivered him over to Satan." The sayings about the unpardonable sin were scratched heavily out; so was "He will have mercy on whom He will have mercy." In the midst of these fantastic scrawls there appeared here and there a carefully written comment. Against "God shall be all in all" was written in a small, sedate hand: "Lies," and against "reconciling the world to Himself" appeared, similarly, "Not true."

The fly-leaves, the back of the New Testament half-title, and the spaces between the various books were occupied with longer jottings. The first of these seemed to be a kind of discussion. It was not easy to decipher, but it appeared to be a summing up of the promises of salvation and an *argumentum ad hominem* at the end. But the very end was the words, heavily printed: "I am damned."

This sort of thing, whatever religious mania it suggested, was not of much use to the inspector. It brought him no nearer to discovery why the murdered man, if Mr. Pattison were he, had got himself murdered. Farther on, however, he found himself, at the end of Deuteronomy, confronted with the single word: "Gregory." Nothing followed, but it raised his hopes wonderfully. Still, it was one thing to read "Gregory" and another to prove that Gregory had slain the writer. He went on turning the pages.

At the end of Job there was a whole sentence. "He won't let me go and Jesus won't get me away." This might be Gregory or it might, as the inspector suspected, be meant for the devil. Well, if Mr. Pattison and the devil were on those terms, all wasn't lost yet.

Between two of the minor prophets was scrawled: "I saw

her to-day; so she is out"; after which there was a blank, till, on the back, of the half-title of the "New Testament of our Lord and Saviour Jesus Christ," there came this longer note:

"I will put it all down. I am James Montgomery Pattison. I am forty-six years old, and I know that the devil will kill me soon. I have done his will against my wishes too long and I cannot get away from him now. When I heard Mr. Macdermott preach I thought my heart was opened and the Lord had come to me and saved me, and I testified to my master, who was a worse sinner than I. But he has me too fast and I cannot escape. I have served him and the devil together for twenty-four years, since he caught me robbing him. I have done forgery and worse. I have stood by and seen him swear the woman I seduced into prison for soliciting him; and now I cannot get free. He is going to kill me; it is in his eyes and face." There came an outburst of appeals to God and to Christ, and the record resumed. "He had Louise put into prison to torture me. It was him all through." There was a blank space, and then, written in the steady, sedate hand, "I have gone back to him altogether, and he will kill me. This is what comes of God."

On the very last page of the book, enclosed in a correct panel, with decorative curves flowing round it, was printed in clearly and precisely: "Mr. Gregory Persimmons, Cully, Nr. Fardles, Hertfordshire."

The inspector shut the book and went into the kitchen to make himself tea.

Chapter Fifteen

'TO-NIGHT THOU SHALT BE WITH ME IN PARADISE'

Lord Mayor's Street in the evening seemed always, if by any chance it could, to attract and contain such mist as might be about. A faint vapour made the air dim, especially round the three shops, and caused passers-by to remark regularly either that the evening was a bit misty or that the evenings were drawing in or that there might be something of a fog by the morning. But for Gregory Persimmons, as he came swiftly into it about nine o'clock on the same day, the chemist's shop rode London like a howdah on the back of an elephant, the symbol and shelter of the prince that ruled the armies of the air. He reached the door, which was still ajar, pushed it open, entered, and closed it after him.

The shop was dark, after the street light a few paces away outside, but the gleam of a light came from the inner room. For the first time since Gregory had known it the Greek was not there, but as he hesitated a voice sounded from within.

"Is that you, Gregory?" Manasseh called.

"It is I," Gregory answered, crossed the shop, and went in.

The room was bare and dirty. On a table under the window and exactly opposite the door in to the shop, the Graal stood exposed, under the light of a single electric bulb which hung without a shade from the middle of the ceiling. There were no pictures and no books; a few chairs stood about, and in one corner was a high closed cabinet. A dilapidated carpet covered the floor.

The Greek was sitting in a chair on the left of the Graal.

'To-night thou shalt be with Me in Paradise'

Manasseh had apparently been walking up and down, but he stood still as Gregory came in, and looked at him anxiously. "Well," he said, "have you brought the child?"

"Not to-night," Persimmons said. "I thought it better not. You or someone else, Manasseh, have worked wonders. She's almost well again, and wanted to see him. So I promised she should to-morrow, and he's coming to London with me to-morrow afternoon to go to—I forget where he is to go to. It doesn't matter. When do we leave England?"

"The day after," Manasseh said. "I'm supposed to go down and see the woman again that morning. But as things are I don't know . . ."

"Send them a wire in the morning," Gregory suggested. " 'Detained till this afternoon.' We shall be at Harwich by then."

"I don't know why you're so keen on the child," Manasseh said morosely. "You won't have him—interfered with at all, even to make the journey easier?"

"The journey will be all right," Gregory said. "Jessie's coming too. Jessie is the girl who looks after him. It's quite safe—she doesn't know exactly, but she *will* come. She's got no relations near at hand; she's a sensuous little bitch, and she has her wanton eyes on Mr. Persimmons of Cully. She'll hope to be compromised; I know her. And she knows she may have to go on a journey, but not where or why."

Manasseh nodded. "But why take him?" he insisted.

"Because I owe him for a debt to the Sabbath," Gregory answered. "Because we haven't often the chance of such a pure and entire oblation. It's wonderful the way he's taken to me, and I think we shall make him a lord of power before we have done. Isn't that worth more than sending him silly? And Jessie can be dropped anywhere if she's inconvenient." He walked across to the table. "And what about you?" he asked. "Do we take this with us, or do you still want to destroy it now?"

'To-night thou shalt be with Me in Paradise'

"No," Manasseh said. "I have thought of it, and we will take it. There may be something in what you said."

"What I said?" Gregory asked, whistling softly as he surveyed the Cup.

"We may be able to use it for destruction—to destroy *through* it," Manasseh said. "I have dreamt that we might learn to destroy earth and heaven through it, or at least all intelligible experience of them among men. It is death as well as life, and who knows how far death may go? They talk of their Masses, you talk of your Black Mass, but there may be such a Mass of Death said with this as shall blast the world for ever. But you and I are not great enough for that."

Gregory answered softly, "I think you may be right, Manasseh. Bear with me, for I am young in these things. I know the current of desire in which all things move, and I have guided it a little as I will. But I see there are deeper things below." He looked at the Greek. "And what do you say," he asked, "who are older than we?"

The Greek answered, his eyes fixed on the Graal: "All things are indivisible and one. You cannot wholly destroy and you cannot wholly live, but you can change mightily and for ever as any of our reckoning goes. Even I cannot see down infinity. Make it agreeable to your lusts while the power is yours, for there are secret ways down which it may pass even now and you shall not hold it."

Gregory smiled, and filliped the Graal with a finger. "Do you know," he said, "I should like to annoy the Archdeacon a little." He stood still suddenly and cried out: "And there is a way by which it may be done. I have tried it, and I know. This is the circle of all souls, and I will gather them and marry them as I please. I will bring them from this world and from another and I will bind the lost with the living till the living itself be lost."

Manasseh moved nearer to him. "Tell me," he said; "you have a great thought."

'To-night thou shalt be with Me in Paradise'

"I have a thought that is pleasant to my mind," Gregory said, "and this is what we will do. There went out from among us lately by my act a weak, wretched, unhappy soul that sought to find its god and in its last days returned to me and was utterly mine. It was willing to die when I slew it, and in the shadows it waits still upon my command. We will draw this back, and we will marry it to this priest, body and soul, so that he shall live with it by day and by night, and come indeed in the end to know not which is he. And let us see then if he will war against us for the Graal."

"This you can do if you will," Manasseh said, "for I have seen spirits recalled, though not by means of the Graal. But can you bind it so closely to the priest?"

"Assuredly you can," the Greek said, "if you have the conditions. But they are exact. You must have that body here into which you will bring that soul in contact—I do not know if it could be done at a distance, but I do not think it has been done, and I am sure you have no time to try. And you must have that soul at your command, and I think you have. And you must have a means of passage, and you have it in this Cup. And you must have a very strong desire, and this you have, both of you, for this is at once possession and destruction. And you are the better for knowing the worst, and this I do, and I will set my power with yours if you choose."

"We must have the body here," Gregory said. "But—will he come?"

"I do not see why he should not come if he is asked," the Greek said. "Cannot Manasseh bring him with some tale of the woman?"

"To-morrow night is the last night we can be sure of having in England," Manasseh answered, "if we wish to escape with both the Graal and the child. But he might come for that."

They were silent, standing or sitting around the Cup, where it seemed to await their decision in a helpless bondage. They

were still silent some minutes later when a sudden knock
sounded on the door of the shop. Gregory started, and both he
and Manasseh glanced inquiringly at the Greek, who said
casually: "It may be someone for medicine or it may be they
have followed Gregory. Go you, Manasseh. If they ask for me,
tell them I am away from home to-night; and if for Gregory,
tell them he is not here."

Manasseh obeyed, pulling the door to behind him. Gregory
smiled at the Greek. "Do you really give them medicine?" he
asked.

The Greek shrugged his shoulders. "Why not?" he said. "I
don't poison ants; they may as well live as die. But there are
not many who will come."

They heard Manasseh cross the shop and open the door,
then several exclamations at once in different voices. Then a
gay voice, at the sound of which Gregory started and looked
round, said: "Why, if it isn't the doctor himself! Now this is
fortunate. My dear doctor, we've been talking about you all
day. Let's see, were you properly introduced to the Duke?
No, oh, no, don't shut the door. No, I beg you. We've come
all the way from Fardles—Castra Parvulorum, you know; the
camp of the children—to ask you a question—two questions.
Is Gregory here by any chance? That's not one of them. No,
really—sorry to push, but . . . Thank you ever so much; you
can shut it now."

Under this rush of talk had sounded Manasseh's exclamatory
protests and the scuffle of feet. Gregory put out a hand to the
Graal, but the Greek made a motion with his hand and
checked him. "How many are there?" he asked softly. Gregory
tiptoed to the narrow opening and peeped through. "Two, I
think," he whispered, returning. "Mornington and the Duke.
I can't see or hear anyone else. Hadn't we better move
that?"

The Greek turned a face of sudden malignity on him. "Fool,"
he said, "will you always run from your enemies?" He stood

up as he spoke and began to move the few chairs noiselessly back against the wall.

In the shop, Mornington was plying Manasseh with conversation. "We felt so curious about the Graal," he said, "and, to tell you the truth, so curious about what you'd done to Barbara Rackstraw, that we simply had to come and ask you about it. The Duke's done nothing but rave about it ever since. Unrecognized genius, you know—Mrs. Eddy, Sir Herbert Barker. You took the Graal, so you must have done something. Manasseh is an honourable man." He stopped suddenly and sniffed. "I'm sure you've got Gregory here," he said. "It smells like a dung-heap. You don't mind me going in?"

Manasseh apparently had jumped in his way. There was a slight scuffle, then Kenneth said pleasantly: "Hold him, Ridings. Bring him along too and let's look round."

The Greek stooped down, took hold of the carpet, wrenched it from the occasional nail that held it down, and flung it to one side of the room. The floor beneath was marked with what looked like chalk in two broad parallel lines running from about two-thirds of the depth of the room to the two posts of the communicating door. At the end of the room these two lines were joined by a complicated diagram, which Gregory seemed to recognize, for he caught his breath and said: "Will it hold him?"

The Greek threw a cushion on the floor between the diagram and the table on which the Graal stood, and sank down on it. "This is our protection," he said. "Call to Manasseh that he does not enter, for this is the way of death. I have charged these barriers with power, and they shall wither whoever comes between them. Open the door, stand aside, and be still."

Gregory went to the door and drew it open by reaching to the top till the handle came within reach; he seized it and pulled it back till the whole entrance lay open between the equal lines. The Greek peered forward into the little dark shop,

and saw dimly Kenneth's figure opposite him at the same time
that Kenneth saw the Graal.

"My dear Ridings, he's been admiring it," Mornington said.
"The workmanship, probably. It was Ephesus, I fancy, that
the dear delightful Gregory told us it came from. There's a
gentleman here sitting on the floor who may be the carrier.
Hobson, you know, and John what-you-may-call-him in that
very disastrous Christmas thing of Dickens's. Or perhaps
they've been having their favourite food. The Graal, I remember, in a charming way always provided you with that. What is
yours, doctor? Something Eastern, no doubt. Rice? What a
horrible thing to waste the Graal on!"

He had come to the doorway as he spoke, and drew a
revolver from his pocket. "The Duke's really," he went on.
"One of those little domestic utensils you can pick up for
almost nothing at a sale. Have you got him, Ridings? There
seems to be a pavement-artist somewhere in this establishment;
the most original little sketches adorn the floor."

"Take care," the Duke's voice cried. "There is hell near us
now."

"I think it very likely," Kenneth said, "but you can't expect
me to think much of hell if Gregory is one of its kings." He
took two or three swift steps into the room, flung a quick
glance behind him lest he should be attacked from the wall he
passed, and, even as he did so, staggered and put his hand to
his heart. The Duke heard him gasp, and, still clutching
Manasseh, pushed forward, to see what was happening. Kenneth had reeled to one of the white lines and was stumbling
blindly, now forward, now backward, drawing deep choking
breaths. The Greek had thrust his face out, and as the Duke
saw it in the full light he gave a little gasp of dismay. For the
face that he saw looked at him from a great distance and yet
was itself that distance. It was white and staring and sick with
a horrible sickness; he shut his eyes before this evil. All the
gorgeous colours and pomps of sin of which he had been so

often warned had disappeared; the war between good and evil
existed no longer, for the thing beneath the Graal was not
fighting but vomiting. Once he realized that his eyes were
closed he forced himself to open them, saw Kenneth almost
fall across the space between the lines, and called to him. Then
he flung Manasseh from him to the floor, cried out on God
and the Mother of God, and sprang forward; but as he reached
the doorway he felt his strength oozing from him. Hollows
opened within him; he clutched at the doorpost, and, as he
touched it, seemed to feel this also drag him sideways and
downward. He crashed to the floor while Kenneth, gathering
all his life's energy together, forced himself two steps nearer his
aim, moaned as even that energy failed, dropped to his knees,
and at last, choking and twisting, fell dead on the diagram
before the Greek.

Manasseh had got to his feet, but he remained leaning
against the door of the shop as Gregory against the wall of the
inner room. The Duke, unable to move, lay prostrate across
the threshold. So, as they watched, they saw the body of the
dead man shiver and lift itself a little, as if moved by a strong
wind. Gradually there appeared, rising from it, a kind of dark
cloud, which floated upwards and outwards on all sides, and
was at last so thick that the form itself could no longer be
discerned. Manasseh watched with eyes of triumph. But
Gregory was curiously shaken, for he, less instructed in the
high ways of magic, recoiled, not from the destruction of his
enemy, but from the elements which accompanied it. He
shrank from the face of the sorcerer; like the Duke, he found
himself in a state for which he had not been prepared and at
which he trembled in horror. A sickness crept within him; was
this the end of victory and lordship and the Sabbath, and this
the consummation of the promises and of desire? The sudden
action had precipitated him down a thousand spirals of the
slow descent, and he hung above the everlasting void. He
sought to keep his eyes fixed on the symbol of triumph, the

dark cloud that streamed upward from floor to ceiling in front of him, but they were drawn back still to the face which dominated it and him.

Slowly, as they watched, the pillar of cloud began to sink, withdrawing into itself. The colour of it seemed to change also, from a dense black to a smoky and then to an ordinary grey. Quicker and quicker it fell, hovered for a few minutes, and at last collapsed entirely. There remained, in the place where the body had been, nothing but a spreading heap of dust.

The Duke, defeated in mind and body, and with too young a soul to dare the tempest, made yet some effort to assert the cause in which he believed. He raised himself on one hand as he lay and cried out in the great Latin he loved—loved rather perhaps as literature than as religion, but still as a strength more ancient and more enduring than himself. "Profiscere, anima Christiana," he stammered, "de hoc mundo, in nomine Patris. . . ."

"Be silent, you!" Manasseh snarled, and, with one of those grotesque movements which attend on all crises, took from the counter a small bottle as the nearest missile and flung it. It smashed on the floor, and the Greek's eyes moved toward it and came to rest on the Duke. He stood up with an effort, and motioned to Gregory to draw the carpet again over the magnetized passage of death. When this was done, the three gathered round the Duke, who half rose to his feet and was overthrown again by the touch of the Greek's hand.

"Will you not destroy him also?" Manasseh asked, half greedily, half timidly.

The Greek slowly shook his head. "I am very weary," he said, "and the strength is gone from the figure. If that other had not despised us, I do not know whether I should have won. And, since he is here, unless you will kill him yourself, you should use him for what you desire to do."

"How can we use him?" Gregory asked, meditatively prodding the Duke with his foot, his momentary fear gone.

"Let him write and tell this priest whom you hate that he and the Graal are here—and that which was the other—and that he must come quickly to free them."

"But will he write?" Gregory asked.

"Certainly he will write," the Greek said, "or one of us will write with his hand."

"Do you write then," Manasseh said, "for you are the greatest among us."

"I will do it if you wish," the Greek said. "Lift him partly up, and give me pencil and paper."

As Gregory tore a page from his pocket-book, Manasseh dragged and pushed at the Duke till he sat at last leaning against the door. The Greek knelt down beside him, put one arm round his shoulders, and laid the right hand over his. To the Duke it seemed as if an enormous cloud of darkness had descended upon him, in the midst of which some unknown strength moved him at its will. In the conflict of his inner being with this tyranny the control of his body was lost; the battle was not in that outer region, but in a more central place. Ignorant and helpless, his hand wrote as the Greek's controlling mind bade, though the handwriting was his own.

"Come, if you can by any means," the letter ran, "for That and we are here. The bearer of this will tell you as much as he will, but believe him if he says that without you there is an end to all.—Ridings."

The Greek released the Duke and rose. Gregory took the note, read it, and shook his head. "I do not think he will be deceived," he said doubtfully.

"But what can he——" Manasseh began, but the Greek silenced him with a gesture and said, "He will do what he must do. There is more than we and he which moves about us now. I think he will come, for I think that the battle is joined, and till that which is with us or that which is with them is loosened it cannot end. Take care of your ways to-morrow."

"And who is to be the bearer?" Gregory asked.

'To-night thou shalt be with Me in Paradise'

"That you shall be," the Greek said.

"But how much shall I tell him?" Gregory asked again uncertainly.

The Greek turned upon him. "Fool," he said, "I tell you you cannot choose. You will do and say what is meant for you, and so will he. And to-morrow there shall be an end."

Chapter Sixteen

THE SEARCH FOR THE HOUSE

Tea, tobacco, meditation, and sleep brought the inspector no nearer a solution of his problem. On the assumption that J. M. Pattison was the murdered man, there had still appeared no reason why Gregory Persimmons should have murdered him. It was true that so far he knew nothing of their relations. If Pattison had been blackmailing Persimmons now—but then why the scribblings in the Bible? Some ancient vengeance, he rather desperately wondered, some unreasoning hate? But he could not get away from a feeling that, even so, it was the wrong way round. Small nonentities did sometimes murder squires, bankers, or peers, but it was not normal that a squire should murder a small nonentity. Besides, religious mania seemed to come into it somewhere. But whether Mr. Persimmons or the deceased was affected by it, or both of them, the inspector could not decide. And why the devil? Why, in God's name, the devil? The inspector's view of the devil was roughly that the devil was something in which children believed, but which was generally known not to exist, certainly not as taking any active part in the affairs of the world; these, generally speaking, were run by three parties—the police, criminals, and the ordinary public. The inspector tended to see these last two classes as one; all specialists tend so to consider humanity as divided into themselves and the mass to be affected. Doctors see it in the two sections of themselves and patients potential or actual; clerics in themselves and disciples; poets in themselves and readers (or non-readers; but that is the mere wickedness of mankind); explorers in themselves and stay-at-homes; and so on. The inspector, however, was driven by the definitions of law to admit that the public was not as a whole and altogether criminal, and he inevitably tended to consider it more likely that Mr. Pattison should be guilty than that Mr. Persimmons should be. Only someone had strangled Mr. Pattison, and Mr. Pattison's own expectation seemed to point direct to Mr. Persimmons.

Colquhoun went over in his mind the incidents which had led him to this point—his failure to connect anyone directly with the crime, his irritation with Stephen Persimmons and Lionel Rackstraw, his anger with Sir Giles, his discovery of Gregory's connection with Stephen and Sir Giles, his not very hopeful descent on Fardles. His conflict with Ludding had relieved, but not enlightened him. He came to the events of the morning and the way in which the young stranger had recognized him. Of course, more people knew Tom Fool . . . no doubt, but he had a feeling that he knew the face. He thought of it vaguely, as Mrs. Lucksparrow and Ludding had done, as a foreigner's. The Duke had thought of it in connection with the high friendships of his Oxford days; Kenneth as related to his intelligence of the Church and its order; Sir Giles had seen it with equal curiosity and fear—but this was almost purely intellectual, and did not suggest the revival of some past vivid experience. Gregory and the Archdeacon had answered to it more passionately, as somehow symbolical of a mode of real existence; as Barbara had recognized in it at once the safety and peace which had succoured her in the house of the infernal things. Nor, had Gregory remembered it—but the crisis of Kenneth's death had put it out of his mind—was it without significance that the Greek had seemed to feel a power moving under and through the activities of his opponents.

But these things were not known to Colquhoun, who, nevertheless, found himself trying to recollect who the stranger was. He had met foreigners enough in his life, and he was driven at last to believe that it must have been on a visit of the Infanta of Spain some time before that their meeting had taken place; he had interviewed enough members of the Spanish police then for more than one face to have been seen and since forgotten, till chance rediscovered it. Chance also had directed the conversation with Mr. Batesby to fear and his past experiences, and so to the appeal of the late James Montgomery Pattison. At least, chance and the stranger between them, for it had been he who had asked the occasional helming question. He tried to consider whether this stranger could have had anything to do with the murder, but found himself foiled; when his mind brought the assumed Spaniard into relation with any other being one of them faded and was gone. It was chance, of course; and chance had done him a good turn—up to a point, anyhow.

He took his troubles to the Assistant Commissioner the next morning, who listened to his report carefully, and seemed disposed to make further inquiries. "On Monday," he said, "Colonel Conyers mentioned Gregory Persimmons to me as having taken part with him in a curious little chase after a chalice which had been more or less stolen by the Duke of the North Ridings and the Archdeacon of Fardles. This Persimmons assured us he wouldn't prosecute, and that made it very difficult for us to move. But I went to tea with the Duchess on Tuesday and had a chat with the Duke."

"And did he admit that he'd stolen it?" the astonished inspector asked.

"Well, he seemed to think it really belonged to the Archdeacon," the Assistant Commissioner answered, "but he was rather stiff about it, told me he had reason to believe that the most serious attempts were being made to obtain possession of it, and even talked of magic."

"Talked of *what*?" the inspector asked, more bewildered than before.

"Magic," the chief said. "*The Arabian Nights*, inspector, and people being turned into puppy-dogs. All rubbish, of course, but he must have had *something* in his mind—and connected with Persimmons apparently. I had Professor Ribblestone-Ridley tell me what's known about Ephesian chalices, but it didn't help much. There seem to be four or five fairly celebrated chalices that come from round there, but they're all in the possession of American millionaires, except one which was at Kieff. I did wonder whether it was that—a lot of these Russian valuables are drifting over here. But I still don't see why the Duke should have bolted with it, or why Persimmons should have refused to get it back. Unless Persimmons *had* stolen it. Could the deceased Pattison have been mixed up in some unsavoury business of getting it over?"

"Bolsheviks, sir?" the inspector asked, with a grin.

"I know, I know," the Assistant Commissioner said. "Still, 'wolf,' you know . . . there *are* Bolshevik affairs of the kind."

"I suppose it's possible," Colquhoun allowed. "But, then, did Pattison mean the Bolsheviks by the devil?"

His chief shook his head. "Religion plays the deuce with a man's sanity," he said regretfully. "Your clergyman told you he thought he was saved, and in that state there's nothing people won't say or do."

"It might be one of the American chalices," the inspector submitted.

"It might," the other said. "But we should have been warned of the theft from New York, probably. It might also be the Holy Graal, which Ribblestone-Ridley says, according to some traditions, came from Ephesus."

"The Holy Graal," the inspector said doubtfully. "Hadn't that something to do with the Pope?"

"It's supposed to be the cup Christ used at the Last Supper —so I suppose you might say so," the Assistant Commissioner answered almost as doubtfully. "However, as that Cup, if it ever existed, isn't likely to exist *now*, we needn't really worry about that. No, Colquhoun, I lean to Kieff. I wonder whether the Duke would tell me anything." He looked at the inspector. "Would you like to go and ask him?" he finished.

"Well, sir, I'd rather you did," Colquhoun said. "I like to have some hold on people when what I'm asking them is as vague as all that—it seems to help things on."

The Assistant Commissioner looked at the telephone. "I wonder," he said. "We don't know much, do we? A chalice and a Bible and a clergyman. What an infernally religious case this is getting! And an Archdeacon on the outskirts.

"Perhaps Persimmons has killed the Archdeacon by now," he added hopefully as he took off the receiver.

The Duke, it appeared, when he got through to the butler, was not in London. He had been up for two nights, but had returned to the country on Wednesday—yesterday—morning. He had been accompanied (this when it was understood who was inquiring) by the Archdeacon of Fardles and a Mr. Mornington. They had both returned with the Duke. Should Mr. Thwaites be called to the telephone? Mr. Thwaites was— no, not his Grace's secretary; no, nor his Grace's valet; a sort of general utility man to his Grace, in the best sense, of course.

The Commissioner hesitated, but he didn't want to seem to be asking questions about the Duke, and decided to try Ridings Castle first. He asked for the trunk call, and sat back to wait for it.

"It all seems to be mixed up together, sir," Colquhoun said. "There was a Mr. Mornington at those publishing offices; it may be another man, of course—but there's a Persimmons and a Mornington there, and a Persimmons and a Mornington here."

"And a Bible all written over with Persimmons there, and a chalice that Persimmons stole or had stolen here," the other said. "Yes. It's odd. And a corpse there. We only want a corpse here to make a nice even pattern."

Scotland Yard not being usually kept waiting for its trunk calls, they had not broken the few minutes' silence by any further remarks before the housekeeper at Castle Ridings had been notified that she was wanted at the telephone. No, the Duke was not in the country. He and Mr. Mornington had left for London last night. By train—the car had been away for a day for some minor repairs. No, nothing was known of his Grace's return. He had said he should be at Grosvenor Square. What had the Duke's movements been yesterday? He and Mr. Mornington had arrived, unexpectedly, for lunch. They had gone out walking in the afternoon, and the Duke had said they might not be back. Where had they gone? She did not know; she had heard the Duke say something about a Mrs. Rackstraw to Mr. Mornington after he had told her they might not be back. Yes, Rackstraw. Could she give any message?

The Assistant Commissioner rang off and looked at the inspector, who was in a state of some excitement.

"That *damned* Rackstraw," he said. "He's always coming in. He lunches out with Sir Giles Tumulty and a man gets killed in his room. The Duke goes out to call on his wife and the Duke disappears."

"I wonder if we've got the other corpse," his chief said. "I think, Colquhoun, we might go and see what this Thwaites fellow can tell us. It's all right, no doubt, but I don't seem quite to like it."

Thwaites, when at Grosvenor Square he was summoned to the presence, seemed at first, if not recalcitrant, at least reluctant. He disclaimed any knowledge of the Duke's whereabouts; he thought his Grace would not be at all pleased if they were brought into publicity. Why? Well, he had an idea that his Grace wished for privacy. Yes, he admitted gradually, he *had* seen a chalice in the Duke's possession on Monday. Considering that on the Monday night he had been awakened to watch in front of it after the other three had retired, content to believe the Archdeacon's assertion that the attack had failed, this was a restrained way of putting it. But it had been indicated to him that the Duke desired secrecy, and secrecy

Thwaites was trying to maintain. But he became anxious when he heard of the disappearance, or at least of the non-appearance, of his master and admitted more than he altogether meant. He admitted that the chalice was not now in London; the Duke and his friends had taken it with them on the Wednesday. This was Thursday, he pointed out, to himself as well as the visitors, so the Duke's absence had not yet lasted for much over twelve hours—not so very long.

"Say four o'clock to twelve-twenty," the inspector said.

"Well, not twenty-four," Thwaites answered. "Only a night, you might say. Not so long but what, if his Grace was busy with something, he mightn't easily be away."

"Does the Duke often stay away without warning?" the Assistant Commissioner asked.

Not often, Thwaites admitted, but it had been known. He had gone for a sort of a joy-ride once and not been back for the whole twenty-four hours. Still, his Grace had been very anxious about something, something private, he didn't know what, but something to do with the chalice, on the Monday and Tuesday.

The Duchess, Thwaites thought, had not been told, since the Duke was not much in the habit of telling his aunt anything; and he very strongly dissuaded the visitors from making any inquiries there. Her Grace, he hinted, was a notorious chatter-box, and the incidents they were investigating would be discussed in a thousand drawing-rooms. If inquiry must be made, let it be conducted by the police along their own channels.

It was, however, exactly the method of conducting it which was annoying the Assistant Commissioner. He exhorted Thwaites to let him know immediately the Duke returned, or if news of him arrived, and to report to him by telephone every two hours if the Duke had not returned. He then withdrew with the inspector.

"Well," he said when they were in the street again, "I think you'd better go back to Fardles, Colquhoun, and see if you find out anything there. You might, in the circumstances, have a chat with the Archdeacon, and keep an eye on Persimmons's movements. I'll send another man down to help you. There's only one other thing that occurs to me. When Colonel Conyers was up on Monday he asked about the Duke and the Archdeacon and the others, and also about some North London Greek who had got Persimmons this accursed chalice. I'll put a man on to *him*. Ring me up later and tell me what's happened."

Towards evening the Assistant Commissioner received three telephone reports. The first was Thwaites, with the usual "Nothing has happened, sir. His Grace has not returned and we have received no information." This time, however, he added, "The Duchess is becoming anxious, sir. She is talking of consulting the police. Shall I put her through to you, sir?"

"No, for God's sake," the Commissioner said hastily. "Tell her something, anything you like. Tell her to ring up the nearest police station. . . . No, she won't do that as she knows me. All right, Thwaites, put her through."

The Duchess was put through, and the Commissioner extracted from her what he really wanted—permission to investigate. He then pretended to be cut off.

It was some minutes later that he received a call from Colquhoun.

"The Archdeacon isn't here, sir," the inspector reported. "He left for London just before lunch, about when we were at the Duke's. They don't know when he'll be back. Mr. Persimmons also left, just after lunch. I must have passed him in the train. Rackstraw is here and his wife, in a cottage in Persimmons's grounds. They apparently have a small boy, but he's been taken to London by a maid of Persimmons'. I knew Rackstraw was in it somehow."

"Family man, Persimmons," the Assistant Commissioner said. "Pity you couldn't have let us know he was coming, and I really think we'd have had him covered."

"Well, sir, both he and the Archdeacon were away before I got down here," the inspector said forbearingly. "Shall I come back?"

"No, I think not," his chief said. "Stop to-day, anyhow, and let me hear to-morrow if there's anything fresh. I've sent Pewitt to Finchley Road, but he's not reported yet. It's all pure chance. We really don't know what we're looking for."

"I thought we were trying to find out why Persimmons murdered Pattison, sir," the inspector answered.

"I suppose we are," his chief said, "but we seem rather like sparrows hopping round Persimmons on the chance of a crumb. Well, carry on; see if you can pick one up and let us guzzle it to-morrow. Good-bye."

He sat back, lit a cigarette, and turned to other work, till, somewhere about half-past eight, Pewitt also rang up. Pewitt was a young fellow who was being tried on the mere mechanics of this kind of work, and he had been sent up to the Finchley Road not more than two hours earlier, having been engaged on another job for most of the day. His voice now sounded depressed and worried.

"Pewitt speaking," he said, when the Commissioner had announced himself. "I'm—I'm in rather a hole, sir. I—we—can't find the house."

"Can't *what?*" his chief asked.

"Can't find the house, sir," Pewitt repeated. "I know it sounds silly, but it's the simple truth. It doesn't seem to be there."

The Assistant Commissioner blinked at the telephone. "Are you mad or merely idiotic, Pewitt?" he asked. "I did think you'd got the brains of a peewit, anyhow, if not much more. Have you lost the address I gave you or what?"

"No, sir," Pewitt said, "I've got the address all right— Lord Mayor's Street. It was a chemist's, you said. But there doesn't seem to be a chemist's there. Of course, the fog makes it difficult, but still, I don't *think* it is there."

"The fog?" the Commissioner said.

"It's very thick up here in North London," Pewitt answered, "very thick indeed."

"Are you sure you're in the right street?" his chief asked.

"Certain, sir. The constable on duty is here too. He seems to remember the shop, sir, but he can't find it, either. All we can find, sir, is——"

"Stop a minute," the Commissioner interrupted. He rang his bell and sent for a Directory; then, having found it, he went on. "Now go ahead. Where do you begin?"

"George Giddings, grocer."

"Right."

"Samuel Murchison, confectioner."

"Right."

"Mrs. Thorogood, apartments."

"Damn it, man," the Commissioner exploded, "you've just gone straight over it. Dmitri Lavrodopoulos, chemist."

"But it *isn't*, sir," Pewitt said unhappily. "The fog's very thick, but we couldn't have missed a whole shop."

"But Colonel Conyers has *been* there," the Commissioner shouted, "been there and talked with this infernal fellow. Good God above, it must be there! You're drunk, Pewitt."

"I feel as if I was, sir," the mournful voice said, "groping about in this, but I'm not. I've looked at the Directory myself, sir, and it's all right there. But it's not all right here. The house has simply disappeared."

"That must have been what just flew past the window," the other said bitterly. "Look here, Pewitt, I'm coming up myself. And God help you and your friend the constable if I find that house, for I'll tear you limb from limb and roast you and eat you. And God help me if I don't," he said, putting back the receiver, "for if houses disappear as well as Dukes, this'll be no world for me."

It took him much longer than he expected to reach Lord Mayor's Street. As his taxi climbed north, he found himself entering into what was at first a faint mist, and later, before he reached Tally Ho Corner, an increasing fog. Indeed, after a while the taxi-driver refused to go any farther, and the Assistant Commissioner proceeded slowly on foot. He knew the Finchley Road generally and vaguely, and after a long time and many risks at last drew near his aim. At what he hoped was the corner of Lord Mayor's Street he ran directly into a stationary figure.

"What the hell——" he began. "Sorry, sir. Oh, it's you, Pewitt. Damnation, man, why don't you shout instead of knocking me down? All right, all right. But standing at the corner of the street won't find the house, you know. Where's the constable? Why don't you keep together? Oh, he's here, is he! Couldn't even one of you look for the house instead of holding a revival meeting at the street corner? Now for God's sake don't apologize or I shall have to begin too, and we shall look like a ring of chimpanzees at the Zoo. I know as well as you do that I'm in a vile temper. Come along and let's have a look. Where's the grocer's?"

He was shown it. Then, he first, Pewitt second, and the constable last, they edged along the houses, their torches turned on the windows. "That's the grocer's," the Commissioner went on. "And here—this blasted fog's thicker than ever—is the end of the grocer's, I suppose; at least it's the end of a window. Then this must be the confectioner's. I believe I saw a cake; the blind's only half down. And here's a door, the confectioner's door. Didn't you think of doing it this way, Pewitt?"

"Yes, sir," Pewitt said, "the constable and I have done it about seventeen times."

The Assistant Commissioner, neglecting this answer, pushed ahead. "And this is the end of the confectioner's second window," he said triumphantly. "And here's a bit of wall . . . more wall . . . and here—here's a gate." He stopped uncertainly.

The Search for the House

"Yes, sir," Pewitt said; "that's Mrs. Thorogood's gate. We called there, sir, but she's an old lady and rather deaf, and some of her lodgers are on their holiday and some haven't got home from work yet. And we couldn't quite get her to understand what we were talking about. We tried again a little while ago, but she wouldn't even come to the door."

The Assistant Commissioner looked at the gate, or rather, at the fog, for the gate was invisible. So was the constable; he could just discern a thicker blot that was Pewitt. He felt the gate—undoubtedly it was just that. He stood still and recalled to his mind the page he had studied in the Directory. Yes, between Murchison the confectioner and Mrs. Thorogood, apartments, it leapt to his eye, Dmitri Lavrodopoulos, chemist.

"Have you tried the confectioner?" he asked.

"Well, sir, he wouldn't do more than talk out of the first-floor window," Pewitt said, "but we did try him. He said he knew what kind of people went round knocking at doors in the fog. He swore he'd got two windows, and he said the chemist was next door. But somehow we couldn't just find next door."

"It must be round some corner," the Assistant Commissioner said; and "Yes, sir, no doubt it must be round some corner," Pewitt answered.

The other felt as if something was beginning to crack. Everything seemed disappearing. The Duke had not come home, nor Mornington, whoever he might be; the Archdeacon and Gregory Persimmons had left home. And now a whole house seemed to have been swallowed up. He went slowly back to the corner, followed by his subordinates, then he tried again —very slowly and crouched right against the windows. On either side of the confectioner's door was a strip of glass without blinds, and he dimly discerned in each window, within an inch and a half of his nose, scones and buns and jam-tarts. Certainly the farther one no more than the first belonged to a chemist. And yet for the second time, as he pushed beyond it, he felt the rough wall under his fingers and then the iron gate.

The Directory and Colonel Conyers must both be wrong, he thought; there could be no other explanation. Lavrodopoulos must have left, and the shop been taken over by the confectioner. But it was on Monday Colonel Conyers had called, and this was only Thursday. Besides, the confectioner had said that the chemist's was next door. He felt the wall again; it ought to be there.

"What do you make of it, Pewitt?" he asked.

Out of the fog Pewitt answered: "I don't like it, sir," he said. "I dare say it's a mistake, but I don't like that. It isn't natural."

"I suppose you think the devil has carried it off," the Assistant Commissioner said, and thought automatically of the Bible he had studied that morning. He struck impatiently at the wall. "Damn it, the shop must be there," he said. But the shop was not there.

Suddenly, as they stood there in a close group, the grounds beneath them seemed to shift and quiver. Pewitt and the constable cried out; the Assistant Commissioner jumped aside. It shook again. "Good God," he cried, "what in the name of the seven devils is happening to the world? Are you there, Pewitt?" for his movement had separated them. He heard some sort of reply, but knew himself alone and felt suddenly afraid. Again the earth throbbed below him; then from nowhere a great blast of cool wind struck his face. So violent was it that he reeled and almost fell; then, as he regained his poise, he saw that the fog was dissolving around him. A strange man was standing in front of him; behind him the windows of a chemist's shop came abruptly into being. The stranger came up to him. "I am Gregory Persimmons," he said, "and I wish to give myself up to the police for murder."

Chapter Seventeen

THE MARRIAGE OF THE LIVING
AND THE DEAD

While Inspector Colquhoun had been discussing the Pattison murder with his chief that morning, the Archdeacon of Castra Parvulorum had been working at parish business in his study. He hoped, though he did not much expect, that Mornington would call on him in the course of the day, and he certainly proposed to himself to walk over to the Rackstraws' cottage and hear how the patient was progressing. The suspicions which Mornington and the Duke had felt on the previous day had not occurred to him, partly because he had accepted the episode as finished for him until some new demand should bring him again into action, but more still because he had been prevented by the Duke's collision with him from seeing what had happened. He supposed that the new doctor had been able to soothe Barbara either by will-power or drugs, and, though the doctor's mania for possession of the Graal appeared to him as bad-mannered as Gregory's, that was not, after all, his affair. The conversation of the previous night he kept and pondered in his heart, but here, again, it was not his business to display activity, but to wait on the Mover of all things. He went on making notes about the Sunday school register; the Sunday school was a burden to him, but the mothers of the village expected it, and the Archdeacon felt bound to supply the need. He occasionally quoted to himself "*Feed my lambs,*" but a profound doubt of the proper application of the text haunted him; and he was far from certain that the food which was supplied to them even in the Sunday school at Fardles was that which Christ had

234

intended. However, this also, he thought to himself, the Divine Redeemer would purify and make good.

Mrs. Lucksparrow appeared at the door. "Mr. Persimmons has called, sir," she said, "and would like to see you for a few minutes, if you can spare the time. About the Harvest Festival, I think it is," she added in a lower tone.

"Really?" the Archdeacon asked in surprise, and then again, in a slightly different voice, "Really!" Mr. Persimmons's manners, he thought, were becoming almost intolerable. He got up and went to interview his visitor in the hall.

"So sorry to trouble you, Mr. Archdeacon," Gregory said, smiling, "but I was asked to deliver this note to you personally. To make sure you got it and to see if there is any answer."

The Archdeacon, glinting rather like a small, frosty pool, took it and opened it. He read it once; he read it twice; he looked up to find Gregory staring out through the front door. He looked down, read it a third time, and stood pondering.

" 'Sihon, King of the Amorites,' " he hummed abstractedly, " 'and Og, the King of Basan: for His mercy endureth for ever.' You know what is in this note, Mr. Persimmons?"

"I'm afraid I do," Gregory answered charmingly. "The circumstances . . ."

"Yes," the Archdeacon said meditatively, "yes. Naturally."

"Naturally?" Gregory asked, rather as if making conversation.

"Well, I don't mean to be rude," the Archdeacon said, "but, in the first place, if it's true, you would probably know; in the second, you probably wrote it; and, in the third, you probably and naturally would read other people's letters anyhow. Yes, well, thank you so much."

"You don't want to put any questions?" Gregory asked.

"No," the Archdeacon answered, "I don't think so. I've no means of checking you, have I? And I should never dream of relying on people who made a practice of defying God—in any real sense. They'd be almost bound to lose all sense of proportion."

"Well," Gregory said, "you must do as you will. But I can tell you that what is written there is true. We have them in our power and we can slay them in a moment."

"That will save them a good deal of trouble, won't it?" the Archdeacon said. "Are you sure they want me to interfere? 'To die now. 'Twere now to be most happy.' "

"Ah, you talk," Gregory said, unreasonably enraged. "But do you think either of those young men wants to die? Or to see the vessel for which they die made into an instrument of power and destruction?"

"I would tell you what I am going to do if I knew," the Archdeacon answered, "but I do not know. You are forgetting, however, to tell me where I shall come if I come."

Gregory recovered himself, gave the address, reached the door, remarked on the beauty of the garden, and disappeared. The Archdeacon went back to his study, shut the door, and gave himself up to interior silence and direction.

Gregory went on to Cully. The slight passage at arms with the priest had given him real delight, but as he walked he was conscious of renewed alarms stirring in his being: alarms not so much of fear as of doubt. He found that by chance he was now in touch with two or three persons who found no satisfaction in desire and possession and power. No power of destruction seemed to satisfy Manasseh's hunger; no richness of treasure to arouse the Archdeacon's. And as he moved in these unaccustomed regions he felt that what was lacking was delight. It had delighted him in the past to overbear and torment; but Manasseh's greed had never found content. And delight was far too small a word for the peace in which the Archdeacon moved; a sky of serenity overarched Gregory when he thought of the priest against which his own arrows were shot in vain. He saw it running from the east to the west; he saw below it, in the midst of a flat circle of emptiness, the face of the Greek spewing out venom. Absurdly enough, he felt himself angered by the mere uselessness of this; it was something of the same irritation which he had expressed to his son on the proportion of capital expended on the worst kind of popular novel. Enjoyment was all very well, but enjoyment oughtn't to be merely wasteful. It annoyed him as his father had annoyed him by wasting emotions and strength in mere stupid, senile worry. Adrian must be taught the uselessness of that—power was the purpose of spiritual things, and Satan the lord of power. He turned in at the gates of Cully, and saw before him the window where he had talked with Adrian's father. "A clerk in a brothel," he thought suddenly; but even the clerk desired power. And then, in a sudden desperation, he saw that unchanging serenity of sky, and even the flames of the Sabbath leapt uselessly miles below it. Here he had met the young stranger: "only slaves can trespass, and they only among shadows." But he was not a slave—that sky mocked him as the boast swelled. Slaves, slaves, it sounded, and his foot in the hall echoed the word again in his ear.

He inquired for Jessie and the boy; they were in the grounds, and he went out to find them, looking also for Lionel and Barbara. But these he did not meet, although he eventually discovered the others. Adrian, apparently resting, was telling himself a complicated and interminable story; Jessie was looking into a small stream and pondering her own thoughts —Gregory smiled to think what they probably were. He very nearly addressed her as "Mrs. Persimmons," remembering that she probably knew nothing of his wife in the asylum, but refrained.

Barbara, it seemed, was as well as ever; she had spent an hour with Adrian before Mr. Rackstraw had made her go away. Then they—Jessie and Adrian—had come out into the grounds, and there had met a strange gentleman who had talked and played with Adrian for a little while. Gregory raised his eyebrows at this, and Jessie explained that she had not approved, but had not been able to prevent it, especially since Adrian had welcomed him so warmly that she had supposed them to be old friends.

"But what was he doing in the grounds?" Gregory asked.

"I don't know, sir," Jessie answered; "he seemed to know them, and he told me he knew you."

Gregory suspected that this was the only cause of her frankness, but it was hardly worth troubling to rebuke her. Within a week Jessie might find herself only too anxious to make friends with strangers in Vienna or Adrianople, or somewhere farther east.

"What was he like?" he said.

"Oh, quite young, sir, and rather foreign-looking, and dressed all in grey. He and the boy seemed to be talking a foreign language half the time."

Gregory stood still abruptly, and then began to walk on again. What had Sir Giles said about this stranger? And who was it the stranger reminded him of? The Archdeacon, of course; they both had something of that same remote serenity, that provoking, overruling detachment. In the rush of the previous day's excitement he had forgotten to consult Manasseh; that would be remedied before night. But the talk of a foreign language disturbed him a little, lest Adrian should have a closer and more intimate friend than himself or than he had known. If there were anything in Sir Giles's babblings . . . He gathered himself together and turned sharply to Jessie.

"We shall go to London," he said, "I and Adrian and you to look after Adrian, directly after lunch. To-morrow we may go abroad for a little. It's sudden, but it can't be helped. And it's not to be chattered about. See to it."

It chanced therefore that, by the time Inspector Colquhoun had finished making inquiries of Mrs. Lucksparrow at the Rectory, Gregory, with Adrian and Jessie, had reached Lord Mayor's Street. The shop was closed, but Manasseh admitted them, and Jessie was shown, first the kitchen and afterwards the small upstairs room where she and Adrian were to sleep. She was not shown the cellar, where the Duke of the North Ridings lay bound, and she and Adrian were rushed swiftly through the back room, where the Archdeacon was looking pensively out of the window. He glanced at them as they went through, but neither face conveyed anything to his mind. Gregory had provided Adrian with two or three new toys, but it was intimated to Jessie that the sooner he was put to bed the better, and that she had better stay with him, as it was a strange room, lest he woke and was afraid.

The captives thus disposed of, Gregory went back to his friends, who were in the shop. The Archdeacon had left off looking out of the window and was reading the *Revelations* of Lady Julian close by it.

"He has come, then," Gregory said.

"He has come," Manasseh answered; "didn't you expect him?"

"I didn't know," Gregory said. "He didn't seem at all sure this morning. And I don't know why he has come."

"He has come," the Greek said, "for the same reason that we are here—because in the whole world of Being everything makes haste to its doom. Are you determined and prepared for what you will do?"

Gregory looked back through the half-open door. "I have considered it for many hours," he said. "I am determined and prepared."

"Why, then, should we delay?" the Greek said. "I have hidden this house in a cloud and drawn it in to our hearts so that it shall not be entered from without till the work is done."

Gregory involuntarily looked towards the window, and saw a thick darkness rising above it, a darkness not merely foglike, as it seemed to those without, but shot with all kinds of colour and movement as if some living nature were throbbing about them. The Greek turned and went into the inner room, and the other followed him. There the darkness was already gathering, so that the Archdeacon had ceased to read and was waiting for whatever was to follow. All that day, since he had talked with Gregory in the morning, he had been conscious that the power to which he had slowly taught himself to live in obedience was gradually withdrawing and abandoning him. Steadily and continuously that process went on, till now, as he faced his enemies, he felt the interior loss which had attacked him at other stages of his pilgrimage grow into a final overwhelming desolation. He said to himself again, as he so often said, "This also is Thou," for desolation as well as abundance was but a means of knowing That which was All. But he felt extraordinarily lonely in the darkness of the small room, with Persimmons and Manasseh and the unknown third gazing at him from the door.

The Greek moved slowly forward, considered for a moment, and then said: ";Do you know why you have come here?"

"I have come because God willed it," the Archdeacon said. ;"Why did you send for me?"

"For a thing that is to be done," the Greek said, "and you shall help in the doing." As he spoke, Manasseh caught the priest's arm with a little crow of greedy satisfaction, and Gregory laid hold of his other shoulder.

"You shall help in the doing of it," the Greek said, smiling for the first time since Gregory had known him, with a sudden and swift convulsion. "Take him and bind him and lay him down."

It was quickly done; the Archdeacon was unable to resist, not so much because of the greater strength of his opponents as because that interior withdrawal of energy had now touched his body and he was weakening every moment. He was stretched on the ground, and Manasseh tore at his clothes till his breast was bare. Then the Greek lifted the Graal from the table by the window and set it on the priest, and still the darkness increased and moved and swirled around them. The Archdeacon heard voices above him, heard Gregory say:

The Marriage of the Living and the Dead

"Are there no markings and ceremonies?" and the Greek answer: "We are retired beyond such things; there is only one instrument, and that is the blood with which I have filled the cup; there is only one safeguard, in the purpose of our wills. For your part, remember the man you slew; keep his image in your mind and let it be imposed on this man's being. For through this Manasseh and I will work."

The darkness closed entirely over, and as the Archdeacon lay he knew for a while nothing but the waste of an obscure night. Then there became known to him within it three separate points of existence and energy about him, from each of which issued a shaft of directed power. He was aware that these shafts were not yet aimed directly at him; he was aware also of a difference in their nature. For that which was nearest him was also the least certain; it shook and faltered; it was more like anger as he had known it among men, red and variable and mortal. This anger was the effluence of a similar centre, a centre which was known on that earth they had left as Gregory Persimmons, and trembled still with desires natural to man. So far as in him lay, the Archdeacon presented himself to that spirit and profession as a means whereby the satisfaction of all desire might meet it; not by such passions was hell finally peopled and the last rejection found.

But this procession was not alone; it was controlled and directed by mightier powers. From another centre there issued a different force, and this, the victim realized, it would need all his present strength to meet. There impinged upon him the knowledge of all hateful and separating and deathly things: madness and tormenting disease and the vengeance of gods. This was the hunger with which creation preys upon itself, a supernatural famine that has no relish except for the poisons that waste it. This was the second death that cannot die, and it ran actively through that world of immortalities on a hungry mission of death. What that mission was he did not yet know; the beam played somewhere above him and disappeared where a central darkness hid the Graal. But he knew that the mission would be presently revealed, and he asserted by a spiritual act the perfection of all manner of birth.

Even as he did so the act itself quivered and almost died. For the third stream of energy passed over him, and its very passage shook the centre of his being from its roots. This was no longer mission or desire, search or propaganda or hunger; this was rejection absolute. No mortal mind could conceive a desire which was not based on a natural and right desire; even the hunger for death was but a perversion of the death which precedes all holy birth. But of every conceivable and inconceivable desire this was the negation. This was desire itself sick, but not unto death; rejection which tore all things asunder and swept them with it in its fall through the abyss. He felt himself sinking even in the indirect rush of its passage; here, if anywhere, the foundation of the universe must hold them firm, for otherwise he and the universe were ruining together for ever. But that foundation, if it existed, had separated itself from him; he cried desperately to God and God did not hear him. The three intermingling currents passed on their way, and, fainting and helpless, he awaited the further end.

There came for a little a relief. He was dimly aware again for some moments of external things—a breath above him, the slight feeling of the Cup upon his breast, the pressure of the cords that held his arms to his sides. Then slowly and very gently these departed again and he felt himself being directed towards—he did not know what. But he was, as it were, moving. He was passing to a preordained tryst; he was meeting something, and he grew dreadfully afraid. Marriage awaited him, and the darkness above him took shape and he knew that another existence was present, an existence that hated and strove against this tryst as much as he hated and strove against it, but which was driven as he was remorselessly driven. Nearer and nearer, through ages of time, they were brought; desire and death and utter rejection gathered

The Marriage of the Living and the Dead

their victims from the various worlds and drew them into union. His body became aware again of the Graal, and from the Graal itself the visitation came. He felt that no longer the Graal but a human being was there; he saw a weak, anxious, and harassed face look on him despairingly. He saw it float about him, and his very consciousness, which had taken in all these things up to then, began to feel them differently. Some entry was being forced into that which was he; in that Vessel which had held the Blood which is the potentiality of all he and this other were to be wrecked in each other for ever. Then this knowledge itself was withdrawn and no function of his being recorded any more.

It was at this moment, when he had been driven beyond consciousness, that the masters of the work above him concentrated their utmost resources for the purpose they had in hand. The Graal vibrated before them in the intensity of their power.

In obedience to the Greek's direction, Gregory had concentrated his consciousness upon that being whom he had, not so very long ago, slain; partly for safety, partly for mere amusement, partly as an offering to his god. He set before himself the thought of the wretched man's whole life, from the moment when the discovery of small thefts had put him in his power, through his years of service and torment, through the last effort towards freedom, through the last deliberate return. Pattison had returned to his death and had died, obeying minutely all the orders that had been given him; clean and unmarked linen, no papers, his few belongings left in a bag at some Tube station, and the ticket destroyed —he had seen that all was done under the fascination of his master's law. And now that law was to do something more with him; it searched for him in the place of shadows where his uncertain spirit wandered; it explored the night beyond death to recover him thence. Gregory held the knowledge of the man's soul fast in his mind, and from his own solitary wanderings in the abyss that soul began to return to its lord. Upward now, his image began to rise, as some few days since the wraith of the child Adrian had floated, but even more swiftly by virtue of the triple call. A fantastic bubble of tinged cloud seemed to appear, moving upward from the Graal, and the bubble thickened and became mist and shaped itself into a form and face. The Graal was dimly visible in a faint green light, through which and over which the recalled spirit took on a mortal covering. Gregory involuntarily smiled at the appeal on the face that was momentarily visible, and renewed his effort to offer up both the captives in sacrifice to the tremendous power he adored. Slowly the strength of the three prevailed. Little by little that shadow sank and spread itself over the motionless form on the floor, little by little it flowed round it and into it. Gregory, almost exhausted with the effort, would have ceased, contented, as the last faint coils of mist faded from the light that shone, like a light of decay, from the Graal. But the knowledge and energy of his companions insisted, in the continuous force they expended, that nothing but a mental haunting, a perpetual obsession, had yet been achieved. Something further yet was needed for the final and perfect marriage of these two victims; and in an instant something further came.

The faint glow round the Vessel faded and vanished; and all the moving darkness of the room seemed to direct itself towards and to emerge from that thickest core of night which beat in the Cup, as if its very heart were beating there. One moment only they heard and felt that throbbing heart, and then suddenly from it there broke a terrific and golden light; blast upon blast of trumpets shook the air; the Graal blazed with fiery tumult before them; and its essence, as at last that essence was touched, awoke in its own triumphant and blinding power. None could tell whether light and trumpets were indeed there; but something was there—something which, as it caught and returned upon them the energies they had put forth, seemed also to bestride the prostrate figure on the floor. The Graal was lifted or was itself no more —they could not tell; they were flung back before this lifting and visible form. He over whom it stood returned also from the depths; he looked up and saw it flaming through the scattering night, and heard a litany which changed as it smote his ears from the chant of an unknown tongue into the familiar and cherished maxims of his natural mind.

"Let them give thanks whom the Lord hath redeemed," a great voice sang, and from all about it, striking into light and sound at once, the answer came: "for His mercy endureth for ever."

"And delivered out of the snare of the enemy," it sang again; and again an infinite chorus crashed: "for His mercy endureth for ever."

He moved his arms and the cords that held them snapped; he half arose as the Graal, or he that was the Graal, moved forward and upward. All sense of the horrible intrusion into his nature and essence had gone. He saw somewhere for a moment near him the face he had seemed to see before, but it was free and happy and adoring; he saw Kenneth somewhere and lost him again, and again all round him the litany wheeled like fire:

"He hath destroyed great nations: for His mercy endureth for ever:

"And overthrown mighty kings: for His mercy endureth for ever."

He was on his feet, and before him the room, cleared of light and darkness, showed its usual bare dirtiness. In front of him was the figure of the priest-king, the Graal lifted in his hands. Beyond lay the others—Gregory prostrate on his face, Manasseh shaking and writhing on his back, the Greek crouched half back on his heels.

"I am John," a voice sounded, "and I am the prophecy of the things that are to be and are. You who have sought the

245

centre of the Graal, behold through me that which you seek, receive from me that which you are. He that is righteous, let him be righteous still; he that is filthy, let him be filthy still. I am rejection to him that hath sought rejection; I am destruction to him that hath wrought destruction; I am sacrifice to him that hath offered sacrifice. Friend to my friends and lover to my lovers, I will quit all things, for I am myself and I am He that sent me. This war is ended and another follows quickly. Do that which you must while the time is with you."

The Archdeacon saw Gregory drag himself slowly to his feet; Manasseh was lying still; the Greek crouched lower still on the floor.

"Gregory Persimmons," the voice went on, "they wait for you close at hand. Can a man sacrifice his brother or make agreement with any god for him? Die, then, as this other has died, and there shall be agreement with you also in the end, for you have sought me and no other."

Gregory turned dully to the door and moved towards it. The priest-king turned to the Archdeacon and held the Graal out to him. "Brother and friend," he said, "the rest is in your charge. One of your friends is below, the other is with me. Take your friend and this Cup and return, and I will come to you to-morrow."

The Archdeacon took the Graal with his usual sedateness. It was as tarnished as it had been when he last saw it. He glanced at the figures on the floor; he looked again at the high face of the priest-king, glimmering in the natural dusk; then, gravely and a little daintily, he went out towards the cellars.

In the room above, the maid Jessie was awakened by what seemed the light of a shaded lamp. She saw the stranger with whom Adrian had played that morning standing by her. "Come," he said, "your master is in the hands of the police, and we return to Fardles to-night. Do not disturb yourself about the child; he will not wake." He gathered the sleeping Adrian in his arms, wrapped some dark covering round him, added: "Come; I shall wait for you at the doors," and left the room.

How Jessie got back to Cully she was never very clear. She had a vague impression of moving through country lanes, and supposed it must have been in a motor, though, as she afterwards said, to her most intimate friend, "I was so sleepy it might have been an angel, for all I knew. And a mercy the police got Mr. Persimmons in time, for I don't know that I'd have said 'No' if he'd asked me."

"You'd have had the house and a good bit of money, even so," her friend elliptically said.

"What, and be the wife of a man that's been hung?" Jessie said indignantly, "to say nothing of his being a murderer. Thank you for nothing, Lizzie; that's not the kind of girl I am. Why, it'd be no better than selling yourself for money."

Chapter Eighteen

CASTRA PARVULORUM

The Duke of the North Ridings had spent the night at the Rectory, and both he and the Archdeacon had slept soundly, though it was rather late before they got to bed. They had caught the last train to the nearest junction, which was five miles off; and both in the train and on the walk the Archdeacon had been mildly bothered by the Graal. He had caught up a sheet of paper from the shop when they left it, with some notion of not being a cause of blasphemy to the ungodly by carrying an unveiled chalice, but he had never been able to arrange it successfully, and its ends kept waving about and disclosing the Cup. A cheerful and slightly drunk excursionist in the train had found this a theme for continual merriment at the general expense of the clergy and the Church, and something he had said had caused the Archdeacon to wonder whether perhaps he were being a stumbling-block to one of those little ones who had not yet attained detachment. However, he recovered his usual equilibrium during the walk, and negatived successfully the Duke's feeling that they ought to keep a common vigil.

"I'm extremely sleepy," he said apologetically, but firmly. "After all, it's been rather a tiring day, and—as someone said —I will meet my God with an unclouded mind."

"Doctor Johnson," the Duke unthinkingly supplied the unnecessary information, and then smiled. "I expect you're right," he said. "He gave us sleep also."

"For His mercy endureth for ever," the Archdeacon quite sincerely answered; and they parted for the night.

Barbara awoke early that morning in her cottage; she had

taken a dislike to sleeping at Cully, and, without disturbing the sleeping Lionel, wandered out of doors. The first person she saw was Adrian playing on the grass with the young man she had tried to recognize on an earlier day, and she ran over to them with exclamations. Adrian, fresh and energetic, hurled himself at her with tumultuous shrieks of greeting and information, and she looked laughingly to the stranger for an explanation.

"Gregory Persimmons has been arrested," he said, "on his own confession, for murder; and, as I was there, I brought your son back at once. He's slept very well, and we've been playing out here since he woke."

Barbara, holding Adrian with one hand, pushed her hair back with the other, the long scar showing as she moved her wrist. "That's very nice of you," she said. "But Mr. Persimmons! What a dreadful thing!"

"Do you really think so, Mrs. Rackstraw?" the other asked, smiling.

Barbara blushed, and then looked grave. "No," she said. "Well, at least, somehow I don't feel surprised. Since I met you, I haven't felt quite the same about Mr. Persimmons."

"You may feel the same now," Prester John answered, and was interrupted by Adrian.

"Hush, darling!" his mother said. "Go to church? Yes, if you like. I'm afraid", she added, blushing rather more deeply as she looked at the stranger again, "that we don't go as regularly as we should."

"It is a means," he answered, "one of the means. But perhaps the best for most, and for some almost the only one. I do not say that it matters greatly, but the means cannot both be and not be. If you do not use it, it is a pity to bother about it; if you do, it is a pity not to use it."

"Yes," Barbara said doubtfully. "Lionel was rather badgered into it as a boy, and he almost dislikes it now, and so . . . ."

"One's foes are always in one's own household," the other

answered, with a rather mournful smile. But, as Barbara glanced at him, suspecting a remoter meaning, he went on. "But this morning Adrian is to serve me in the church over there."

"Serve!" Barbara said, aghast. "But he can't do it. He's only four, and he knows nothing about it, and———"

"He can do all I need, Mrs. Rackstraw," her friend said, and was drowned again by Adrian's "Mum-*mie*! and we've been playing cricket, and will you come and play after breakfast?"

"I thought we were to go to church, darling," Barbara answered.

"Oh, after church too," Adrian said. "And will you come?" he asked the stranger.

The answer was delayed by his seeing Lionel wander out of the cottage in pyjamas, to whom he rushed away still full of the importance and immediacy of life. The other two came after him to the door.

Lionel received with a certain shock the news of Gregory's surrender, but it was a shock produced merely by its suddenness. His eyes dropped to Adrian with a certain questioning dread, as if he were wondering what similar fate in after-life already predestined that innocent and ignorant head. And as Barbara, murmuring of breakfast, or at least of some sort of coffee and biscuits before they went over to the church, disappeared into the cottage with her son, the stranger said to Lionel, "Yet he may escape."

Lionel looked up. "Oh, yes," he said vaguely, though he felt the fantasy, as he stood alone with the other, take sharp form within his mind. "Oh, yes—that, but something awaits him surely of ruin and of despair."

"It may be," the stranger said, "but perhaps a happy ruin and a fortunate despair. These things are not evil in themselves, and I think you fear them overmuch."

"I fear all things," Lionel answered, "and I do not understand how it is that men do not fear them more. In the town it is bad enough, but there one is deafened and blinded by people and things. But here everything is so still and meditative, and I am afraid of what those meditations are."

"Is there, then, nothing pleasant in life?" Prester John said.

Lionel answered, almost savagely, "Can't you see that when life is most pleasant one suspects it most? Unless one can drug oneself with the moment and forget."

"I do not think you drug yourself much," the stranger said, smiling. "Are you sure you do not love your fears?"

"No," Lionel said; "I am not sure of anything. I do think I love to feel them though I loathe them, but I do not know why."

"Because so chiefly you feel yourself alive," the other said, "separated from them and hostile and tormented, but alive in heart and brain. You desire death! Your very desire witnesses how passionately you feel these things and how strongly you live."

Lionel smiled a little. "*Heautontimoroumenos?*" he asked doubtfully.

"No, not that," the stranger answered. "But you are afraid of losing yourself in the fantasies of daily life, and you think that these pains will save you. But I bring the desire of all men, and what will you ask of me?"

"Annihilation," Lionel answered. "I have not asked for life, and I should be content now to know that soon I should not be. Do you think I desire the heaven they talk of?"

"Death you shall have at least," the other said. "But God only gives, and He has only Himself to give, and He, even He, can give it only in those conditions which are Himself. Wait but a few years, and He shall give you the death you desire. But do not grudge too much if you find that death and heaven are one." He pointed towards Cully. "This man desired greatly the God of all sacrifice and sacrifice itself, and he finds Him now. But you shall find another way, for the door that opens on annihilation opens only on the annihilation which is God."

Castra Parvulorum

He walked away across the glade, and when Lionel saw him
again it was in the church built above the spot where, tradition
said, Caesar had restored the children to their mothers.

The Duke of the North Ridings, rather more than obedient
to the strict etiquette of his Church, was leaning against the
door-post; the Archdeacon was in his stall. As the other members of that small and curiously drawn congregation came in,
Adrian broke from his mother's hand and ran up the aisle on
small, hasty feet to where, by the altar, Prester John turned to
receive him. To Barbara and the Duke, accustomed to liturgical vestments, the priest-king seemed to be clothed in the
chasuble of tradition; to Lionel he seemed to stand, pure and
naked, in the high sunlight of the morning; what he seemed to
the child none then or ever knew. He sank on one knee to meet
him, opened his arms to Adrian's rush, and then, after a
moment during which they seemed to confer, drew him gently
to the credence table at the side. There Adrian, grave and
content, plumped himself down on a hassock for a seat, and the
priest-king returned to the front of the altar.

The sacristan was away down in the village, but suddenly
above them they heard the noise of a bell, only higher and
more remote and more clear than any bell they had heard
before, as if the very idea of sound made itself felt in those notes,
and withdrew and ceased. The priest-king spread out his
hands and brought them together, and there was a movement
throughout the church, as if a hundred watchers had stirred
and drawn breath at the beginning of the Mysteries. The
Duke leaned a little forward in perplexity; he saw the forms
with which he was acquainted, but here and there, only always just to one side or in some corner, he seemed to see other
forms. They had vanished in a moment, yet they had been
there. He had caught certain of the faces which he knew in the
great gallery of his ancestors in the Castle, and other faces more
antique and foreign than these, a turbaned head, a helmed and
armoured shape, outlandish robes, and the glint of many

crowns. They had vanished, and he saw Adrian plunge to his feet and go to the celebrant's side. And clear and awful to his ears their voices floated.

The voices were clear, but what they said was hidden. To him by the door, as to Barbara kneeling by a chair, there issued sometimes a familiar phrase. "Introibo," he thought he heard, and could have believed that the child's voice answered, "Ad Deum qui lætificat juventutem meam." But he looked in vain for the motions of the Confession; while he looked the priest-king was up the steps by the altar, though he had not seen him go, and about the church rang the *Christe eleison* and died.

Barbara, less adept at ritual, caught only a sentence of the Collect—"to Whom all hearts be open, all desires known"—and then was happily distracted by the sedate movements of her child, till of a sudden the words of the Lesson recaptured her: "And God said: Let us make man, in Our image, after Our likeness . . . in the image of God created He him, male and female created He them." The very sound inclined her ever so slightly towards her husband; her hand went out and found his, and so linked they watched till the end. And the priest-king's voice closed on the Gospel: "Behold, I make all things new."

But the Archdeacon, hearing all these words, trembled a little as he knelt. The thoughts with which he approached the Mysteries faded; the Mysteries themselves faded. He distinguished no longer word from act; he was in the presence, he was part of the Act which far away issued in those faint words, "Let us make man"—creation rose and flowed out and wheeled to its august return—"in Our image, after Our likeness"—the great pronouns were the sound of that return. Faster and faster all things moved through that narrow channel he had before seen and now himself seemed to be entering and beyond it they issued again into similar but different existence —themselves still, yet infused and made one in an undreamed perfection. The sunlight—the very sun itself—was moving on through the upright form before the altar, and darkness and light together were pouring through it, and with them all things that were. He saw, standing at the very edge of that channel, the small figure of Adrian, and then he himself had passed the boy and was entering upon the final stage of the Way. Everything was veiled; the voice of the priest-king was the sound of creation's movement; he awaited the exodus that was to be.

Everything was veiled, but not so entirely that he did not hear from somewhere behind him, in space or in experience, the Duke's voice saying, "Et cum spiritu tuo," or a call from in front, "Lift up your hearts," or again, from behind, Barbara's voice crying, "We lift them up unto the Lord," or, in a higher and more tremendous summons, "Let us give thanks unto the Lord," and, amid the tumult of song that broke out, Lionel's own voice joining in the answer, "It is meet and right so to do."

"It is very meet, right . . ." the priest-king said; the three heard it, and heard no more intelligible words. They saw Adrian moving up and about; they saw his grave and happy face as he turned to some motion of his Lord's; they saw him go back and sit down again on his hassock, cuddling his knees, glance down at his mother, and turn to watch the event. For now the unknown sounds were pealing steadily on; all separate beings, save where the hands of the lovers lingered in a final clasp, were concentrated on that high motionless Figure—motionless, for in Him all motions awaited His movement to be loosed, and still He did not move. All sound ceased; all things entered into an intense suspension of being; nothing was anywhere at all but He.

He stood; He moved His hands. As if in benediction He moved them, and at once the golden halo that had hung all this while over the Graal dissolved and dilated into spreading colour; and at once life leapt in all those who watched, and filled and flooded and exalted them. "Let us make man," He sang, "in Our image, after Our likeness," and all the church of visible and invisible presences answered with a roar: "In the image of God created He him: male and female created He them." All things began again to be. At a great distance Lionel and Barbara and the Duke saw beyond Him, as He lifted up the Graal, the moving universe of stars, and then one flying planet, and then fields and rooms and a thousand remembered places, and all in light and darkness and peace.

He seemed to hold the Graal no more; the divine colour that had moved in that vision of creation swathed Him as a close-bound robe. Beyond Him the church was again visible, and silence succeeded to the flying music that had accompanied vision. Like the centre of that silence, they heard His voice calling as if He called a name. He had not turned; still He faced the altar, and thrice He called and was still. The Archdeacon stood up suddenly in his stall; then he came sedately from it, and turned in the middle of the chancel to face the three who watched. He smiled at them, and made a motion of farewell with his hand; then he turned and went up to the sanctuary. At the same moment Adrian, as if in obedience to some command, scrambled to his feet and came down towards his mother. At the gate of the sanctuary the two met; the child paused and raised his face; gravely they exchanged the kiss of peace. Before Adrian had reached Barbara the other began to mount the steps of the altar, and as he set his foot on the first sank gently to the ground.

On the instant, as they gazed, the church, but for them and the prostrate form, was empty. The sunlight shone upon an altar as bare as the pavement before it; without violence, without parting, the Graal and its Lord were gone.

They knelt and prayed, and only stirred at last when, with the natural boredom of childhood, Adrian said in a minute to his mother: "Shall we go home now?" The words dissolved as by a predestined act the forces that held them. Barbara stood up, looked once at Lionel, smiled at Adrian, and went with him out of the church. The Duke came up the aisle.

"Will you tell his people or shall I?" he asked Lionel, and Lionel answered with an equal normality, "As you like. I will stay here, if you will go."

"Very well," the Duke said, and paused, looking at the body. Then he said, smiling at Lionel, "I suppose they will say he had a weak heart."

"Yes," Lionel answered, "I expect they will." He felt suddenly the joy of the fantasy rise in his mind; he walked to the door and watched the Duke crossing the churchyard, and waited till beyond the hedge he saw Mr. Batesby hurrying to the church. Then he went out to meet him.

"Dear, dear," Mr. Batesby said, "how truly distressing! 'In the midst of life' . . . The Archdeacon too. . . . Cut down like a palm-tree and thrust into the oven. . . . No doubt the knock on the head affected it rather much."

THE END